I0452948

The Secret Ecology of Sex

The Secret Ecology of Sex is a work of fiction. The characters and dialogue are not to be construed as real. Any resemblance to actual persons, living or dead, is entirely coincidental.

Printed in the United States of America

First Printing, 2015

ISBN 978-0-9961821-0-2

Magic Door Publications

Cover image courtesy of NASA/JPL-Caltech
Cover design by Steven Luna

*To friends, lovers, and mentors, past and present,
and especially to S. Bazik, who patiently gave me support through
my hours hunched over the keyboard.*

The Secret Ecology of Sex

R. Vania

Prelude

Like a deeply creased mahogany figurehead on the prow of a ship, she sat motionless, staring far into the distance, farther than her eyesight could discern, but not farther than her hopes. Wisps of gray hair fluttered by her eyes, pointing toward the deeper waters.

"Tibu! Come on!" the younger voice behind her called. "Why do you stay here every day anyway?"

"I'm waiting."

"Tibu! What are you going to do when the storms come? You can't sit here then. What will you do when *marawa* covers your feet?"

"What are *you* doing for that day?" Tibu asked back.

"What can I do? I can't stop it."

"Then when *marawa* covers my feet, I will wait for it to cover my eyes."

Lila sighed in exasperation.

"You'll see. He'll come," Tibu added.

"Why do you think he'll come?"

"Because he knows I wait for him."

"And then what? Will he save you? Will he save me? Will he save any of us?"

"It depends on what you mean by 'save,' my young Lila," she whispered to herself as she rose.

Lila motioned her grandmother to come with her. "Well, maybe he'll come. But right now I really need you to help with dinner."

Tibu smiled. To some, Lila seemed flighty—even giddy. Tibu knew that joyful lightheartedness was not the only Lila. She was a human chameleon. On the job, she was a sophisticated professional when she needed to be. And then there was the sensitive and caring Lila that really needed no help with the cooking.

Tibu worried that Lila would not be able to keep the old values if she had to leave. "I want to be buried in Tungaru," Tibu reminded Lila.

"Not that again. Remember? There is no Tungaru."

"Don't be silly. If there was no Tungaru, it couldn't be our home."

"Exactly. Never mind. Besides, none of us will be buried here. The bodies will just float away."

"Float back to Tungaru. That's good. I would like that. That's what I will do."

"I give up. Come on, Tibu. Do you want to take a little nap before we start dinner? You didn't get much sleep last night."

Tibu slept. She dreamed visions of a home. The waters rose, but it didn't sink. It wasn't washed away. As it rocked on the waves, the home became radiant with light. Breadfruit and papaya trees flourished near her door. Tibu picked each one with loving gratitude and knew she was in a new Tungaru. The same but not the same. This Tungaru was the paradise it once had been, but without the worries for its future.

"Lila! I've had a vision."

"You were sleeping. It was just a dream."

Tibu was wide awake now. "Of course it was a dream."

Lila rarely lost patience with her. Amused, Lila said, "You're not making any sense again. Or is it me?"

"Yes. I don't make sense to you because you can't see it too."

"You sound like one of those new age books the tourists keep leaving at the hotel." It was the kindest reply Lila could come up with at the moment.

They smiled at one another. Lila sometimes wondered if Tibu had wisdom beyond the ordinary, or just ordinary dementia. But then again, what was the difference? Lila forgot to ask what the dream was about.

Lila tried to keep Tibu focused in "reality." "Here; help me cut this up for dinner, please?"

Part One

Laurel was shocked but not as panicked as she was the first time she got the call from the ER—she had been through this once already. She grabbed her things and got to the hospital as quickly as possible.

She went directly to the ER reception. "My husband, Mark Bradford, was brought here..." She expected a room number in reply, but the look from the woman at the desk drove a wedge into her confidence. Laurel was told to sit and wait for the doctor. The doctor's explanation was too short and too simple. She was too late. He was gone.

"He was discharged?" she stammered in confusion.

"No. He passed away about 15 minutes ago."

Laurel sat. At the age of 42, her home, her perfect little world had vanished, imploded into a sudden sinkhole, as cold as the late fall day that was darkening on the horizon.

A disembodied sound forced its way into her consciousness. "Can we call someone for you?"

She could think of no one. She couldn't think of what to tell Mark's aging parents, nor his far-away siblings. Her own parents were miles away on vacation. She couldn't think of what to tell herself. Megan. It was the only name that came to her.

Laurel remained motionless—inside and out. Time did not exist before Megan arrived. There was a flurry of meaningless words before she was gently scooped up and driven home.

Megan and Rachel tried to stay the night with her, but Laurel refused. She was floating in a void and needed to focus on what had just happened. She needed to make it real so that she could deal with it. Logic and reason had been her coping techniques before. Those and lists. They were all she could count on now. Maybe logic could lift the fog that encased her brain and her heart.

It was a long and sleepless night in the big empty house. She remembered when working as a "personal banker" at the Bank of Plymouth, she had dealt with Mark's sensible account choices so many years back when they first met. *Was it really six years ago?*

Just before their wedding, she and Mark had purchased this "modern colonial" brick house in an upscale area. They thought it ideal as a long-term investment. The price had been very good—no one else wanted it because of its history. It had been built by a conspiracy theorist who had taken ill and died when, in distrust, he refused to get medical attention. Mark, ever the businessman, was unmoved by the tales of the previous owner when he heard the price. Laurel thought having an unusual story behind its sale added to its charm. She imaged it would be amusing to tell people as she gave friends and family a tour of their new home.

With all the hopes and dreams of a financially secure young couple, they had also chosen a home that would be perfect for the rest of their lives together. There were three bedrooms, a three-car garage, and a large yard. The side and back yards had perennials in the landscaping and were enclosed by a wrought iron fence with decorative touches at the gate and corners. Tiny lilies of the valley hid amongst the lush shade-loving ferns that flourished in the north-facing front. It maintained the traditional appearance from the road with all the up-to-date details, garages, and decks out of view in the back. The best part, in Laurel's opinion, was a small "mother-in-law apartment." It was connected to the main house by a passageway behind the garages—separate but accessible. It would be perfect for guests, an aging parent, or maybe even a restless teenager in need of privacy. Laurel left her job at the Bank of Plymouth to dedicate herself to her new life with Mark.

Laurel thought back, trying to discern when that "perfection" had all begun to crumble. After their marriage, as before, sex had been an expression of their love for one another. Laurel had never considered it could be anything else for them. Partly out of consideration for Mark's ego, she had, more than once, faked an orgasm. Besides, Laurel knew that whatever he was doing at those times would not bring her complete satisfaction, no matter how long he kept going.

She had sometimes wondered if her frequent inability to reach a climax was somehow her fault—that there was something wrong with her. Whether or not that was true, at those times she had resigned herself to appreciating the closeness they shared.

Was that, so far back, the beginning of the end of that storybook life of mine?

Before her marriage, her life had been a smooth ride down a flat and familiar road in a sensible sedan. It had always suited Laurel well enough. Now it felt like it had been a New England boiled dinner; nourishing, but bland. That early upbringing left her with no compass to direct her in times like these.

Guess I'm going to have to chart a new course from here on, she thought. *I just don't know...*

But Laurel did know two things: she had intelligence, and she had solid finances. It was a starting point she would grab like a drowning person grasps a lifeline.

Her monetary security came from Mark's business, the Bradford Village Furniture Company. He had taken it over a couple of years before when his father's store expanded and was divided into two stores. Pouring more and more of his own life blood into it, Mark had transformed it into a well-established and prosperous business. It was everything he could have hoped for.

And what good did it do him? thought Laurel. *I don't know how to run the company. When it folds, so will my income.* Her despair deepened.

Mark had not directly included Laurel in the business, but there had been enough dinner conversation to give her a feeling she knew what was going on at the store. She had been in charge of entertaining in their home for business networking, and by picking him up for lunch, she'd developed a familiarity with his staff.

A regular little Suzy homemaker, she mused to herself.

She had "worked" for Mark by keeping the home ready for unexpected visitors and business contacts. She kept herself ready to be an attractive companion at events that strengthened Mark's position in the community. She cultivated side interests of her own, as long as they didn't interfere with her primary "occupation." Laurel thought she was on her way to fulfilling her aspirations for personal growth to be an exemplary wife and mother.

How could I have ever thought that! she wondered as she sat in the big living room chair in the dark.

The fact that she and Mark had never succeeded at having children had driven a series of wedges into their relationship. Laurel remembered how nothing had worked. In vitro fertilization, tests, medications; all had failed. Her increasing frustration was met with Mark's steely patience. This had only made her quietly angry. After all, he had his career and all the outside events and activities to maintain his success. She, on the other hand, had little more of significance to fret about than the absence of a child and, consequently, her inability to excel as a mother.

When Laurel was given a diagnosis of "unexplained infertility," she blamed herself and fell into the silent rage of a depression. She had refused to take it out on Mark in any way and would not interfere with the energies he had to direct towards the growing business.

She had lapsed into a contradictory state of acceptance of her barrenness and "feathering her nest" for some future concept of "family." She repainted, remodeled, and redecorated room after room, in subdued neutral tones, all as perfect as the displays in her husband's furniture store. When that was done, she had thrown herself into tending her gardens. The flowers became elaborate bouquets for the house that withered in their vases. The fresh fruits and vegetables did, however, prompt a new interest in cooking. As winter closed the garden, Laurel would turn to perfecting her culinary skills.

She had expanded her outside activities as well, while avoiding those that involved children's causes. Her most consistent efforts were with charities that required her to become knowledgeable about the environment and global issues of sustainability. She continued with these but never took a serious leadership role.

Approaching her later 30s, both Mark and Laurel had stopped discussing having a family. The sex had slowed, but their relationship remained an affectionate one. While Laurel had settled into her creative outlets and community projects, Mark's approach was less healthy. He eagerly ate all Laurel's new savory dishes and calorie-laden desserts, telling himself it would be good to encourage her.

I thought it was going well...but it was just another step in the decay. She was missing no point that would serve to drive her depression deeper yet.

As he ate more, Mark had begun to drink more as well. In addition, he was burying himself in ever-expanding company obligations, traveling for purchases, going to business meetings and advertising opportunities—all providing situations for more eating and drinking.

Laurel had told herself that his growing absences were necessary for Bradford Village Furniture, but she became concerned about Mark's increasingly ingrained habits of overindulgence. Mark did admit his weight was getting out of hand, but he was still active and only seemed adversely affected in minor ways.

Laurel remembered clearing the dinner table one night. She had thought it was again time to talk to Mark about taking a real vacation from work. A couple of weeks. Some place warm where they could reconnect and just enjoy each other's company.

Mark had stood in the doorway, interrupting her just-forming plans. "I'm going to run over to the store to pick up some catalogs. I have to be ready Monday morning to re-evaluate our present stock and order new styles."

"Isn't it time to give yourself a break? You never take a vacation."

"I wish I could, but that's how I keep the business on top. I just need a couple of hours right now, and I'll be back. Love you. Bye."

Laurel had resigned herself to the "privilege" of basking in his success and finished up in the kitchen. She realized now that she had been kidding herself. There never would have been any reconnecting.

Within six months of that conversation, Mark's health could no longer be minimized. He had been on the golf course for the first time since last fall, attempting to close a contract with the CEO of a firm that was building an entire new subdivision and needed to furnish three model homes. He had become short of breath and had felt his heart racing. No longer able to stay on his feet, he fell to his knees with a thud.

The emergency room physician had informed Mark and Laurel that it was not a full-blown heart attack but did involve a "cardiac event." It would be imperative for Mark to get a full examination from his family doctor.

Mark grudgingly made the appointment, fully expecting to be scolded for his excess weight. After extensive tests, he and Laurel were given more information than they were prepared to hear. Mark was now classified as "morbidly obese" and was told, "That alone, with its complications, could kill you." As the two were still reeling from that diagnosis, they barely processed the other words: fatty liver, possible cirrhosis, type 2 diabetes, possible sleep apnea, hypertension, high cholesterol. . .

At first stunned, they had gone home in silence. It was Laurel who had managed to start them down a productive path. She quickly organized and devised a plan to approach the monumental task of returning Mark to a healthier, safer state. First, she had researched each diagnosis. She then prioritized the severity of each one, concentrating on the most problematic maladies first and evaluating which actions they could take that would be of benefit to more than one illness at a time. She had grabbed one of her small 6 by 8-inch notebooks and her laptop and had gotten to work.

Mark had let Laurel be in charge of whatever she could do to help his health while he took his typical business approach to his life. Realistically, he admitted to himself he could not maintain the professional pushing and overworking. He was also aware this left him and Laurel very vulnerable from a financial standpoint. Mark had gotten his legal affairs in order and had begun to prepare Laurel the only way he knew how. Now, every new conversation with her began with, "If I can't work for a while..." or "If anything ever happens to me..." Laurel hadn't seen his point and took his comments as rhetorical expressions.

He had not only tried to prepare her for handling financial matters but had also begun to pull away emotionally. Laurel knew some of the medications he was on had a negative impact on libido and performance, but it was more than that. Was he intentionally distancing himself from her? Was it really his health, or was it another woman? She had dismissed the thoughts but kept them in the back of her mind. In any case, Laurel did not bring it up, thinking Mark would talk to her when he was ready.

At work, Mark had begun to train his employees to take more and more responsibility. His assistant, Megan Yates, was a capable and confident choice. He had meticulously educated her on the fine points of every aspect of the company. Nearly every night, he would come home late, elated by Megan's latest accomplishment.

Mark began taking Megan to the Better Business Bureau meetings, the Lions Club, and Rotary Club events. The evenings with Megan turned into buying trips to Drexel, Stickley, Baker, and Century Furniture, where she met all his contacts in person. Megan had been given power of attorney to sign paychecks and other documents in Mark's absence. She could legally make decisions when necessary as well.

While this seemed a sensible approach, Laurel had begun to wonder more about Mark's true relationship with Megan. Laurel and Megan had met once or twice before. Megan was younger and attractive. She was trim and fit with naturally curly, honey colored hair. It was just long enough to tie back when she jogged or as a sort of "tell" when she needed to concentrate on difficult concepts, as if her hair got in the way of her thoughts. After another mention of long hours at work, Laurel had tried to sound casual when she asked, "Is Megan married?"

"Yes. Her wife owns a jewelry import business and does a lot of international traveling, so Megan is more than willing to put in extra hours to become successful in her own right."

Little did I know then how important Megan would be to me, Laurel thought.

Relieved at Mark's reply, Megan became a regular topic at the dinner table. Laurel could see Mark's anxiety ease in direct proportion to how well Megan was able to take command. Before the summer was over, Megan and her wife had been asked to dine with Mark and Laurel. Megan was delighted at the invitation and quickly checked with Rachel to make sure she would be available.

Laurel had no idea what to expect of the evening, nor of the interaction with the women who were coming. She had prepared a simple but superb meal that would not tie her up in the kitchen for long periods of time.

Laurel knew she must have expected something, due to her shock at what walked in when Mark answered the doorbell. Rachel's long black hair with its soft curves hung well below the shoulder. She had olive skin and almost-green hazel eyes that showed a light but effective hand with makeup. She was impeccably dressed in a finely woven linen tunic that flowed gracefully over steel grey silk slacks. The lines and fabrics were flawless—and clearly expensive. As Rachel came closer, Laurel saw the tunic's exquisite touch of white-on-white embroidery.

"Hi, Laurel!" Megan had called as she bounced past Mark. "I want you to meet my wife, Rachel Zemfira. Rachel, this is Mark's wife, Laurel."

Rachel had extended her hand to Laurel first. "So happy to finally meet you!" And turning to Mark, "To meet you both!"

Laurel had taken a closer look when the conversation turned to Mark. The jewelry Rachel wore was some she had found in Indonesia—uncomplicated exotic swirls of burnished silver hung from her ears with a matching design engraved on a wide bracelet. There was no scent from perfume or lotion.

Hah. And I thought a woman wasn't well dressed without perfume.

Rachel had moved with the confidence of a successful entrepreneur but was warm and clearly keen to know these two people from Megan's world. And she was older than Megan, nearer to Laurel's age.

Laurel had found Megan to be a delightful guest. During dinner, when Mark began a discussion about work, Megan diplomatically led the subject back into topics to include Laurel. Megan was energetic, but not irritatingly so, and quick to smile without being silly. Laurel liked her more than she had anticipated, and Megan seemed to feel the same about Laurel.

After finishing the meal, Rachel had followed Laurel into the kitchen, empty dishes in hand, while Megan and Mark discussed the business. "That was a lovely meal! I'll have to get the blend of seasonings on that roast. Not that I cook that much! That requires the privilege of being able to stay at home long enough to build some skills!"

Laurel knew Rachel had eaten in fine places all over the world. "Thank you. But it's not complicated," she answered blandly as she put dishes into the dishwasher.

Rachel gauged Laurel's subdued reaction and went on. "Sometimes the simplest spices and tastes can be the most elegant. Flavor is only part of the total meal experience. Meat must be tender but still have some 'tooth' to it. The choice of wine that complements the other flavors is critical. Then there's the total presentation of colors and textures that all must come together with a creative appearance. But you obviously understand all that!"

Laurel closed the dishwasher, stood up, and looked directly at Rachel. "Would you like some fresh coffee? Or brandy? Better yet, I make a hot coffee drink with coffee liqueur that you might like."

"Sounds perfect!"

"Would you please ask Megan and Mark if they'd like some too while I get it started?"

"Sure!" Rachel smiled as she turned to check with the others.

Laurel reached out and touched Rachel's arm. "Thanks."

Laurel comforted herself with these memories. *Sweet Rachel.*

~

As days became weeks, Megan and Rachel socialized with Mark and Laurel several times. Laurel learned that Rachel had begun her business via an early understanding of Internet potentials. Rachel and Megan had met through mutual friends several years before, at a time when neither was looking for a relationship. They became closer and more trusting of one another, but it was a casual camping trip that had turned the tide. Both women had brought their dogs and, though different breeds and sizes, the two thoroughly enjoyed the company of another canine. Play dates for the dogs eventually turned into play dates for Megan and Rachel.

Laurel remembered watching Megan and Rachel's relationship. They seemed close and were attentive to each other. They were verbally affectionate but rarely touched one another when with others—though once, while they were waiting on the deck alone, Laurel saw Rachel step closer to Megan. Their faces were barely inches apart. Laurel had recognized the intensely direct way they had looked at each other, and their suggestive smiles. She had a hard time remembering when she and Mark had last shared such a moment.

Laurel thought Megan and Rachel had been at ease answering any questions, even Laurel's naive ones, about being "out" as a couple. Since neither were in fear of losing their job if they went public, it was a non-decision. No, neither was worried about the other's fidelity when they were often separated by time and distance. It was not what had been said but more the inferences drawn that had led Laurel to believe the lack of jealously came not from a firm belief in the limits of behavior so much as a more casual and open attitude towards discreet encounters. It was a thought Laurel had stored away for further future evaluation.

Was it because I was distracted by this new social life? Is that why I let worries about Mark's health, and the growing gap between us, give way to habit and complacency?

Maybe that was why it was so jarring when Mark had collapsed this second time a year later.

~

As it often happens after a death, it was all a rapid blur. Laurel and Megan had quickly gone to Mark's desk to find his address book with the numbers of his business associates and relatives. Along with it, they found a folder labeled "In the event of my death." Mark had already made arrangements. The cremation and memorial service had already been paid for and the urn had been picked out by Mark at that time, all unbeknownst to Laurel.

Megan, with Rachel's help, was indispensable. She was compassionate but directive. "Should I call..." would not work at this point. Asking Laurel what she wanted would only elicit an "I don't know." Instead, Megan cued Laurel, phone in hand: "Do you want to call Mark's brother, or should I? Maybe you should," and "Shall I inform the employees about the memorial service, or do you want to?"

The relatives, both his and hers, arrived in town and, though more than willing to help, found there was no need. Laurel's parents clung to her with encouraging words that penetrated her groggy perceptions but had little effect. Laurel let things whirl around her, barely noticing Megan's expert directives.

Only as she lay in bed alone after the funeral could Laurel think at all. She watched the past year stream by her inner eye once more as she waited for dawn, running her palm over the flat, cold sheet beside her.

Laurel was now sure Mark had known his time was short. She was positive that instead of pulling closer to her for his own comfort, he had tried to get her accustomed to being alone. In her jumble of emotions, she felt both cheated and grateful. She was better prepared to be alone, but she was also angry that, without her knowledge or input, he had taken away over a year of himself from her.

Well, she thought, beginning an unprecedented level of introspection, *maybe he actually began pulling away—maybe we* both *began pulling away—when we gave up on having a family.*

Through the first month after Mark's death, she cried, she raged, she became alternately hyperactive and inert. Megan supported Laurel but let her go through what she needed to without trying to manage her.

Laurel got to a point where she thought she was doing well. She was back into her usual activities of spending most of her time tending to the house and garden but little else. She wasn't attending her community groups because she didn't want the drippy sympathies of other married women.

Then it would happen. Once, she was moving a big overstuffed chair to vacuum behind it. There she saw Mark's favorite pen that he'd had for years and then lost. She remembered how he fussed about it for a week. She burst into tears and was barely able to get out of bed for several days.

Another time, she let a small bush die because it was one Mark cared for. She pulled it out by the roots, screaming at it, "See? He thought he had us all set to go on without him, but he let you die, didn't he?!"

Nothing was ever the same again, yet nothing changed. The sun still came up every morning, and there was still laundry to be done and bills to be paid. Laurel's goals and directions in life had been cemented in the home. But if not a family, "home" had at least meant "husband." Laurel no longer knew who she was, nor why she was here.

~

Perhaps it was a blessing that Laurel had to get up, get dressed, and hear what Megan had to say that chilly winter morning. She had given Laurel an hour's notice by phone that she was on her way to the house to talk to her.

Megan was treading on open wounds and tried to do so with care. "Mark left everything to you because he loved you, and so that you would always be financially secure. But in doing so, you are now in a position that requires you to sign business documents and make decisions about the company—decisions only you can make. I know you don't feel ready, but you'll need to start coming in to the office. I think you'll find you already know more about it than you think."

Laurel sat for a moment, weighing the words. Yes. She would have to move on this eventually. But she hadn't done much of anything since the funeral, and that was weeks ago. By the time Laurel gave her attention back to Megan, she was hearing, "So I will be here to pick you up at 9:00 tomorrow morning."

As sole owner of the company, Laurel knew she was everyone's superior without having the knowledge to carry it off. Megan began with a simple but thorough tour, as she would have with any new employee. Laurel met people, putting faces with names and stories she had heard in the past. Smiling and grasping her hand, they seemed happy, even relieved, to see her there.

Megan had shown Laurel hints of her coming obligations but had only one task for her to complete that day. "In order for everyone to be paid tomorrow, these paychecks need to be signed today. You can sit right here, and I will be at my desk just around the corner if you need any questions answered."

Laurel sat and stared at the pile of checks. Signing them was an obsolete system, but it was more personal. She hesitantly lifted her gaze to study the desk and the room. It had been Mark's. She knew that, but the chair seemed new, and the desk had been tidied. Two pictures on the wall and some decorative items had been replaced. His, but not his. She casually signed the first check, and then another, and another. She began to feel she needed to get on with it. People's lives were depending on these checks. They were depending on her. She needed to do this.

Laurel took the signed checks to Megan. "Is there anything else I should do?"

Megan said, "There are some things tomorrow. I want your opinion on some new living room stock that needs to be bought. I have some catalogs for us to go through. And when you come, you might want to let me take you around so that you can give the checks to each employee individually. Just this once; I think it would help them feel more confident that the company—and their jobs—are still here. Can you be here by 8:30 tomorrow?"

Laurel was grateful for Megan and for the extra training Mark had given her. But Mark was gone. Impulsively, Laurel said to Megan, "I want to ask you something, but I don't know how to say it so that it won't come out in a way I don't intend."

"Of course. Go ahead," said Megan, expecting a company-related query.

"Do you and Rachel ever miss not having a man around the house? You know, for repairs and maintenance things and such? Well, for anything?"

Stunned only for a split second but keeping her composure, Megan replied, "Not really. If there's something we don't know how to do, we learn. There are do-it-yourself books, and the people at home supply stores are very helpful. Online videos fill in, too. Sometimes women without a male around can be targets for unscrupulous businesses and whatnot. But being aware of that possibility and being prepared for it is usually enough. Like when we buy a car. You can just hear the salesman thinking we don't know anything. If they start by asking if we have a particular color in mind, we know he's that type!

"So far, we've been able to handle just about everything except heavy lifting—like appliances. We hired movers to do that.

"Don't get me wrong—it hasn't all been rosy! The most heated arguments we've ever had have been about how we should be doing maintenance or repairs. You should have seen us trying to retile the bathroom floor! But we're getting better with that.

"And as far as the relationship itself, well, I can't imagine how any two people of opposite gender could be that close. Men and women are so different. Being the same, we have so much more in common."

"Thanks," was all Laurel said, but her mind was spinning. So was Megan's.

Through the weeks to come, Laurel would cling to Megan's reassuring reply like a child to a security blanket. She went over Megan's words in her head over and over until they were worn out. The only thing left of them would be the easy courage Megan had handed to Laurel.

Within a few days of beginning her work in earnest, Laurel was off to a local book store chain, and she left with a bagful of publications on how to run a business and how to be a supervisor. She read them in the evenings but was not entirely what she specifically needed or wanted to learn from them. So she read them all. Every word. Some reminded her of many of Mark's descriptions of what was going on at work. She began to realize she did know more than she had given herself credit for, just as Megan had said. But she had never had to apply any of that knowledge, nor had she been in a managerial position, other than with the few bank tellers that had been under her direction years ago. She hoped she knew more about being a leader than she thought, too.

~

"Where are you going to at this hour?" Lila asked.

"I'm going to be the first person on earth to see the New Year being born."

"I'm up now; I might as well tag along."

At the first hints of dawn, Tibu began to dance…slowly at first, but gaining energy with the increasing light. The old dances effortlessly came back to her arms.

"I don't know why you're so happy. This year doesn't look like it's going to be any more promising than the last."

"Have you tried to change that?" Tibu asked back.

"What can I do?"

"You'll see. Today is a new year. A new time. Dance with me. Can you do that?"

Lila brightened. "Of course! You taught me well!"

"And you learned well," Tibu assured her.

"So what do you think this new year will bring for us, Tibu? Will this be the year to flee?"

"Not if you keep learning. Hold your feet still unless it's time to move them." Tibu directed.

Lila wasn't sure if Tibu meant in the dance or something else. Or both.

~

Laurel had initially thought she wouldn't have time or energy to go to the store every day, forty hours a week. She had always been busy at home, running the household. Now she was busy at work instead, sometimes bringing reports and flow charts home while continuing her self-directed studies. She grabbed breakfasts on the run and had working lunches at restaurants near the store. She improvised at dinner time, but even that was often taken up by business-related meetings.

As Laurel's foundation of knowledge grew, she was able to use logic and reasoning more and more, needing Megan's help less and less. Nonetheless, her remaining dependence on Megan was nagging.

"Megan, we've been doing this a full forty hours a week for weeks now. I'm still learning and I feel, well, awkward."

"Don't worry; you're doing fine! You're picking all of this up much more quickly than I expected."

"What I'm learning and how fast I'm learning it isn't the problem. I own this company now. That means you work for me. But here you are, the expert, teaching me. It doesn't feel right."

"The fact that you're aware and want to discuss it should show you how well equipped you are to do this job—to take over the position. You're being sensitive to your employee's feelings while still being able to take the reins. Trust me. We'll be over this awkward phase in no time."

Laurel did trust Megan. Mark had done well to choose her.

~

Rachel greeted Megan at the door. "How was work today?"

"Fine, but Laurel and I reached a turning point."

"How so?"

"Well, when she first started coming to work, she was focused on knowing about the business. She still is, but now she's thinking about taking over. She's finding it strange that I'm training her, but as soon as she knows enough, she'll be my superior. She's going to want to get out of this dependency on me as soon as possible. I honestly hadn't thought about it before, and now I'm finding it strange, too."

"But you're okay with it, right?"

"Of course. But what if she decides to take over before she's ready? I'm not finished with training her yet, and what if she flops? It will be my fault."

Rachel took Megan affectionately by the shoulders. "Megan. I know you. Would you ever be finished? Would you ever think she knows enough or is ready? And do you really think Laurel—or anyone else—would blame you? Stop being such a mother hen! You're going to have to learn to let go."

"You're right. She's been in this orientation process for a few months now. She began back in the winter, and here it is, spring. She'll be fine."

Rachel poured two glasses of wine. "Come on. Let's sit on the *flokati* in front of the fireplace for a bit before dinner."

They were a good match. Each balanced the other. Rachel didn't speak again until Megan's tensions from her day at work had melted in the warmth of the flames.

~

After two or three weeks of particularly long hours at the store, Laurel planned to spend the weekend catching up at the house. She needed to plan meals so that she could make the grocery list. There was cleaning, laundry, and shopping to be done.

Saturday morning found Laurel about to spring into action. She was up, showered, and dressed well before 8:00. She grabbed some yogurt and toast and sat down to begin the menus. She made it to day three before she burst into tears. Without thinking, she had automatically planned meals for two.

The rest of the chores went no better. Laundry had barely piled up, and there was little out of place in the house—no one had been there.

Something about the undisturbed dust reminded Laurel of the local historical society's museum.

She needed time to think, to get herself together, to focus. How much of the whirlwind was she using as a distraction rather than making real headway? She usually drank tea at home, but coffee had become her new best friend at work; the pot was never empty, and employees seemed to live on the stuff. She rummaged about the kitchen cabinets until she found the coffee and coffee maker that had been untouched since Mark's last meal at home with her how long ago? It seemed so long ago now. Or was it just yesterday?

Making the coffee took an eternity. Laurel had to choose the type of coffee she wanted: caffeine or decaf, favored or not flavored, the minimum number of cups the pot could handle or more to have ready for later, filtered water or tap water, a tall mug, a short, fat mug, or a cup and saucer that matched her china set. It wasn't this complicated when she'd made it for Mark. There weren't choices to make then. She knew what he liked and what he wanted.

Laurel loaded the pot, chose a mug, and, having no half and half, got some whipping cream out of the refrigerator. She had gotten it a few days before to make strawberry shortcake that had never materialized.

She leaned on the counter and waited. A small, steamy gurgle was the first sign. Laurel listened intently as the disturbance grew to a torrent of sound and smell. The thin drizzle of dark, hot fluid fell into the shiny, clear pot, churning up short-lived bubbles. The level in the pot rose. Then stopped. The noise exploded in a last effort to push any remaining steamy drops of water up into the system. Then silence.

Laurel remained motionless, staring at the pot. "Meditation in motion." That was the phrase a friend had used when he was telling Mark and her about a Tai Chi class he had begun. At least making the coffee took less energy than Tai Chi.

Laurel sat down with her full mug. *Now it's official*, she thought to herself. *I am alone. And so responsible for so much.*

Tears welled up. It took several seconds for them to spill quietly over onto Laurel's motionless cheek. When she passed out those first paychecks, she thought one of the older men there was about to cry. "Oh, thank you! We were so afraid the company might close..." His voice seemed to run out of air and fade away. With nothing to lose, he had spoken his mind.

"My God!" she yelled out loud. Before, she had only been responsible for Mark and his surroundings. Now she was responsible for the very lives of so many employees at the company. "What am I going to do?! What THE HELL am I going to do?!"She had asked herself this before. But it was different this time. It was a simple question. There should be a simple answer.

Laurel picked up the mug and paced it back and forth across the kitchen, first at a near run, eventually slowing to a determined stride, over and over, sipping as she went. It was much better than the coffee at work. And that was the answer she needed. At work. Concentrate on the company. Household duties were minimal, and she could always get help with those if she really needed it. She reached for her notebook and began writing furiously.

~

Mark's leadership style had tendencies toward a "beneficent dictator." Maybe that was too harsh a description, but he had definitely been in charge. Laurel couldn't pick up where he left off. She didn't know how to take complete command in that way, nor did she want to.

In the six months since Mark's death, Laurel was becoming a part of the company, making decisions, learning the nuances of being a leader—by example of her effort and determination, if nothing else. She would go on, and so would the company. Maybe even better and stronger than it had before. She would take the wheel and call for a general meeting. She spent the rest of that Saturday and half of Sunday planning how to say what it was she wanted to communicate. In the end, it would be short and to the point. She knew she had to be confident—in her company, in its people, and in herself. "Fake it 'til you make it," she said to herself, but she couldn't remember where the quote had come from.

Monday morning, she quickly found Megan. "How long would it take for you to announce a meeting? It would have to be first thing in the morning before the store opens and before the delivery drivers go on the road. I want everyone there. Everyone."

"Okay..." Megan was trying to think faster than she needed to talk. "I'll tell the office to change any early deliveries that might be scheduled and make sure we have a space ready and..."

"And tell them breakfast will be served. People are always in a better mood if they have a full stomach. I'll arrange for Breakfast and Beyond to cater it. As soon as you tell me when it can happen, I'll call them. No. I'll go there to deal with them in person. Let's have it Thursday or Friday. No, Friday. That will give me time to go through some things with the financial records, too."

At first, Megan thought it sounded like Laurel might want to thank employees...but why would Laurel be so preoccupied and unwilling to discuss it all? And what about the finances? "Is there anything I can help with or anything else you want me to do?" Megan managed without screaming, "What the hell are you doing? What's going on?!"

"No, but thanks. At least not for now." Laurel turned back to Megan, "Please understand. I feel I must try to start doing things on my own, even if it's just getting a meeting together, and even if I do it badly."

Megan only relaxed slightly and couldn't wait to talk to Rachel about this, but she was on a buying trip. This left no sounding board for Megan, who tried to predict Laurel's next move. When no more information came from Laurel by Tuesday afternoon, Megan point blank asked Laurel what she had planned.

"I just need to say a few things to everyone."

Rachel was still out of the country, but on Wednesday, Megan did manage a poor phone connection. Only the basics got through before the line went dead. No help there. And no more from Laurel either, who had come in as usual but then said she would be gone for the rest of the day. And maybe tomorrow.

~

Laurel headed for the bank. The Bank of Plymouth felt warmly familiar as Laurel walked through the double glass doors and up the half-flight of steps. The rhythmic clacking of her sensible heels on the old, solid marble floor announced her arrival to the receptionist. Laurel was promptly taken in to John Renson's executive office. He was an older man who couldn't stop himself from standing and extending his hand when a "lady" appeared.

"So glad to see you again! You look well! What can I do for you today?" He gestured toward the large chair with padded arms in front of his desk and did not sit down until Laurel was seated. He offered her coffee or tea without waiting for a reply to his previous question.

"No, thank you. As you know, I now have Bradford Village Furniture; I need to get a better handle on the helm, so to speak. I need to understand the finances as much as possible and as quickly as possible. I know it will take some time to be fully versed on all aspects and how it all works, but right now, I need a crash course."

"Of course you do! Mark worked with three bankers here beside myself. Any one of them could help you, but how soon were you wanting to begin?" Renson sensibly inquired.

"Immediately. Today, if I can. I know that might not be possible, but how soon could I begin?"

"Hmmm. Let me think a minute. Chuck is already tied up for the day. Jason is at a meeting with the town council. Let me see if Tony can help. I will be right back."

Laurel was more than ready to take the task on and felt a glimmer of hope that it might actually happen within minutes.

Renson went into Tony's office. "I have Mrs. Bradford here, Laurel Bradford. She inherited Mark's business but doesn't have the foggiest how Mark was handling anything as far as the finances. Is there a chance you can have Emma clear your calendar for today—and maybe tomorrow—so that you can be of complete service to her? It's going to be somewhat complicated for her since she wasn't part of her husband's business before, but she is an important client for us. Understand?"

He did. Completely. "Give me five minutes, and I'll be there," he said as he lifted the phone on his desk to give instructions to his assistant.

Renson returned to his office. "We're in luck. Antonio Moreno will be able to go through things with you. Tony will be available to you for the rest of the day, but if you feel you need more time with him, he'll be able to give you some tomorrow as well. But don't decide now. You also might want to stop at a point, digest, apply that much, and then evaluate what you need from there. Whatever we can do..."

When Tony took Laurel into his office, she pulled out a pen and a small spiral bound notebook from her tote bag. *I must look like a total idiot,* she thought to herself, but she kept hold of her notebook anyway.

Tony began by giving Laurel the generalities as simply as he could. Mark, or more recently Megan, had made the deposits that were divided into specific accounts. First, he explained, a set amount went for the expenses of running the day-to-day functioning and general overhead of the store, including utilities, salaries, purchases, property taxes, delivery truck maintenance, and other predictable needs.

A secondary account went for future expansion, advertising, and other long-range plans. Mark had talked about some of this with Laurel in the evenings. He had hopes of opening another store, depending on the market, with a different line or different style of furniture and more decorative items.

A third account was for any funds that had not been put in the other two accounts. This was Mark's slush fund for bonuses, holiday parties, and anything else that was non-essential or purely morale boosting. Being the conservative that he was, he had not dipped into this fund often or deeply. Laurel understood his motives. She remembered how, on the anniversary of the 9-11 attack on the Twin Towers, Mark confidently told her about a cash cushion that would see them through until any economic crisis was past. There were some minor sub-accounts that took care of specific needs as well, he said; country club and other business promotion expenses that didn't fit neatly into the other account categories.

Laurel asked about the two company credit cards and was told one was for the first account and one was for the third. Mark had treated the second one as more of a savings account and had not requested a credit or debit card for that.

Laurel listened intently, taking notes as she sat across the desk from Tony. He went into more and more detail as the afternoon progressed. Since Laurel didn't ask many questions, he felt she was probably overwhelmed by the deluge of information. More than once, he had asked Laurel if she wanted to stop and come back at a later time, but Laurel had told him, "No, you're able to give me this time now, so I think I should take advantage of the opportunity."

A half hour before closing time, Laurel decided they should stop. She thanked him for being so thorough and giving her so much vital information.

"It was my pleasure, and I'm sure you'll find some of the application of all this confusing. So don't hesitate to call for a follow-up appointment with me. My assistant, Emma, will help you set it up when you're ready." He was positive she would be on the phone in the next few days, or certainly within two weeks. When no call came, he smirked to himself, assuming she had become so bogged down by her lack of experience that she wasn't ready to handle any more.

~

On Wednesday, Laurel asked the custodian-handyman, Gus Tapia, to take charge of making an "appropriate" space for the breakfast and handed him a company credit card to cover expenses. This request was out of his league by far. There wasn't much time to figure out what to do, and being entrusted with the credit card was a bit terrifying. "Is it okay if I ask my wife, Rosa, to help me? Not for pay, just to help."

"Of course. That would be fine."

Gus brought Rosa with him to work the following day. The two of them worked together, adding tables with tablecloths and chairs facing a low platform in part of the warehouse section. The industrial atmosphere was minimized by setting up folding screens that were already part of the inventory.

Laurel spoke with Gus while Rosa attended to some final touches. "Gus, could Rosa come tomorrow for breakfast? I'd like to thank her in person for all she's done here." Gus was taken aback but happy to oblige.

Gus was well into late middle age and had been with the store for a few years, but Laurel hadn't met Rosa before. Both Mark and Megan had mentioned Gus, saying he was dedicated and thorough. Mark had called him "one of the few men of integrity left in this world."

Laurel had always liked Gus. But he didn't seem at ease with her or Megan. When asked to do something, he would never say, "Okay." It was always a quiet "Yes, ma'am." She assumed it was a cultural dictate of some sort, but this was America, the land of equal opportunity. It made her uncomfortable.

Laurel walked around the warehouse after everyone left, not only to do her usual last-minute checks, but also to see what Rosa had done.

The warehouse was always spotlessly clean, and a burned bulb was never out more than ten minutes, thanks to Gus. But it felt different tonight. It was hard to say why at first, but the subtle changes were there. The tables had small but lovely centerpieces, and a carpet runner had been put at the doorway, leading in. The screens that hid the guts of the storage area were not a man's idea. Where screens couldn't be used, stock was shifted out of sight; not hidden and hard to find for the next person, just not immediately visible for the breakfast goers. It could only have been Rosa's touch.

Walking back to her office to pick up her things, Laurel checked her mail box one last time for the day. There was a white envelope with her name in neat cursive, written in pencil. The note inside was short. "Dear Mrs. Bradford, I found this while moving things for the breakfast and didn't know who it belonged to. Rosa."

Folded inside the note was a twenty-dollar bill.

~

Friday morning, everyone arrived for the meeting on time. Both fear and curiosity had insured that. Megan had been instructed to inform everyone to enjoy their breakfast and that Laurel would be joining them shortly.

The caterers were ready. Laurel had opted not to have boxes of bagels and donuts left for the grabbing. She wanted these people to be respectfully served.

After about twenty minutes, Laurel came in and joined them. She was given a plate and a token amount of food. She made a point of finding Gus and Rosa. She also searched out the older man who had seemed so relieved when she handed him his paycheck. She had found out who he was and addressed him by name. Shaking his hand, she said, "Mr. Harris! So glad to see you again!"

Laurel had no microphone. She could speak in a strong enough voice without shouting. Besides, the shiny warehouse floor would reverberate her words so that she would easily be heard by all as they sat with their nearly empty plates. She had been reminding herself for days: she couldn't show the least bit of nervousness, nor could she overcompensate and seem arrogant. There were no enemies here. All would be well. She needed only to be herself.

Laurel began predictably enough. She thanked them for welcoming her so warmly and for providing such a positive atmosphere as she learned the business. She was learning their names, and she wanted them to know that she knew they were all oarsmen on the company ship—and that included Mrs. Tapia, who had graciously volunteered to help her husband prepare the area.

Then she paused. She took a slow breath while looking downward. Those in front of her had been listening to her, but now they were listening to her silence. Was she about to become overly emotional? Was she going to tell them the company was closing? Megan knew no more than anyone else. Her fork froze in midair.

Laurel lifted her head and spoke without notes.

"Mark left us this legacy. But Mark also left all of us with a responsibility. The Bradford Village Furniture Company is just a small island in a sea of modern commercialism. In a very real sense, our lives depend on its survival.

"Once I understood that, with your help, I knew I had to take a hard look at the company's present state of heath and its prognosis for the future. The company is, for the moment, very healthy."

There was an audible mass sigh of relief.

"I knew my husband was sensibly frugal, but I had no idea how he applied that to the company. So I went to the financial advisors at the bank that had worked with Mark. I left with even more respect for Mark's business sense than I had before. The company's profits have been going to an account for the usual overhead of running the business, but there is more. Mark had set up a second account to plan for growth and expansion. Then, there was a third fund for unexpected or unplanned things along the way—like a breakfast! So thank Mark for this, not me!"

More at ease now, there was a ripple of polite chuckles across the small sea of attentive faces.

"I have worked out the finances and am happy to tell you that the 'breakfast account' will be able to cover a thank-you and end-of-year bonus for all—5% of your annual salary."

Laurel had expected immediate clapping or cheering, but there was stunned silence. She was just about to go on when a salesman in the back raised a fist toward the ceiling, stood straight up, and shouted, "YES!" There was laughter and applause from all.

Relaxing, Laurel went on. "But bonuses aren't raises. Raises must have the extra funds year after year, regardless of how the business does. And after the recession, we all know there is no guarantee how the economy will affect us. Even severe weather events could affect the business. So I've come up with an idea: profit sharing. Salaries will not go up without a great deal of thought, but when the business thrives, every employee can share in those profits. If the business hits a bad spot, your pay will not go down, but the profit sharing will be very little or nothing.

"So, how do we get our profits up and growing? It's up to every one of us. And I do mean *every one*. I now have control over the store, but I have no idea what kind of engine oil goes in our delivery trucks. Only the drivers know the ins and outs of the maintenance on those vans. Every one of you is an expert in your own position.

"So let's start with a simple suggestion box. Every suggestion or idea will be taken seriously. If it is used, you will be given a reward in proportion to the savings or gains. Big ideas or little suggestions are all welcome. With your continued support, and the help of our financial advisors, we can succeed. With your continued efforts, the company can turn a profit to insure profit-sharing payments for all. We cannot just survive, but grow into the future and whatever that may bring. We sink or swim together.

"So, with that, I'll turn it over to all of you. Any comments or questions?"

There was a buzz of people talking to each other. As Laurel looked across the faces, they seemed to be having positive reactions. Then the first question arose.

"What size of a cut will we get for those money-saving and profit-raising suggestions?"

Before Laurel could get her eyes fixed on the spot where the voice came from, another was heard. This time it was Megan.

"Sorry to interrupt, but I have a suggestion!" The crowd responded with polite amusement, and Megan went on. "I'm sure everyone has questions. I know I do. I suggest we get the box up in the staff lounge area in the next day or two, and then everyone put your questions in there, along with ideas and suggestions. That way, we can work out the answers and put together a newsletter announcement sort of thing."

Megan had come through for Laurel once more. Laurel had asked for questions and expected to answer them on the spot. However, this would give Laurel time to confer with Megan and the bank, or to do research on her own to devise careful answers.

"Perfect!" she called back to Megan. "So! Let's all get to work!"

~

At first there were a few tentative and conservative ideas, invariably folded and refolded before being dropped in the box. Laurel wasted no time in projecting savings or profits, and then rewarding the contributor with 10% of the amount saved or gained in the space of one year. Once the announcements were posted, more creative, less cautious ideas were submitted.

Suggestions were as varied as the personalities in the store. One that initially sounded too expensive worked out well when the math was done. Discontinuing use of an outside company to control vending machines meant paying a surprisingly large sum of money up front for Bradford's own machine. But not only would it be profitable over the course of a year, it would also be an excellent motivational tool. Every clink of a coin was a reminder to the employees that they did have a voice. That, in turn, encouraged more participation and bolstered morale.

One salesperson wanted to take out the paper towel dispensers and put in blow-driers. There was no doubt it would save money, but everyone hated the thought. As a compromise, Laurel rewarded the employee with a gift card for a local restaurant. She knew it was something Mark would not have done. For the first time, Laurel began to see some of Mark's policies as less than ideal. Her approach was not only building morale and saving money, it was fostering a newfound self-confidence in Laurel's leadership abilities, as well as employee loyalty.

Tony had given Laurel an excellent foundation as far as the company's finances, especially from the bank's perspective, but now she wanted to build on that knowledge and get a firmer grip on the smallest details of the systems within the store. Over the next few days, Laurel waded through the company's books over and over. There were discrepancies that were so small, she thought at first it was a math error on her part. She tallied and subtracted over and over, but the figures remained the same. And those figures were short—never by large amounts, and rarely the same. From month to month, it might only be $10 or $20, and it was never more than $247. Still, over time, it added up. It was not the amount of money that bothered Laurel so much as the evidence of a disloyal and dishonest employee in their midst.

Laurel told no one for the moment. She didn't have enough information, and she had to re-think her evaluations of those she thought were people of integrity.

I could take Tony up on his offer to go over the books in more detail, she thought. *No. I have to check the books at work more thoroughly first.*

If she didn't track down the culprit immediately, it certainly wouldn't bankrupt the company. Like the meeting, this was something she would tackle on her own.

Laurel began to play amateur detective, but with little success. She did background checks on those she didn't know well. When that failed to produce anything, she started checking those she thought were beyond reproach. That, too, revealed nothing suspicious.

She began to piece together the multitude of paths every cent in and out could take, along with all the recording and paperwork involved. It was consuming a disproportionate amount of time and effort. Laurel decided to keep working at it, but only when she had all of her over tasks and duties completed for the week.

~

Laurel's inability to solve the problem of the missing funds quickly added to her growing concerns for general security, something that had never before entered her mind. Mark had either taken care of such matters or made her feel safe simply because he was there.

She was on her way to work on a Friday morning, listening to her usual NPR radio station, when the local news came on. There had been another home invasion. Laurel concentrated on maneuvering through the congested narrow streets just blocks from the store. That is, until she heard "...Lighthouse Road..." True, there was a Lighthouse Road in nearly every town in every state that bordered the coast. But her attention was now locked on the newscast. It was the house three doors down from her own. Someone had broken in after dark when no one was at home.

When she arrived at work, she phoned the security company that had equipped the store with cameras and alarms. They could be at the house Saturday morning. When she took her lunch break, she drove to a nearby hardware store, where she purchased four timers to put on lamps in the house.

Laurel arrived at home after work and immediately placed the timers in different rooms for different times. There would be at least one light on all through the night. She closed the blinds so that no one could see in, but the light would still be visible. She thought this was a good plan to deter any culprits lurking around the neighborhood and assure her a good night's sleep. She was wrong.

It was after midnight when she was able to laugh at herself. She felt so smug in her solution, she had forgotten that she hadn't had a good night's sleep since Mark had died. *Whatever made me think I would now?* she wondered.

The alarm company was right on time Saturday morning. A security sign was stuck in the front garden by the walk, and cameras were positioned to cover the front and back doors. Upgraded door alarms were installed at the front door, the back door, and the door that led in from the garage. Laurel felt like the house was as well-protected as a little prison. Even so, it still did not help her to sleep any sounder.

~

Laurel awoke before dawn Monday morning. Unable to go back to sleep, she decided to get up and go to work. The missing money, and her lack of getting a handle on it, was nagging at her like a festering hangnail.

I'll put myself on flex hours, she thought as she went into the building. When she opened the door to her office, the morning sun gave the air a glow. She sat, absorbing its comforting warmth, when the door opened.

"Oh! I'm so sorry. I didn't know you were here. I was just going to vacuum." Gus stood there, vacuum wand in hand.

"Oh, Gus; no, *I'm* sorry. I should have told you I was coming in early today. Why don't you skip my office this morning?"

"Of course, ma'am." Gus noticed there was no sign of any work on Laurel's desk. "Is there anything I can do for you?"

On impulse, Laurel answered, "Well, maybe so. I know your hours are shifted earlier than anyone else's, but what time is it that you leave?"

"3:00."

"Do you think you could come to see me for a few minutes at 2:30?" Laurel saw Gus's face take on a concerned look. "I want your advice on something," she added.

The concern turned to puzzlement. "Yes, ma'am. Of course."

"Good! Thanks, Gus. I'll see you then."

Laurel wasn't sure what Gus could do for her, but she trusted him and Rosa. He wouldn't think it frivolous of her to be concerned over her security, and he just might have some answers for her. She would have several hours to think about it before he returned.

Feeling a lack of security and safety both at home and at work, Laurel felt even more vulnerable than she did when Mark first passed away. She spent a good part of the day learning more about the company's books and deposit system and billing. It seemed casual, and even somewhat disorganized, but she thought it might have been due to her lack of familiarity with it all.

Funds primarily came from the day's sales and payments by buyers who had in-store financing. The money that went out was far more complicated. There was the drinking water delivery, the company that provided clean carpet mats at the doorways, paper towels and soap for the restrooms, office supplies, travel expenses for buying stock or going to business association meetings, snow removal, landscaping and lawn care, IRS employer contributions, estimated annual tax installment payments, and so much more. Could there be a false expense hidden in that endless list?

Laurel was appreciating Megan even more. As much as Laurel wanted to solve the mystery on her own, she admitted to herself that she might have to check with Megan at some point concerning how she felt about the ethical standards of the financial people in the office. It would be an ideal point for funds to be siphoned off. But the small size of the repeatedly missing money had her stumped.

Gus returned promptly at 2:30. She was ready for him. "Please, have a seat. I remembered when I asked you to set up things for my first meeting, you had asked Rosa to help you. Did that mean she isn't working?"

Still unsure of what was happening, Gus explained, "She used to work, but the family she worked for had some money problems, and they had to let her go. She's been picking up shorter jobs here and there."

"Do you think she might be up for working part-time again?"

"Oh, yes! But we're getting older, and she can't do all the things she used to."

Laurel noted Gus had asked no questions, but only gave information. "I think she could handle what I have in mind. Let me explain my situation. Ever since Mark passed away, I have been alone in the house. It wasn't easy for me, but I did all right until a few days ago when I heard that a house, just three doors down from mine, was broken into. I had a security system put in, but I know wires can be cut.

"Besides that, I'm spending more and more time at work and less and less time with housekeeping. I thought if Rosa could do a little light housekeeping for me while I'm at work, she would be there to keep an eye on the house at the same time.

"I still need to think about what to do about feeling more secure at night. If you have any ideas about that, I'd love to hear about them."

Gus was looking much more relaxed now. "I am pretty sure Rosa would agree to that, but I'll talk to her about it tonight. Do you want me to tell her to call you or come in tomorrow?"

"Why doesn't she come in so we can talk in person? If she can, of course. Any time will do. I'll tell Megan to watch for her. If she can't come tomorrow, you can let me know."

"Okay. And maybe I can help with the other thing, too. It's not good to trust people or electricity to keep you safe. I know about a man—a good man—who trains guard dogs. Rosa knows him too. He's the son of a friend of hers. A dog is reliable. You can count on a dog. Not like a person. And it will start barking before anyone comes near. That scares bad people away. But talk to Rosa about him. She knows more than I do."

Laurel was nervous around big dogs. The idea of a trained guard dog sounded even scarier. But it was better than having someone break into the house. Someone who might be armed and do who-knows-what to her. She would talk to Rosa.

Rosa called the office before she came in to ask about coming at 2:00 PM. Laurel was informed and agreed. Laurel liked that. Rosa understood personal boundaries and proprieties.

Rosa arrived on time and was shown into Laurel's office. Laurel had arranged the upholstered chairs so that she could sit with Rosa. "I'm sure your husband filled you in on our conversation."

"He told me you need someone at your house during the day, and you would want me to do some housekeeping while I'm there."

"Yes. That must sound a bit odd, my asking you to just be there first, and then the housekeeping second. There is plenty for you to do there, but nothing out of the ordinary. Since I'm alone, it wouldn't be like keeping house for a whole family. Could you do the laundry as well as cleaning? The laundry room is off the kitchen, not in the basement, so there would be no stairs to climb."

"Of course!"

"How about watering the garden? Would that be something you've done before?"

"When the kids were young, we used to grow many of our own vegetables. I miss a garden now that it's just the two of us and we're in an apartment. I'd like that."

"I suppose we could work out the details of other tasks as we go along. If we agree on salary, are there questions you have before you decide?"

"Well, yes. You want me there because there have been problems for your neighbors. And everyone knows your house is empty, so I'm a little afraid to be there too. But Gus said he talked to you about a dog. I would feel very safe there with a dog."

"You know about getting a guard dog? Gus said you knew someone."

"I do. A good man with good dogs. Very well trained. No one would dare come in with one of those dogs."

"Well, honestly, I find the idea of a big guard dog that's trained to attack people almost as frightening as a stranger breaking into the house."

"No, no. They are dogs you can trust. You know the police dogs? You know they go home with the policemen and live with their families? They're like that. Bad for strangers, but good for their people."

"I'm sure they are supposed to be, but..."

"I can take you to meet the man. He can explain how they are trained. And you can see for yourself. If you still don't like the idea, we can think of something else."

Laurel agreed to go with Rosa. The wild barking as they entered the property did nothing to allay her fears of them. Rosa boldly marched in and announced herself. The nice young woman behind the counter introduced herself as Blair and told Rosa and Laurel they were expected. Blair would show them in. When she rose to escort the two women, Laurel heard a soft, high-pitched whimpering. "Oh, Rex. Don't be silly. I'll be right back," she said.

Laurel looked over the counter and down to the floor, expecting some fluffy lap dog. A worried face looked up at her, but it belonged to a German shepherd that looked exactly like the one on the company's poster in their window.

"Was he a class dropout?" Laurel asked with a smile.

"Him? Not at all. He graduated top of his class. He's just very bonded to me and my family. He thinks he should be protecting us every second and gets nervous if I'm not within sight of him," she answered. "He's our baby. Our big ferocious baby. Zack's office is this way."

It was clear Rosa had talked to her friend, who then informed her son who ran the security dog business. His sales pitch was thorough and reassuring without being frightening.

Zack explained, "These dogs are from Europe—pure lines and no inbreeding like here in the States. And they come to us with some training. Since their first handlers spoke German or Dutch to them, we keep several of those commands, paired with hand signals.

"We won't sell them without training for the new owner. We also hold reinforcement classes regularly so that the dogs will still react properly to situations that they might not have experienced in their new homes. For example, we hope you won't have any break-ins, but if you do, the dog will have had supplemental training often enough to react appropriately. You can literally bet your life on it.

"I can guarantee complete satisfaction with any of our animals as long as you are also trained and you keep the dog coming to refresher sessions."

Laurel still had doubts but was interested. Then she heard their "usual" price. It was thousands of dollars more than she had any idea of paying.

"I don't doubt the dogs are worth it—especially if they ever need to spring into action. But it *is* expensive!"

Rosa, invested in her own safety, and trusting dogs, bluntly asked, "Aren't any on sale? Mrs. Bradford's alone and needs protection. Can you give her some kind of discount?"

Laurel was no longer surprised by Rosa's constant point-blank view of how to handle situations. But she fully understood why these animals were so expensive. Laurel was ready to start thinking about another way to handle the potential dangers of being alone when Zack began talking.

"Well, I think I can do better than a discount. I might have the perfect dog for you. And she comes at a perfect price." Laurel noted the mention of the fact she was a female. Somehow, that alone made the idea of having her more tolerable. "Her name is Greta, and she was a brilliant student. Very smart dog. But she has a characteristic that prevents us from selling her. She will, of course, protect you with her own life if necessary. She will bark alerts, and if that doesn't work to scare someone off, she will attack and hold them with one of the strongest grips I've ever seen.

"So here's where the flaw comes in: She either never got the right idea or just refuses to actually try to tear anyone to pieces. No one gets away from her, but no one dies. I'm not saying she won't break an intruder's arm or leg from the sheer strength of her hold—and her teeth—but she will not go for the throat or shred them. So she's on sale."

"Can we see her?" Rosa blurted out enthusiastically before Laurel had a chance to think.

"Of course. I'll have Blair bring her in." Zack called to the receptionist, who quickly rose to fetch the dog.

"Won't Greta have a problem with Rex out there?" Laurel asked, trying not to show her nervousness.

"Not at all. There is no threat, so neither dog will respond without a specific command from me or Blair."

Laurel could already hear heavy breathing and rapid clicking on the floor in the hall. She glanced at Rosa, who only beamed with delighted anticipation.

The two came in, and Blair immediately said, "*Zit!*"

The dog planted herself so quickly, Blair hadn't even finished the word. Greta was large and emitted an intensity of spirit. She was nearly seventy-five pounds and almost two feet tall at the withers.

Zack asked, "Would you like to hear how she would sound if she heard a stranger approaching?'

"Yes, yes!" Rosa nearly yelled.

"Okay. You two ready? Greta, *blaffen.*" Greta emitted a loud, rumbling growl from deep in her throat. "That was step one. Now for the second command. Greta, *blaffen, blaffen*!" Rousing to a stand, the dog's loud and instantaneous response reverberated off the hard, solid walls of the room to a deafening and intimidating volume.

Blair saw the two women jump, wild-eyed. "Greta, *Af*!" Greta fell silent and planted herself on the floor.

When Greta panted, her open mouth and substantial teeth reminded Laurel of a bear trap she once saw hanging in an old barn. Zack said her genetic herding instinct was still intact. He brought her home at times, to keep her socialized, where she would round up all the kids in the yard.

"Rounded them up for her dinner?" Laurel tried to sound like it was a joke, but her concern could still be heard.

When Laurel spoke, Greta turned to her, glued her eyes there, and barely blinked. It didn't seem to Laurel to be a threatening stare. What was it?

Before Laurel could ask, Zack said, "Oh look. She thinks it's your turn to tell her what to do."

"But I literally don't speak her language. Why isn't the training in English? What were those words?"

"She came speaking Dutch. She was used to that, so we kept it to make the transfer as smooth as possible. It's not because a stranger might give her a command that will confuse her; she will only follow our commands, and yours. She knows the difference between 'friendlies' and suspicious strangers. I'll spell a word for you so she won't hear the command from me. Say her name first and tell her s-t-a-a-n."

Laurel looked Greta straight in the eye and tried to sound in charge. "Greta, *staan!*" Greta popped up like a cork in the ocean.

"So how much?" Rosa piped up.

Since she was not fit to be chosen by those wanting killer security dogs, the owner said he would not only give her up for half price, but also set her up at Laurel's with an outdoor pen and shelter. It sounded too good to be true to Laurel, but the owner knew if he couldn't get this woman to take Greta, he would probably have to pay to have her put down. All things considered, it would not be good advertising to deal with this dog in any other way than to make a customer satisfied.

Zack turned to Laurel. "Your relationship with her will be all about taking confident control. Begin with her name to get her attention, and then tell her h-i-e-r. It's pronounced just like the English word, h-e-r-e."

Laurel expected the dog to respond by coming and sitting. Greta, however, did exactly what she was told, and there was no added request for her to *zit*.

"Greta, *hier*!" Laurel bravely ordered.

In a brown, furry flash, Greta was in front of Laurel and still standing, resting her damp chin in Laurel's lap. Without thinking, Laurel locked eyes with her and stroked Greta's big head murmuring, "That's a good girl." It was a moment that had not gone unnoticed by Rosa's sharp eye.

Laurel was still hesitant about price until the owner said there would also be handler training for her and Greta, and she was under no obligation to buy until after she and Greta had this training time together. Laurel decided she would sign the contract on the condition that Rosa, if she agreed, would also be trained and would agree to regular "refresher" sessions. Rosa jumped at the chance.

~

Training went better than Laurel expected. As an added bonus, she and Rosa got to know each other on the neutral territory of the kennel grounds. Rosa usually deferred to Laurel, even though it was Rosa who took to bonding with Greta like a duck to water. Greta, in turn, would take Rosa's orders with full enthusiasm and bounding energy.

At first, Laurel was less sure of herself with Greta. Greta seemed sensitive to Laurel's feelings, never coming toward her too quickly or with too much force. Sometimes, growing impatient with the kindness of the trainer, Rosa would tell Laurel, "Tell her like you mean it!"

Laurel knew Rosa was right, and as Rosa would be muttering "Sorry, sorry, sorry," to her, Laurel would be thanking Rosa for keeping her on track.

When graduation day came, Rosa beamed as she took Greta through her paces. Then it was Laurel's turn. Laurel took Greta, noticing Rosa's flat expression. She briefly wondered at Rosa's apparent concern. Greta had, after all, just followed Rosa's every command to perfection. Step by step, Laurel and Greta performed each task flawlessly. At the end, Rosa never noticed she was the only one there clapping and yelling, "Bravo! Bravo!" Laurel looked back at Rosa, who was not watching Greta. Rosa was clapping for Laurel.

~

Laurel took advantage of Rosa's skills with Greta and assigned her the task of getting Greta acclimated to her new shelter with its own high fence enclosure that was positioned around the back door of the house. Greta was trained to patrol the yard, which had already been fenced in with shorter, more attractive landscaping fencing. Greta could clear it with little effort but knew her boundaries well. When the chores were done, Rosa tossed a ball over and over for Greta in the warming early summer air.

If Laurel knew just how much time Rosa "exercised" Greta, she wouldn't have done it again after dinner. But Rosa never mentioned it, and Greta seemed so anxious to run, fetch, and return yet another soggy, pulverized ball. Leashed together, Laurel began jogging around the neighborhood with Greta as well.

Rosa arrived at the house every morning just before Laurel left for work. Rosa had always called Laurel "Mrs. Bradford." It was a title that felt increasingly awkward for Laurel. Not knowing a better approach, she asked Rosa to call her by her first name. Rosa froze for a moment, and then replied, "Okay. Miss Laurel."

Not long afterward, Rosa stopped Laurel before she left for work one morning. Motioning at Laurel's large and bulging handbag, Rosa blurted out, "You can't go walking around the streets like that. Carry your cards and cash in a pocket or money belt. Your phone, too, if it will fit. Use a purse only for things that can be stolen from you. A little cash for the day, your tissues." And, as she turned to begin her work day, "Nothing too important."

Laurel took Rosa's advice to heart. The following weekend, while shopping for a new carry-on sized bag, she saw the display of the usual travel items next to the luggage. There were two different money belts and a pocket that anchored between bra straps and tucked into the center cleavage. Thinking she wouldn't have much room there for such a gadget, she tossed one of the money belts in with her other purchases.

A week later, Laurel had a business event to attend in downtown Boston. Thinking it a good opportunity to try out the money belt, she took it out of the packaging for the first time. The elastic band that went around her waist was easily adjusted for length. The zippered pocket was lightly padded on the back with a soft fabric covering. An additional smaller zippered compartment on the front was the perfect size for credit cards and a driver's license. It was surprisingly comfortable and undetectable when tucked down inside the front of her slacks. Laurel noticed the adjustment buckle and zippers were plastic—no problem in places with metal detectors.

Laurel left early in the morning for the convention. She enjoyed driving and had no desire to spend the night in Boston before coming back home. The meetings went well, and she took the opportunity to network with others in the fields of interior decorating and furniture. She decided to stay and accept their invitation to have an early dinner at the hotel with them before driving home.

The day had been a positive one. She had a handful of business cards to go through and organize with notes tomorrow. Car keys in hand, she started out the door, mentally planning alternative driving routes in case the traffic was snarled on her way home. Out of nowhere, she felt a sharp, hard jerk. Her purse was gone. She quickly looked in every direction, expecting to see someone running so that she could at least give a description to the police. Everyone was walking at a normal pace. Panic began to set in. Then she relaxed. She pulled her phone from her pocket and called Rosa.

"Rosa, I'll be later than I expected. I'm going to have to make a police report. No! I'm fine, thanks to you. My purse was snatched, and all I lost was a bunch of junk, a little notebook, and my favorite traveling bag…you're the one who told me to keep everything important in my pockets or money belt. No, I haven't even called them yet. It happened just a minute ago. Yes, it would be great if you could stay until I got home. I would rather not walk into an empty house tonight. Why don't you call Gus and invite him for dinner. Look in the freezer and fridge. Have whatever you want. No, I really mean *whatever.* Don't be shy. I owe you for this. It could have been so much worse. Okay. Thank you…I'll call you when I'm about an hour from home. Oh! And could you feed Greta her dinner, too? Thanks. Bye."

When Laurel arrived that night, both Rosa and Gus were running into the garage before the door was fully up. She was exhausted but still operating on adrenaline. She was touched by their concern for her and their offer to stay the night. Laurel did feel less and less safe, even with Greta right outside. Even so, she declined their offer but added, "Maybe when I have to go away for an overnight trip, the two of you could stay in the...the little attached apartment. It's not big, but I think you'd find it adequate." She could not use the term "mother-in-law apartment." It was never that. It never would be.

Gus and Rosa readily agreed. Rosa added, "Like everywhere else, our neighborhood is changing too. It's not as safe anymore. Gus and I have even talked about moving. I would like to be here with Greta. I would like that very much. Any time you want. You too, Gus?"

Gus agreed wholeheartedly.

"I have to tell you, I've never touched that apartment. I thought I'd wait to see what we needed it for and then decorate it accordingly. So there's nothing but white walls there right now. How about this: I have two extra rooms in the main part of the house, so I don't see anyone using that apartment but you two. What if I give you a credit card and a list of price ranges for paint, furniture, bedding, kitchen things, and whatever else it needs? Since I don't know when you'll be staying here, I suppose we should get on this as soon as possible. Rosa, if you'll pick out paint colors, I'll pay Gus overtime to paint it."

Gus looked lovingly at Rosa. "Do I have to go with the colors *she* picks out?"

Rosa grinned back at Gus.

"I think I'll let you two work on that!" Laurel answered.

"Okay. We'll start this week," said Rosa.

~

Laurel drove to work musing at the ups and downs of life's changes. Just eleven months ago, she felt completely alone and lost. Now she had Greta, Rosa, and Gus there to help her. She had a new career with Megan to support her at work. Even the sugar maples in the back yard were showing off vibrantly happy hints of reds and oranges on the tips of their branches.

Soon it would be the first anniversary of Mark's death. She promised herself she would ask Rachel and Megan to go out to dinner with her. Not to start mourning all over again, but to thank them and to celebrate her own progress since that day.

She had gotten her morning cup of coffee ready and sat down at her desk when Megan tapped on her open door, an unusual gesture at this stage of their working relationship. It was an alert…but to what, Laurel had no idea.

"Can I talk to you for a few minutes? Or is this a bad time?"

"What's wrong?"

"Well, I hope nothing, but there are some changes we'll need to address."

"Grab a cup of coffee and have a seat."

"Thanks, but I'm off coffee for a while. I've switched to herbal teas. But anyway, Rachel and I have some news that's going to impact my work schedule."

Laurel asked, "Do you need to go part-time? Whatever it is, I'm sure we can figure something out."

"Well, no. I'll be needing a leave of absence—for a few months, but not right away. I'm pregnant."

"Oh my gosh! That's wonderful news! Rachel must be thrilled! When are you due?"

"Not until the end of May. I know it seems like a long time away, but there's a lot to be done before then! And between being so tired and the morning sickness, I'll need some time off right away. Or just be able to come in later."

"Of course you can. How exciting! Decorating the baby's room? I know where you can get some great furniture."

They were both giggling like school girls, but Megan changed the mood. "Laurel, I'm going to be out of the office for some time, and you're going to need a replacement."

"Yes, but I can't think of anyone I can take out of their present position. We are already giving the employees enough responsibility. Can you think of anyone? And while you're at it, sometimes I feel like I could use a bodyguard! This parking lot is dark when I'm here late. I know it might sound like paranoia, but I still ruminate about being robbed right on a busy street in the city…and I can't forget the neighbor's break-in either. But I'm getting off track!"

"Actually, Rachel and I have already talked about that. Rachel knows a man that she has often hired to be a security escort. He knows the business world as well. Hopefully, I'll be here for a few months, so I could train him to be a sort of replacement, consultant, and security person. We would never recommend him if we didn't have past experience with his work and have complete confidence in him."

"He sounds intriguing, but how is it that he's available just when we need him? What does he do for a living?"

"He's a professional escort. But..."

"Wait a minute! You mean an escort like a *gigolo*?!"

"Well, yes, but hear me out."

"You want me to trust a gigolo with both my company and my life?! And what else? Get a little sex as a bonus?! What are the two of you thinking?!" Laurel was crushed at the thought.

"It's not like that! *He*'s not like that! Rachel goes to all sorts of places here and abroad. She's alone and, well, attractive. She hires him to take care of the trip planning, reservations, and then as a sort of a subtle bodyguard. She doesn't use him for sex!"

"No. I apologize. I didn't mean to imply that, but how can he be an escort if that isn't part of the job?"

"Well, sometimes it is, with some women. But sometimes it isn't. Look. Before I mess this up any more, promise you'll talk to Rachel about him."

"I fail to see what difference that would make."

"Fine. Then if it won't make any difference, you have nothing to lose by talking to her. Right? Think about it. Where are you ever going to find someone who can come in here and help with the business? Even if you do, that still leaves you without anyone to make you feel safer and more secure on the streets.

"I'll bring Rachel by after dinner tonight. You can be pissed at her instead of me then."

~

Rachel could see Laurel was in no mood for light chitchat and got right to the point. "So Megan tells me you are dead set against hiring this man I use."

"The gigolo? No, I don't want to hire him."

"So tell me why. Are you morally or ethically against that part of his career?"

"You make it sound so...what—normal? I don't need those services. I don't *want* them."

"Of course not. But do you object to him on moral grounds?"

"Well, I don't think I could honestly say I do. What consenting adults do in the privacy of their own space is very much their own business."

"Okay. So you don't hold that part of his service—that he offers to *other* women—against him. So put that completely aside. You wouldn't be hiring him for that, and he wouldn't expect it. It's really a small part of who he is. Megan and I can tell you from personal experience that he would never make an unwanted pass at you. So let's just look at the rest.

"You know I travel alone all the time. I've hired him as a multi-tasking assistant many times. I tell him where I want to be and when. He goes to work setting up the flight itinerary and all my accommodations, ground transportation, and visas. He comes with me and offers excellent suggestions for choice of my jewelry and takes care of the import-export details."

"But I don't need any of that."

"Maybe not, but it does give you an indication of what his capabilities are. Besides, you *do* take business trips. And he's an excellent bodyguard. He's well-trained but looks like nothing more than an attractive companion. He even carries packages and will, if pressed, cook a dinner or two for you.

"He also knows his boundaries, in part because he needs his clients to have boundaries, too. He understands confidentiality on a personal level."

"Sounds like you've known him for some time."

"I have. *We* have."

"So when you travel, how does he protect you in hotels? Does he stay in the same room with you?"

"Oh my god, no. He takes an adjoining room. The door is unlocked, but he never walks in without knocking and waiting for a reply—unless he hears me yell, or there's something else that doesn't seem right. When I've been in places I'm really not sure of, I've left the door ajar so he can hear every sound. But he always respects my privacy.

"Think about this," Rachel went on. "Where are you going to find a bodyguard that can actually function as someone in your furniture business, too? You know Megan can train him for that. And even if you did find someone for the business, where are you going to find one more highly recommended? He's not the cheapest person to hire, but it would be a lot cheaper to hire him than to hire two or maybe even three people to fill all the roles. And then you still wouldn't be completely sure of any of them."

"Are you sure he would understand the limits of his duties and the need to keep his other services under wraps?"

"We can guarantee it. I had to talk to him about his availability, but I didn't tell him who the potential client would be. He understands perfectly.

"How about this? We'll set up a meeting with him—an interview. You have nothing to lose. Absolutely nothing."

"It sounds harmless enough. Especially since there is no agreement to hire him. I have to admit, I am curious."

Rachel was satisfied. "Great. You won't be sorry. But there are some things you have to keep in mind. He must guard his privacy, too. His business depends on reputation and anonymity. So no personal questions, and no questions about specific past clients. He will tell you everything you need to know. And what he does tell you will always be truthful. He's honest but he can also carry off a cover story flawlessly. And don't forget, he would only be there until Megan comes back to work."

Laurel was still not completely sold on this solution. "Okay. But, I swear, if he shows up looking flashy and slick, this interview will end before it starts."

"You mean looking like a common street pimp?!" Rachel laughed as she hugged Laurel.

"Wait! Do you know he'll be available for that long a time?" Laurel asked.

"I do. I checked with him."

"We're talking about a period of months! Does that mean nobody else wants him?"

Unable to stay quiet at that question, Megan was quick to answer. "No. He prefers the steady longer commitments. He just won't schedule anything else for the time he works for you. But even then, he will need certain times off. Even *I* get weekends!"

Sighing in resignation, Laurel asked, "When will you bring him here?"

"Oh, no! He won't be coming here! Remember, this is job interview. Besides, you never want to bring a stranger, male or female, to your home until you are completely sure of them. Let's pick a safe public place so you can see how he handles himself in public too," Megan interjected.

"How about The Chef's for dinner?"

"That might sound more like a date than an interview," laughed Rachel, trying to keep the mood light. "Where could you go just to talk business with someone?"

"I don't know. A nice coffee shop with a quiet corner?"

"Perfect! How about that one near the library? It won't be crowded unless it's lunch time. Megan and I will be there to ask questions you might not think of. We'll tell him to meet us there on Thursday at 9:30, but we can meet there at 9:15 just to be ready."

Laurel was far from convinced this would work, but there was still an opportunity to call it off when she met this shady character. As Rachel said, what did she have to lose?

~

Over the next few days, Laurel tried to keep track of questions that came to her, writing them in the small notebook that she kept in her purse. There weren't many; she didn't know enough about escorts and bodyguards to know what to ask. She had an easier time when she stayed with purely work-related questions as if it would be a "normal" job interview.

As the day approached, Laurel became a bit more anxious but still confident knowing she could stop the process before it began. She did admit she still needed to feel more secure and protected and did need a temporary replacement for Megan. But finding someone who could do all of that at once—and have a compatible personality—seemed very unlikely.

On Thursday morning, Laurel couldn't decide what to wear. Shaking it off, she fortified herself in a nondescript cream colored blouse with a Mandarin collar and long sleeves. She grabbed whatever slacks would work, slipped into a pair of plain, closed-toe pumps with a sensible two-inch heel, and left to meet Rachel and Megan.

"It's quite simple," Megan began. "I listed the roles we need him to fill and some of the skills he needs to fill those roles. He has to learn the basics of the business, but you'll be a backup with that. He'll have to be a social escort at functions, and he has to provide security for you. That might sound like an impossible combination, but, if you think about it, it's what many people do who work for embassies or for heads of state or even major business magnates. I think you'll find this one can do it. And I think you'll find his personality acceptable as well. It wouldn't matter how well he could do the job if he couldn't get along with you."

Laurel let herself become lost in the conversation and, concentrating on the preparation, failed to watch the time. She startled when a man greeted the other two women, his arms open wide and smiling as he hugged each one of them. He then turned to her and said, "You must be Laurel Bradford. "

"Yes!" she said, stammering only slightly. Laurel saw he had not extended his hand, but not before she was already thrusting hers awkwardly forward. He responded easily. It was a firm but not overpowering grasp.

Megan introduced him as Dak Gordon and began the "polite conversation" phase while Laurel tried to take an objective look at him. He was only a couple of inches taller than she was and didn't look very imposing—not at all what she imagined a trained bodyguard to look like. It was hard to imagine him being threatening; his features were fine enough to have an undertone of femininity.

His clothes were well-chosen for such an interview. He was dressed as one might expect for a first meeting at a coffee shop, but one notch up. His soft, woven tan shirt was fashionably loose. The top three buttons were left undone, and the sleeves were rolled up to just below the elbow. It would have been a bit too casual if it had not been what appeared to be silk. The material clung just enough to reveal a muscled body. The slacks were a deeper brown with a slightly nubby weave. Laurel noticed the colors reflected his skin tones. He wore no jewelry whatsoever—not even a metal buckle on the smooth dark belt that perfectly matched his shoes. Conservative choices. This was not the sleazy gigolo that Laurel expected.

She examined his face. He had a somewhat Asian look but could have been anything from Native American to Peruvian to Middle Eastern. Perhaps a mix. He had attentive, dark, oval eyes and black hair. The soft curls were accented by strands of gray. The style was longer than Mark used to wear. Still, it looked as though it had recently been trimmed. His bare forearms were a smooth milk chocolate and nearly hairless. He was nothing short of attractive. Lovely, even.

The gray hairs made it no easier for Laurel to estimate his age, but she guessed he must have been in his mid to late 30's. This "Dak" was no twenty-something boy-toy; he was a mature man.

Laurel began noticing other details while Megan and Rachel held him in conversation about a recent trip to the Florida Keys. His nails were trimmed short but not straight across, the way most men awkwardly wield a set of clippers. The corners were rounded. And there was no scent from him whatsoever—no aftershave, not even soap. He exuded pure cleanliness.

"Of course we'd like to ask you a few questions, but only those that pertain directly to the job. If they are too personal, feel free to say so," Megan said, giving Laurel her cue.

Laurel had more or less rehearsed for this interview with Megan and Rachel. She felt prepared to find out what she needed without prying into the spaces considered confidential. "I'm sure you already know that I have become concerned about my personal safety. Do you feel you would be able to offer effective protection?"

Dak did reveal he had worked as a bodyguard before and was proficient in martial arts. "Since I can't ask for references from past employers, I would be willing to have you come to a local martial arts dojo for a demonstration of my training."

"I don't think so, but it does sound interesting," Laurel mused. She went on to talk about the needs and expectations of the position and allowed Dak to make replies of his choice.

He was assessing her with equal concentration. He was impressed by her ability to get the information she needed without questioning him too directly. She was organized, and the questions showed intelligent planning.

Laurel was intrigued by with the way he was able to give her all the work related particulars about himself that she needed without exposing any way of tracking down where he lived, where he was from, or any other facts that would leave him vulnerable. This ability could serve them both well when he needed to face questions from those at work and at work-related activities.

She wondered if she sounded like she accepted all this craziness.

"So," said Laurel, slipping badly in her newly-learned method of communicating, "how long have you been working as an escort?"

Before Dak could form a smile, both Rachel and Megan jumped on her. "Laurel! You know you can't ask personal questions!"

"But I asked about his work!"

"No. You asked about *him*. If you want to ask about the business, ask about the *business*!"

Laurel looked a bit confused, but Dak wondered if this was not part of her interview to see how he would react. "I thought I was," Laurel mumbled.

"If you think it really matters for this position, ask how long escorts work before they retire or what is an average length of time they stay in business or even if all escorts get paid for sex. But don't ask about him personally."

Dak had been sitting silently, with the hint of a smile, watching the little drama unfold before adding, "I think if I gave you a specific time span, you would feel that your curiosity hadn't been satisfied. First, ask yourself what it is you really want to know. Then, ask me as though you were wanting to know about someone else."

He wasn't scolding or being coldly didactic. Laurel was soothed and calmed by his tone, his attitude—like a kind guiding hand. It was a response Dak took note of.

This was requiring a sort of convoluted introspection and conversational logistic that was completely unfamiliar to Laurel. Several minutes passed while the other three chatted before Laurel finally formulated her real question. "Do women ever mind that their escort has been, or may be, sleeping with a number of other women?"

"Excellent question," Dak replied. He understood, better than Laurel herself, that this question was a huge leap for her. It left her emotionally exposed and vulnerable while momentarily suspending her own belief in a moral system that had served her well her entire life.

Dak went on, keeping his reply focused only on the question at hand, much like a parent answering a child's question about sex and not wanting to give more information than the child is ready for. "By the time women get to the point of having sex with an escort, they know there is complete confidentially, and they know that it is not an emotional commitment to—or from—the escort. The women also know there is always an unwavering dedication to personal health and cleanliness. So they are confident being a client."

Client... thought Laurel. That was the buzz word in so many businesses now. People were no longer customers or patients. It was the politically correct term that was supposed to be free of unspoken prejudices.

Laurel said no more about Dak's escort services. That one question had been enough to set the progress of their relationship to a much slower pace. They both knew it.

"You already know my fee, thanks to Rachel's acting as a go-between for us. You need to know that my prices are fixed no matter what services you are hiring me for. It's an all-inclusive payment. I have found that works better because, invariably, my tasks and assignments change. For example, right now you primarily need an escort, a bodyguard, and someone to help fill in while Megan is out on maternity leave. But, as time goes by, you might find you want my services as a driver or to accompany you during business trips abroad, which I can also arrange. I can organize buying trips to places that are unfamiliar to you and take care of the required visas and reservations—whatever. It's all in the package deal."

Laurel thought *I bet you mean* whatever *I want. Well, fat chance of that.* But she only said, "Yes. I see."

In the split second she let her gaze drop, Dak and Rachel made eye contact.

"Let me ask you something," she continued. "Since you are paid according to time more than task, could you do more than general office work? Could you sit in on business meetings and give me your insights and observations if I asked you to?"

Dak readily agreed, saying, "I am quite familiar with international businesses."

"And are you computer literate?"

"I'm no high-level computer geek, but I am able to do more than the average office employee."

Neither Megan nor Rachel said a word but knew there had to be a point to Laurel's questions.

"I need some time to weigh my choices, but if I decide to hire you, when could you start?"

Without hesitation, Dak said, "I would not be available for two and a half weeks from now. And I would need certain amounts of time off during my work for you. But I would give you plenty of notice when that would be. I wouldn't be at your store 40 hours a week. I would come in identified as a temporary fill-in and consultant with a flexible schedule. But if there was a particular event or other reason for me to be there, I would be. I'm sorry if that sounds vague or loose, but I'm sure we could set guidelines that would be agreeable to both of us."

For Dak to have other obligations made him seem almost legitimate—more like a real person somehow. "Yes. We'd have to be clear about our expectations," Laurel responded.

Laurel observed carefully as Megan talked about the business aspects of being with Bradford Village Furniture. Dak countered with what supportive skills he had and what skills and knowledge he would need. He was most apprehensive about his lack of understanding when it came to the physical construction of furniture—the finer points of structural quality. Considering Dak was interviewing for a position in a furniture store, he sounded honest to a fault. As interviews went, it was rather strangely satisfying and unexpectedly reassuring at the same time. Laurel needed time to think about this.

She had done enough interviews when she worked at the bank. She knew how to tie this one up. "Well, you certainly have presented some intriguing possibilities for being able to handle this position. Hiring someone who has such tight limits as to what he can share about himself is something new to me. I would like to discuss some options with Megan—and Rachel—before making any final decisions. Could I call you in two or three days? Perhaps for a second interview?"

"Of course. That will give me time to think about the information I now have as well."

Dak made a courteous exit, and the three women watched as he disappeared into the crowd outside. It wasn't until he was well out of sight that Laurel relaxed. "So what's the real scoop here? Why is he available for such a long period of time? Is there something about him you haven't told me? I feel like there's more than meets the eye here."

Rachel's response was quick to the point of being an interruption. "Or is it that you've just never talked to anyone like him—anyone with his background—before?"

Megan was right on Rachel's heels. "Remember I told you he prefers long-term opportunities?"

"I have to admit, I can't come up with any major objections right this minute, but give me tonight to think about all this, and I'll talk to you tomorrow."

Laurel thought about nothing else that evening. She knew she had no idea how to interact with a gigolo/security person/ bodyguard/ consultant/whatever he was. She had enough trouble interacting with Rosa when she was newly hired as a housekeeper who, a bit flustered, had refused to eat lunch at the same table with Laurel.

She would have to depend entirely on Rachel's and Megan's word that he was a person of integrity with capabilities to do the job. But, then again, she trusted their judgment.

She would have to polish up the cover story to keep his true identity safe. Laurel would need his expert collaboration for that. Tomorrow she would tell Megan and Rachel that she would offer Dak a trial period—a probationary position. If all seemed to be going well after 30 days, she would officially hire him. Even then, she could always let him go.

Dak blended in as rapidly as a chameleon. Laurel began hearing some of the women speculating about him, but it wasn't until he had been there a few weeks that they spoke to her about him. "Is he married? Does he have a girlfriend?" they eagerly asked.

"No, I don't think so, but I haven't asked him, either."

"Of course not!" one lamented. "His clothes are too nice and he's too cute to be straight!"

"I never thought of that!" was all Laurel said. It was all she needed to say to end their interest in him. And if any of the male employees now became interested? Well, Dak could handle that himself.

~

Laurel and Dak had settled into routines that worked smoothly for both of them. Dak had proven himself competent and trustworthy. Laurel began to relax more with him. It was during the cocktail hour before a meeting of local business owners that a turning point came.

Laurel began cautiously, still clinging to the empty drink glass in her hand. "I haven't asked you anything about your work outside the furniture company. But I'm still curious about it all."

An equally cautious "Go ahead" was all he said, but he had expected her to broach the subject for some time.

It was too late to turn back now, so Laurel hesitantly ventured on. "Since escorts are usually paid by the hour, how much time, on an average, is used for foreplay?" She was remembering Mark's predictable routine in bed. She knew she had missed out on something, and she wanted to know what it was.

Dak knew this was no flirtation on Laurel's part. He took her lead and kept his answer pertinent to escorts and did not respond on his personal behalf. "It depends on the client's reasons for hiring an escort and what she wants. If she wants an escort at a social event and wants to keep sex in the back of her mind as a possibility, the escort will wait until she gives him an indication that sex could be an option. If the woman has hired an escort expressly for the purpose of sex, she is already in the mood, and little, if any, foreplay would be part of the contract."

Laurel's cautious propriety was showing a slight crack. "What if she is willing to consider it but doesn't want to decide right away? What about foreplay then?"

Dak was a skilled dancer being led by his partner. "First, the escort, knowing the sexual experience is still in question, would go ahead slowly, with every chance for the client to gracefully stop the process—or not stop it."

Laurel was more curious than ever but didn't know where to go from there. After a moment, she said, "I'm not sure I understand what you mean. Can you be more specific?"

Dak knew this would either be the beginning or the end of anything to do with sex. She would feel safe here in such a very public place. He was gentle and still maintained a neutral tone in his inflections. "Well, for example, it is Tuesday. If there was a possibility of a sexual experience on the coming weekend, foreplay would start here and now."

"Wait a minute—here and now?" she asked, almost chuckling.

A positive response! thought Dak. "This would be the ideal time and place. The forbidden public setting can add to the excitement. So can the furtiveness. You know the majority of people here, and they can see interactions with everyone else in the room. If I placed a hand on your shoulder while we were having a lively conversation, what do you think they would see the intention as?"

"Well," Laurel spoke slowly while thinking. "It would seem to me to be a gesture to emphasize your intention to get my full attention because you wanted to get a point across."

"Yes! Especially at a business event. Now take a quick look around you. Since we are at the side of the room, only your right side and my left side are visible to others. So, when I put my right hand on your left shoulder like this, and gesture some with my left hand, that is exactly what others see—an intense business conversation. But, while we are still talking, if I move nothing more than my thumb, only you will know."

With that, Dak slowly, and with only the pressure of a passing feather, moved his thumb from the hollow behind Laurel's ear to the valley above her collar bone. He paused only long enough for Laurel's attentive listening to turn into an all-consuming physical reaction that echoed far beyond her neck. He felt it begin under his unmoving palm. And when saw the flush in her cheeks, he knew it was traveling as an intense wave far beyond there.

Before she could think of any verbal response, he added, "If you have any question as to whether or not that is foreplay, I am going to do the same thing again, but this time I am going to move my thumb closer to the front of your neck."

With that short warning, Dak began again, but this time from under Laurel's chin with a hint of more pressure. He hadn't moved his finger down toward her larynx more than an inch or two before she instinctively pulled back in an inexplicable pang of anxiety.

"What happened?" she asked softly.

"There can be less than an inch of space between excitement and threat. The second time, your body knew the move could turn into a life-threatening choke before you knew it consciously. The best foreplay relies on automatic reactions rather than thought out responses too."

"I see..." she said. And much to her own surprise, she did see.

He wondered if he could prove this to her in the future. She wondered what else he knew.

Laurel tried her best to pay attention to the speakers at the meeting, but the sensation came back to her again and again—not her memory of it, but the memory in the cells, in the flesh of her neck.

After the meeting, Dak drove Laurel home. She was quiet in the dark car. Thinking. She couldn't deny her own feelings or her purely physical reaction. Her turning point. Conflicted, she wanted to know more. Maybe even feel more. She also knew she was in a bewildering eddy of disorientation. There would be no answer in the silent darkness.

Laurel's voice sounded small, even to herself. "How does the escort know when a client decides?"

"Just like the speakers judging their audience's reaction tonight, an escort must read emotional responses. But with an escort, he must know his client well enough to be able to read her personal subtleties and nuances, body language, voice inflections."

"It doesn't sound so different than doing an interview for a new hire," said Laurel.

Dak noted that Laurel was now walking that comfort line of hers from all business to sex discussed as business. Her past tugged at her ankles like a riptide below the water's surface. Dak—or was it her own self?—pulled at her like fish on a line. She was being reeled ever closer to the unknown.

~

Dak was busy at work that day. Every time Laurel saw him, he was talking to someone and carrying files and catalogs. *I wonder if this was the way Mark spent his day. No. He was more directive—worked more from his desk.*

It wasn't until just before closing that Dak, papers in hand, poked his head into Laurel's office. "Mind if I stop by a bit after dinner tonight?"

She assumed it had something to do with what had kept him so preoccupied all day and said, "How about around 7:30?" Before she could explain that he might hear a dog barking, he was gone.

Laurel made sure her tea choices were handy and the pot was ready. She heard Greta outside at full alert before the bell rang. *Good dog!* she thought as she answered the door.

"That's quite the alarm system you have," Dak smiled, unbothered by the aggressive sounds of barking and snarling.

"Yes, she's the guard here at the house. She patrols the grounds and alerts me to intruders. And sometimes squirrels!"

"Does she come inside?"

"Mostly when Rosa is here during the day, or when I'm off somewhere for business."

"Could I meet her?"

"If you're not afraid of her." Laurel walked to the back door and let her in. Greta was trained to be protective, but in her mind, she was also part of her owner's pack. If Laurel was relaxed, so was she. "Come on Greta, we have some business to discuss."

Dak pulled catalogs out of his bag as the three of them went back into the living room. Greta sat dutifully between Dak and Laurel.

After giving Greta time to watch him, Dak beckoned Greta while he continued his conversation with Laurel. Greta stared at him without any aggression but stayed glued to the floor. Laurel noticed, and, motioning with a hand, said, "Go ahead Greta. It's okay if you want to." Only then did Greta respond to Dak.

At first, Dak looked towards Greta without giving her direct eye contact. While slowly talking to her, he offered the back of his hand under her chin for her to sniff before softly stroking her shoulder. He looked into her eyes and stoked her head. When Dak stopped, Greta contentedly lay at his feet.

The catalog decisions didn't take long. Dak accepted Laurel's offer for a cup of tea before he left. "You have a lovely house. Did you do all the decorating yourself?"

It was something Laurel would have expected to hear from a woman, or someone in the field of home decor. It never occurred to her that he might have come specifically to see the house. "Thanks. But now it all seems too...well, 'perfect.' It feels sad and dead. Lifeless. I tried putting Mark's urn of ashes away into his—what *was* his—closet, but it didn't help."

"When we arrange our surroundings, it reflects who we are. But it goes two ways. When the house is better, you'll feel better. I think you're right; everything in the house is a bit lifeless. The plants and greenery are artificial, there is no bird bath or bird feeder, no fountain, no pond outside the window to bring healing sounds. But that can be changed. And there's no one here but you; you'll have to start letting others in." Dak added silently to himself, *Yes, it is dead and silent. And you'll need to get out of here before you can become alive.* He had been brutally frank with her, but he had kept his tone academic. It was a calculated risk.

Laurel took it well. "I think you might be right."

Dak gathered his things to leave. He stopped, turned to Laurel, and said, "If Greta is outside, she can't protect you. You have a security system outside to keep the property safe. Greta can keep *you* safe only if she is inside with you—and only if she bonds with you completely. I'll see you at work tomorrow, but I won't be there until the afternoon." He only gave her facts and never directly told her what to do. The choice was completely hers; he was leading the dance without stepping on her toes.

It made perfect sense. Laurel closed the door, locked it, and set the alarms. She turned and looked at Greta, who sat up and slowly swept her tail across the floor, awaiting a command. "Okay, girl. One last sweep outside, and then it's inside with me for the night. We'll see how that goes."

Greta went out while Laurel stood in the doorway watching her. It must have meant something to Greta, because she finished her obligations outside and returned directly to Laurel, sitting without a command. "How about a snack?" Laurel said to Greta, who then followed Laurel into the kitchen.

Laurel spent the next hour or two snacking, getting her clothes laid out for the morning, and preparing for bed. She climbed in, fully expecting her usual nightly routine of tossing and turning, unable to relax enough to sleep until she was completely exhausted. But not tonight.

Ever since Dak had left, Laurel had been talking on and off to Greta. Maybe it was because Greta listened so intently, giving Laurel complete eye contact. As Laurel pulled up the covers, she told Greta, pointing to the rug, "Well, girl, you might as well sleep here on the floor where you can do your job and protect me!" Within ten minutes, Laurel had fallen into a comforting sleep.

In the morning, Rosa arrived as usual. On her way out, Laurel promised Greta she would come home with a proper dog bed. Rosa took note but said nothing. Greta happily went out for the day, and Laurel went to work, feeling more able to face the day than she had since she first went to the office after Mark's death. *Amazing what sleep can do,* she thought.

During the morning, she left work, telling the staff she could be reached by cell phone. The pet store was only three blocks away. Laurel's parents had a small dog when she was in grade school, so she knew this errand would be quick and easy.

Or so she thought.

For a split second, Laurel thought she had walked into the wrong store. Just inside the entrance, there were frilly little dresses, leather biker jackets, and small, colorful boots. Toys of all sorts filled every aisle. It wasn't until she saw the large artificial plant with an opening in the side of the pot that was labeled "Elegant cat litter box hideaway" that she was sure this wasn't a children's store.

She found the dog beds, but, remembering the ragged old quilt folded on the floor in her childhood home, they, too, were nothing she was familiar with. There were heated beds, beds that looked like smaller versions of beds for people, beds with orthopedic mattresses for senior dogs, pink and fuzzy beds, and beds covered in weather-resistant camouflage print.

A clerk offered to help, asking what size bed she needed and what kind she had in mind. By the time Laurel left, she had a large, thick bed with a sensible cover and three padded sides. She juggled that to the car along with the other bags of healthy treats, bowls, mats to put the bowls on, a ball, and a tug-toy—to keep Greta exercised and fit, she told herself, forgetting Greta could "tug" her arm off with little effort if she felt so inclined.

~

At work, Laurel began thinking of Dak as just another employee. At home, she remembered the night at the business meeting. His touch on her neck. He had come to the house and they had shared something. *No. We didn't. He brought something to me, and I was the audience. Or was it bait? Or did I want it to be?*

Consciously or not, Laurel would test Dak; test his integrity, his motives. She was about to open the company's books to him. And then she would watch him very carefully. She caught him as he walked in, and she directed him to her office. She closed the door.

"Remember when I asked you about sitting in on meetings and giving me your insight? I also asked you about computer skills?"

"Yes. I wondered what you had in mind."

"Well, here's the thing," Laurel began. "Before you came, and I was still learning about the company, I thought I discovered some money missing. It was a very small amount, but it would happen every month. Even over the course of an entire year, it wouldn't be a huge amount, but it nagged at me. It still does. I've gone over the books and the processes time and time again, but I can't figure out what's happening to it. If I give you all the stats and figures I have, do you think you could give it a crack?"

"Sure. But what about your employees? Do you suspect anyone?"

"The short answer is no. First of all, the amounts are too small to risk losing your job and being arrested for. Besides that, I've gotten background checks on everyone, and I've known most of these people for years.

"But this would be when you have the time and when you can poke into it without raising suspicion."

"I understand," said Dak. "Give me access to the files you have, and I'll be on it."

~

Over the following days, Laurel almost began to reach a level of ease. There was not the slightest hint that Dak was mishandling his new access to the company's financial information. She had three short business trips coming up, but Dak would be there with her while Rosa and Gus could stay at the house. Between them and Greta, all would be well there.

Rosa and Gus were nearly done with the painting in the kitchen, bathroom, and living room of the little apartment. Laurel's mind wandered. She hadn't interfered with any of the color choices, even though they were much brighter than anything in the main house. She looked around her. The office colors were classic but dull. She had never noticed before.

Then it struck her. These out of town trips weren't going to stop. How could she ask Gus and Rosa to move in and out every time the wind changed? She trusted them, so what was the problem? She would ask if they could just move in. After all, hadn't Rosa expressed her concern about safety in their present place? They would both be there when she got home tonight.

The door was open, but Laurel heard a soft knock. It was Matzak Lazarian. Mat was younger than some who worked for Bradford's, but he had done well there. He presented himself as a professional salesman and was never pushy with the prospective customers. He had an excellent sales record and reputation, but here he was hesitant and soft-spoken.

"Come in, Mat! What can I do for you? Have a seat!"

Getting right to the point, he said, "I wanted to run something by you that might be a thought for the program about ideas that might save the company money and things like that."

"Great! Do you have an idea for something new?" Laurel jumped in, wondering why he hadn't just slipped a note in the suggestion box.

"Not exactly," Mat answered. "I don't even know if this is something that would fit into that or not."

"Well, let's talk about it and see."

"It's the order from the Grayson company. The store has been using them for a long time, and they've been good in the past. But it's this last shipment that came in."

Laurel didn't see the point yet. "Yes?"

"The quality of the workmanship isn't the same. Where they used to put four screws, now there's only three. The furniture used to be all oak, but now they are using white pine in places that don't show. That makes it weaker. There are some other things, too. But the point is, I just thought, if we keep selling this, when it doesn't hold up, we'll have to replace it. Even if we do, we'd still probably lose customers.

"It's not an idea to help make or even save money, but in some ways, I think we would be taking a loss." Mat held his breath for the second following, when Laurel was as still as stone.

"This *is* a surprise. In more ways than one. First, you were very right to come to me with this. And I completely agree with you. We should not—no, *can*not—possibly go ahead with this furniture. I'll get Megan to make arrangements to have it returned.

"This does leave us with a hole in our inventory. And not just for now, but for the future as well. I'll have to think about how we can fix that..." She drifted off into thought.

Mat sat waiting for something. Anything. Was she finished with him? Should he get up and excuse himself?

Laurel suddenly came back. “Mat, may I ask how you found this problem? How you knew what to look for, and why you looked in the first place?” Her tone was not accusatory but one of astonished curiosity.

More relaxed, Mat almost laughed. “Force of habit. I have an uncle that has a furniture workshop in Pakistan. From the time I was about eight, I spent summers working with him there. I called it ‘work’ but everyone else in the family called it ‘character building.’ ‘Matzak!’ my mother would say, shaking her finger at me, ‘You pay attention to your Uncle Ari. He’s a good man. And a clever one, too.’

“Anyway, one of the jobs I was given was to walk with my uncle and take notes while he did his inspections of the pieces—and checked my spelling! He would talk out loud the whole time. I learned a lot. About a lot of things, and I don’t just mean furniture making.”

“Let me get you some coffee. I want to hear more,” Laurel cheerfully said as she walked across the room to her coffee maker.

“Thanks. Just black is fine,” Mat answered.

Laurel brought back two cups and placed them on her desk. “But your family isn’t from Pakistan, is it?” She hoped she sounded interested rather than prying.

“No. We’re Armenians. People without a country. At least that’s true of my family. Armenians went through a diaspora, like so many others. My grandparents on my father’s side ended up in Pakistan.

“They were artisans who made an okay living. When Uncle Ari was old enough to start saving his own money, his parents encouraged him to be creative in other ways. They said he should figure out how to make a business of his own…but always with the welfare of others in mind.

“My uncle saw all classes of society there. Some were wealthy customers, and some were much worse off than he was. He took some savings and hired some of the poorer local men. He bought wood, taught them to carve panels and build screens and cabinets. Some already knew carving, and they taught their co-workers. The business grew, and he became a respected furniture maker. My uncle has been able to help a lot of people while he made a thriving business. They had no children of their own, so my aunt sort of adopted all the employees—or at least that was what my uncle used to say to her when he would tease her.

"Back then we called it 'doing unto others,' but today it's called 'fair trade' and it's quite the thing!"

"Fair trade?" Laurel urged him on, not because she had never heard the term, but because she wanted to know how much Mat knew and how well he could explain it to someone else.

"Sure. That's when, usually...well, let me tell you how it worked with Uncle Ari. He would sell directly to stores in other areas and even other countries. So his prices were lower than wholesalers since he cut out the middleman—and his profits were very good. Some of the profits went back to the workers and to improving their working conditions. He only used what is now called 'sustainable' raw materials and refused to use stains, paints, and chemicals that were poisonous or harmful to his workers or to the environment."

Laurel was listening to Mat with as much attention as she had listened to her bankers and had read her books on management. "You said you learned a lot from your uncle besides furniture making. What did you mean?"

This was something no one outside his family ever asked about before. He went on eagerly. "So much. I hardly know where to begin. For one thing, over the years, I watched the rapport build between my uncle and his workers. We are Christian, but the men who worked there were—and still are—Muslims. One of the first changes my uncle made in his business was to make sure the men had time for prayers when they worked.

"And that isn't a five minute break. The men walk to the mosque around the corner when the call to prayer is heard. Then they wash themselves before going in to pray. Prayers are never rushed, but they never linger longer than necessary, and Uncle Ari has complete trust in them not to take advantage of that time. Not every non-Muslim would encourage the religious practices of their workers.

"I learned patience, too; it took years for Uncle Ari to build the mutual trust he and his workers have. At first, if my uncle would ask about what needed to be improved or changed, they were quiet. But now, they make suggestions. He still tells them over and over that only they know the ins and outs of the job they do and he just keeps it running for them. And for himself, of course!

"But I don't know how much longer that will last. Even though he has a great relationship with his workers and their families, it isn't as safe as it was for Armenians there. Years ago, we had relatives who had to leave Iran, too. But that's another story, and I've already taken too much of your time—and mine!"

"Only for now!" Laurel shot at him as he went out the door. "I'll be picking your brain again in the future!"

Mat turned and smiled over his shoulder as he kept walking back to the showroom.

Laurel thought long and hard about what she had heard from Mat. She saw why the bright young man had applied for a job at a furniture company in the first place and why he had done so well.

The need for a new supplier was an immediate problem. Mat could certainly help find a new and better one. But there was something else here. She just wasn't sure what it was. She had already been building trust and taking ideas from her employees. She had already begun to feel she was running a solid business. So what was it? She needed a sounding board.

~

That evening, Laurel pulled into the garage and went to find Rosa and Gus in the attached apartment. She couldn't help but grin at the nearly florescent yellow in the kitchen. It was going to be a happy place.

"Hi! It looks so cheerful! Could I talk to you two a minute?"

Never one to be anything less than direct, Rosa asked, "Is everything okay?"

"Sure! I just had an idea I want to run by the two of you. We've already talked about your staying here while I'm gone, but I'm beginning to think it would be awful for you to keep moving in and out. What about just moving in permanently?"

Rosa and Gus looked at each other. There was surprise, but Laurel couldn't tell what other reaction they had. She knew this could be good for all three of them, so Laurel charged on. "I know this looks small, but it would come with the third garage space. And there's a storage space above this that you could have, too. There's nothing up there—I've never used it, it was too far out of the way to be useful to me. I don't think the previous owner ever went up there either. There's a pull-down set of stairs in the walk-in closet, but we could put a set of real stairs in somewhere so you could expand up to have a second floor."

Laurel realized she was rambling and had hardly taken a breath. Gus and Rosa had still not spoken. How could they? She hadn't given them a chance. Still unable to stop, she went on. "I'm sure you need time to think about it, and I know it isn't large, but it wouldn't cost you anything for rent. It would be payment to you for watching the property. And you could either buy new things or move your own furniture in—whatever you want. And you'll have privacy. This place is separated from the house, and you'll have your own entrance. I won't be able to hear, no matter how loud your TV is, either."

Laurel wound down and looked at Gus and Rosa intently. They looked at each other again. Rosa spoke in English. "I say yes."

Gus, looking back at Rosa as if Laurel wasn't even there said, "Okay. Yes"

"Great! I'm so relieved! We'll all feel more secure. I'm sure of it."

For now, Rosa had only one question. "While you're gone, is it okay if Greta stays with us? Inside at night?"

"I don't see why not, and I know Greta would love it"

~

The next day, Dak was not at work. He came in mid-morning the following day. "I want to tell you about a conversation I had," Laurel began. Dak sat patiently and listened. She told him how Mat had come in with the quality issue, how the stock would be low, and all about Uncle Ari's business. "There's something else there. A message that I haven't quite got ahold of. It keeps pecking at me."

"Maybe we can figure it out. Do you think it was something in the content of what he said or that it was just such new information that you were fascinated by?"

Laurel took her time and mulled over the possibilities. "No. It's something more complex, more complicated."

"What was his point of coming to you in the first place? Was it pride in sending out pieces that would last? Did he seem angry at the manufacturer?"

Laurel was quick with her first response. "Mat is never angry about anything. He grabs situations and problem-solves. Wait—he *did* begin the conversation by saying something about the incentive program here where compensation is given to those with ideas for making or saving the company money. They get rewards or bonuses in proportion to how much financial good it would be for the company."

"So he wanted a reward of some kind?" Dak suggested.

"That would seem to be the obvious reason, but he never asked about it. Besides, he went beyond the problem with that stock. It was a personal story. It has something to do with that. But I'm not saying he intended to go into it when he came to me. The family information was an outcome of questions I asked him." Laurel's brow was knitting even more.

"Then does it have something to do with *your* personal story?" Dak probed on.

Laurel's frustration was beginning to show. "My God. You sound like a shrink. If I knew, I wouldn't be asking you."

"You're right. I apologize. It's an old habit of mine. But I can't give you quick answers because I don't know what there is in your mind that responded to his story. Let's go back to the beginning and try again. What are you going to do with the problem of the poorly made furniture?"

Laurel shifted gears. "Well, as I said, I told Mat it will be returned. And now we have to find a way to replace it, both for now *and* in the future. We could order more from the other manufacturers that we already use, but that would cut down on variety. And sometimes I wonder if our growth rate is starting to slow down because we already lack styles that are new and different."

They both sat for a few seconds before Dak spoke first. "Let me ask you something. Considering the financial questions about missing funds that have come up lately, do you trust Mat? *Completely* trust him?"

"Absolutely."

"Do you think he learned enough from his uncle to be future management material?"

"I never thought about it before. I haven't been in the job long enough to think about promotions for anyone. But yes, I do. He has a great sales record, he is aware of important details, he has integrity, and he knows the business..." she trailed off. "Why? What are you thinking? You know we don't have an opening for a manager right now."

"I'll get to that in a minute. Let's get back to Mat's story about his uncle. What things impressed you the most about it?"

"The uncle was a survivor. He moved and rebuilt when he had to. And he gave back to his employees. He knew it would be good for the business, and besides, he genuinely cared for them, too. And he used environmentally sound choices for materials. Too bad the political climate there may chase him out."

Dak was more direct this time. "I think you hit on some very important points. We just need to connect the dots. You genuinely care for your employees, too. The uncle took that concern and turned it into a growing business. The idea of environmentally safe and sustainable goods is not only a hot commodity in all markets right now, it's one that will continue to be hot because it is necessary to our survival. You need a new supplier. Why not hop on the green movement? And while you're at it, this is a global topic, not just a local one. If you want new and innovative stock to pull in both new and old customers, think about choosing a manufacturer that is good for the environment, comes from an international source, and is a fair trade supplier too.

"Not only would that be a good choice for all the altruistic reasons, but there are the buyers to consider, too. People like to buy new things and spend money. Give them a cause, and you also give them a new reason to buy from you."

Laurel paused. "I have to think about this. It sounds too good to be true. And you know what they say about things that sound too good to be true. Anyway, where would I begin? It would also toss me into learning about a whole new economic world when I'm still learning the economics of the Bradford Village Furniture Company. I would have to do a lot of research to start with. Would I have to go overseas to shop for a new supplier? Mat could help with that, but would I send him and not go myself? How will I know what will appeal and what won't sell? Would Mat know? What other questions are there to ask myself? Right now, it seems SO overwhelming.

"On the other hand, do I have any other choices? I need a new supplier, and whomever that might be, it could mean a new level of booming sales or a dud that will bring a slow death."

Dak had listened—not only to her words, but to her thought process as well, how she approached new ideas. "It *is* a lot to think about! Why not let it go for a couple of days? Let it sit in the back of your mind. I'll be back day after tomorrow, and we can talk about it again then. What do you think?"

"Yes. Sounds perfect. Thanks for your input on this."

Before Laurel could say any more, Dak was standing to leave. *Where does he go, and what does he do?* she wondered. *Does he have another job? Does he have daily liaisons with clients? No; too many of his disappearances seem like they're on flexible schedules.* It was not the first time she indulged in this line of speculation . . . nor would it be the last.

Dak didn't want to seem like he was rushing out the door, but he didn't want to linger, either. As soon as he was clear of the building's line of sight, he checked his watch and took out his cell phone.

"Hi. It's Dak...sorry about the time. You always say that! I think I have a different sort of opportunity coming out of this position I have now...well, I'm not certain yet, but I know I can use it somehow to our advantage, given some time. I'll talk to you about it as I know more. Maybe you can offer some suggestions. How much I am going to be exposed is always a problem, but there is a good cover with this one...I'll tell you more then." He hung up without saying good-bye.

~

Laurel knew Dak's position with the company was, at first, part of the cover story, but she seriously began to think about his suggestion to get imported, fair trade furniture. Rachel said Dak was familiar with international business and all its tangles of regulations. *He must be able to travel—he travels with her.*

Laurel was glad to be at home. She kicked off her shoes at the door, promising herself to remember to pick them up on her way upstairs later. None of her usual brew tonight. She pulled down a wineglass. She picked a Sauvignon Blanc from South Africa but had chosen a glass for red wines. She filled it nearly half full and, glass in hand, padded to the back of the kitchen. She breathed in the air trapped in the glass and opened the door.

"Come on, Greta. Time for our evening chat. I need your advice."

Greta happily loped in, tail wagging in anticipation of tonight's discussion. As soon as her nose told her the usual coffee smell had been replaced with that other smell, she knew it would be a longer session this evening. Greta sat in anxious anticipation.

While Laurel made their evening meal, she began telling Greta about the conversation with Dak. By the time she had finished that account, Greta had finished her food and had decided to lie on the floor rather than sit at attention any longer, but she kept her gaze focused on Laurel.

Laurel wasn't anthropomorphizing Greta. She really did participate in this nightly ritual. "What do you think about that?" Laurel would ask. Greta would cock her head to one side, and Laurel would say, "You don't know either?"

At other times, Greta had other answers. Sometimes she would suddenly show an open-mouthed smile and put her forelegs straight out on the floor in front of her, leaving her rump high and wagging. "You think that's silly?" Laurel would interpret, clarifying her own thoughts in the process.

Greta was well-practiced at such volleys. She and Rosa "talked" for hours while Laurel was at work. Rosa's bond with Greta was different. Rosa babbled incessantly to Greta, usually in Spanish. Greta quickly learned that most of Rosa's verbiage was not something she needed to, or was expected to, respond to. Rosa used the training words and a tone of voice for commands that Greta recognized easily, and the rest was just friendly noise.

The remainder of the time, Greta took charge of her own responsibilities as expertly as Rosa did hers. Greta would have her breakfast, check the interior of the house, check on Rosa, and go out for the day. An electronically-activated doggie door had recently been installed when Rosa informed Laurel that Greta requested far too many door openings, but declined to say why. Greta had the activating device hanging from her collar, making her independently able to come and go. She would then spend most of the day patrolling the grounds, giving off the occasional warning bark at unfamiliar people and noises.

Rosa talked or sang to herself as she worked. When she dropped something or became frustrated at some task, she would let loose a rant of rapid and loud Spanish that always brought Greta racing through the newly installed doggie dog to check on Rosa's welfare. Greta would not leave until Rosa reassured her that all was well—and sometimes slipped her a treat.

~

Laurel talked to Dak again, this time more seriously, about the conversation with Mat and getting a new, imported furniture line with a foreign, perhaps exotic flair. That is when Dak cautiously brought up the idea of setting up a new store in the future since they couldn't expand their present space. One with a new line. He suggested looking up areas with the highest incomes and the highest growth in home building for a start.

Dak went on to talk about fair trade, semi-native supportive sources, microloans to artisans for interior decor items, and how it would be good for the people and for business. He reinforced the ideas about people not only *feeling* good about buying these products, but actually *doing* good by buying them. It was the perfect excuse for spending too much money.

Dak really did have a feel for business. Laurel was listening, but having taken over the furniture store relatively recently, it was too much too soon for her to properly ingest. Sensing this, he let it rest.

Some of the things he said brought back her time with community activities to help the environment. That part was different for Dak. He was genuinely sincere about ecological causes. This only served to increase her curiosity about who and what he really was.

Dak was having his own thoughts of the future. Were there any signs Laurel was depending too much on him for business expansion and, perhaps, emotional support as well? Megan's return would liberate him from any dependency issues with Laurel, but he knew he must start to prepare her to be on her own with a conscious sense of her own independence and abilities. He still intended to be part of this new business direction. He would have to tread cautiously down a very fine and fragile line.

~

Dak arrived at the office well after lunch. Since he was acting as a temporary assistant and consultant, no one—including Laurel—thought much of the hours he spent there, or didn't spend there.

When Dak was leaving for the day, he asked Laurel, "Do you mind if I stop by for a short while tonight? I want to show you something."

Laurel assumed, like the last time, it was something to do with the furniture business, even though it was Friday and the weekend was about to begin.

Well after dinnertime, Greta was in a guard stance and pointing her nose toward the front door. Dak had't yet shut the motor of the car off. Greta seemed to be deciding whether or not the sound and cadence of the footsteps were familiar when Laurel told her, "It's okay. It's just Dak."

Laurel checked the camera monitor just to be sure and opened the door before Dak could ring the bell. "Greta told me you where here."

Dak smiled, more to himself than to Laurel, as he slipped out of his shoes and put them neatly together just inside the entrance. He had done this before, sparking unasked questions in Laurel's mind about his upbringing.

As Dak and Laurel moved toward the living room, the only sound was Greta's toenails clicking on the tile entrance floor as she followed them. Even that gave way to silence as she stepped onto the carpet.

Laurel sat in the big overstuffed chair. Dak sat on the large sofa, his left foot underneath him, his right foot on the floor.

"What have you got? Furniture catalogs? Price lists?"

"No," answered Dak. "I brought some sounds you might not have heard before."

"What? Sounds?"

Referring to her by name rather than "the dog," Dak said, "Greta will stay hyper-alert if she doesn't get used to sounds in the house. I thought I might try to find something you haven't heard before, just to keep it interesting for you as well."

"That would be easy. I don't listen to music very much at all," Laurel explained. "What did you bring?" Then she added in her head, *Maybe your choice of music will tell me something about you.*

"They aren't all music in the usual sense," he began as he unpacked the messenger bag that had been slung over his shoulder. Dak didn't play each disc in its entirety, but watched Laurel's reactions for indicators. He began with the single sound of a soft Japanese *shakuhachi.* Laurel was spellbound and asked more about it afterward. Dak told her the flute was made of bamboo and was once used by Zen Buddhist monks in their practice of *suizen*, or "blowing meditation." Before Laurel could ask more, the next piece was playing.

This second piece was another flute, but nothing like the first. This was done by a Tibetan man, followed by a recording of an Indian sitar, the unaccompanied song of a single Sufi, wind chimes, singing bowls, and whale songs. Greta listened as intently as Laurel.

Dak then began to play recordings of two sounds at once. Ocean waves were layered with temple bells. Gentle chanting in an unknown language was heard against raindrops. Rhythmic, hollow tappings of sticks could be heard with the sound of dancing bare feet. The final piece was woodland songbirds with leaves rustled by a breeze.

Laurel had stopped asking questions after the third recording. Now she didn't know what she thought or how she felt. She was both totally relaxed and, somehow, exhilarated. She wanted to know so much about what she had heard but didn't want to break the spell that hung in the air like a sparkling, clear-winged dragonfly over a still spring pond. "I don't know what to say..." Her voice trailed off into quietness.

"These are not meant to be talked about, but felt...as healing sounds. Play them for both you and Greta." Pondering those words, Laurel barely noticed when Dak stood up. "Greta will see me out." Right on cue, Greta was up and escorting Dak, her tail swaying with each step.

The next morning, Laurel remembered her thought that she might learn something about Dak by his choice in music. She *had* learned something, but it was as though it was in a foreign language. She had no ability to interpret the information about him.

It wasn't until well after her second cup of coffee that Laurel wondered what prompted Dak to bring those things to her house in the first place. He had said it was to start getting Greta used to sounds in the house, but why that choice of sounds? It was a typically busy day, but that question kept tugging at her attention.

She ran errands and did grocery shopping. When she went home and walked in the door, she was, for the first time, painfully aware of the silence. Only then did she remember what Dak had said about the house being dead. Compared to the strangely compelling sounds last night, it was very dead.

Laurel hurriedly went for the back door and called to Greta. She came bounding so joyfully, she almost misjudged her running speed and skidded the last few inches to sit at Laurel's feet.

~

Dak had been working in the general office area for the past couple of days. Laurel knew he was unobtrusively tracking down any data that would help him to figure out where the missing money was going. And she was watching him in the process. So when he stopped by her office and suggested they go to lunch together, she assumed he had found something.

They found a quiet corner in a familiar cafe within walking distance and ordered. "Did you find out anything new about the missing funds?" she asked.

"Yes and no. I have a clearer view of the systems now and have one or two ideas. I don't want to raise any false suspicions until I know more. But I do feel it's progress."

"How much longer do you think you'll need to be more certain?"

"That's hard to say. It depends on what I find—or don't find—along the way. I can make it more of a priority if you like. The tasks I have taken over for Megan mesh well with my need to examine certain aspects of the financial handling."

"No. It doesn't need to be top priority. You know, it's strange," Laurel said. "I have complete confidence you'll be able to solve this mystery."

"Strange?"

"Well, strange considering what I thought of you before." *And not strange since I haven't seen anything questionable, no matter how hard I've tried*, she added in her own head.

"Before what?"

"Before I met you. I mean my impressions of who you would be before I ever met you. Sort of my views of the generic gigolo."

"Tell me more."

"I thought you would be like the stereotypical flashy pimp. You know, bright, weird colors, flashy jewelry, and cheap aftershave. Certainly not the well-educated kind of person that would understand complex business transactions—and equally complex human transactions. I couldn't have been more wrong!"

"Well, thank you! That is *not* the image I try for."

"Do you *try* for an image, or are you mostly being yourself?" The question slipped out before Laurel had time to consider if it would be too personal.

"Sometimes I don't know where one begins and the other ends. It was easy years ago. I did try for a certain look. But over the years, the image and I morphed into something altogether new. But it does reflect who I am."

"Since I was expecting an overpowering cologne, I couldn't help but wonder why I detected no scent at all. Not even soap. Was that on purpose?"

"Again, years ago it *was* on purpose, but now it's who I am."

"Why? You can't go anywhere without ads about scents of all sorts. Personal, household, 'new car smell' deodorizers."

"That's part of the reason I wear none of that. It's everywhere. You noticed because there was none. But it goes beyond that. First, so many people have allergies these days. It would be insensitive to assume otherwise. Then, artificial smells also mask feelings. Bodies take on different smells because of chemical reactions when you experience fear, anger, or the pheromones of arousal. You might not be consciously aware of it, but your body is. If deodorant is absolutely necessary, it should be without any scent, but better to be clean and allow your body to emit its subtle messages.

"And what if I did wear something, and I chose the wrong scent? Aromas bring up stronger memories than any other sense. Food scents are popular now, but what if I used a green apple shampoo, and that was a smell that brought back memories of your grandmother? Not much of an arousal!"

They both laughed. Laurel tried to remember the last time when she laughed openly and spontaneously like this.

"What if you cooked a wonderful dinner, but the guest next to you smelled of some wonderful perfume? How would the food taste? For the same reason, I would never have a flower arrangement on a dinner table."

"I know all those things—those separate facts—but I never put them together on such a practical level before.

"Do you mind if I ask questions like these while you're still working with me?"

"No. I trust your judgment. And I wouldn't answer anything I thought was too specific or personal anyway." Dak took advantage of the casualness of the moment and added, "You know, you must learn the business—you *are* learning the business—but it is just as important for you to learn to be a whole person again." *Was she ever a whole person?* Dak thought to himself.

Laurel made no reply. She was beginning to realize how much Dak knew about human relationships, the human body, other cultures, and so much more. Conversely, she had to allow herself to admit how lacking her own knowledge was about a world beyond her previous ivory tower.

~

Laurel and Dak had reached a balance with no spoken name, label, or characterization. Causal lunches together no longer needed a designated purpose. She had become adept at asking the scripted non-personal questions and had used the technique in business situations with others with surprisingly good results.

It was another lunch that gave her the opportunity to ask, "Are paid escorts trained like geishas? You know…they know about music, dance, literature, languages, and sex. Do escorts get training too?"

Dak had also been building a rare form of trust in her. She was not the usual female client that needed to be held at a strict arm's length. Besides, many of his new clients needed to talk about sex before they could let themselves relax enough to participate. He kept his tone casually open. "When an escort begins work at some of the better agencies, the men aren't hired unless they are educated, well-spoken, and, sometimes, well-traveled. I suppose that isn't too different from a beginning geisha. There is orientation and training to a certain degree. The agency depends on clients who must be completely confident and satisfied. So confidentiality, personal safety, security, and health are important to know about.

"Explicit sexual training is a bit different. Since most places have laws against having sex for money, an agency can't overtly teach these skills as part of the training. It's unfortunate, because young men often think they are sexually talented just because they're attractive, but they really don't know as much as their clients would like. Sometimes a more experienced escort will mentor them, and sometimes an older woman will help them.

"Men who freelance—that is, work independently without an agency—have usually started in agencies to get an understanding of the business.

"An escort's background culture could mean he already has a view of the fine points of interacting with women. And, of course, there are other male escorts who only deal with male clients, and other escorts who will accept men or women or couples."

Laurel usually didn't ask more than one or two questions, and only when the time was right. She went on with one more. "I keep hearing the word 'security.' But sometimes it sounds like keeping the woman safe, and at other times it sounds like the escort needs to be safe. Why would an escort need to worry about security for himself?"

Dak needed no time to think about this answer. "Sometimes women are less ready for a professional relationship than they think. They could become clingy and possessive. Or they might not be women of integrity. Either way, with any personal information at all, women have been known to track down and stalk an escort, and sometimes even blackmail him, threatening to expose his job to his family or just go public. Going public would mean he could never work again. No client would ever want to be identified as using his services." He sensed it was time to change the subject. "Laurel, I need to ask you—do you think you'll need me for anything this Friday through Tuesday? I know it's short notice, and it's not something I *have* to do; it's just a chance for me to get some personal things done."

"Absolutely no problem! We agreed to a flexible schedule when we started this."

Laurel gave it little thought since Dak came and went irregularly anyway, albeit for shorter periods of time. That was, until she went out to the warehouse area to check on a shipment and overheard him on his cell phone. He was ordering airline tickets to Alaska. *Of all places in the world, why there?* She couldn't imagine why, and she couldn't ask. Her curiosity about him grew with every new bit of knowledge about him. She would have to think about a way to secretly find out more…after she decided if she really wanted to know.

Laurel was far past being just casually curious about Dak's background and personal life. Had he not come so highly recommended by Megan and Rachel, she would never have imagined letting him so far into the business and her personal life. Yet he had proven himself to be honest and trustworthy again and again.

Laurel thought of all those she worked with. She knew Megan very well and had been curious about her background, too. But all the others? She had made it a point to learn something about as many of them as she could. The few facts she could bring up had made them feel personally involved, which was the point. It was good for the business.

Laurel wanted to know specific things about Dak. She was still curious about his background, but she wanted to know *how* he knew the things he knew—enough things about sexuality to be an escort. If she could figure that out, maybe she could figure out how to get that knowledge, too. Was it a simple matter of quantity of experience? *How can I ask him without it being a very personal question?* Asking this question would take some planning, as not to seem prying. It never occurred to her that her question would reveal a great deal of herself to Dak.

PART TWO

The first anniversary of Mark's death had come and gone. It was a difficult time, but it also marked a time for Laurel to reflect on all she had accomplished, all she had become in that first year. The following winter months found her solidifying her progress, reinforcing her trust and ease with Dak, and becoming more ready to move on. Now, the end of winter was in sight.

Laurel felt it was time to move on company matters. She and Dak had been talking about a trip to Bali to scout out merchandise to expand the inventory and rework the store's image.

Unable to give herself any more excuses, she went to Dak. "I think this is a good time to make that trip to Bali happen."

"Do you mind if I call Rachel about it? She's the one with the contacts there. Then I can work on the arrangements and itinerary. Nothing for you to do but pack."

Dak wasted no time.

"So you really got her to agree to go, Dak?"

"We've been talking about it being a good move for the business. And you know she wants—*needs*—the company to be profitable."

"There's my diplomatic Dak," Rachel teased. "We both know Laurel can't admit fear or trepidation in herself to others. It's her way of staying strong."

"You said that, not me."

"I know. You're much too discreet…to a fault sometimes. But back to the point of all this. At least you already know the area. I can give you some pointers on hotels, but what else did you have in mind?"

Dak had already put much thought into this trip. "I need the places I can go to meet, photograph, and buy goods directly from those who make them. No wholesale middlemen. It can be anything, really. Not just furniture. Anything from decor to textiles. Whatever."

"Sure," said Rachel. "I'll get a list emailed to you in the next couple of days. What else?"

"This might be harder, since so much of Bali has turned into a tourist trap. Do you have a contact that can give us access to a private beach area? I want to do some snorkeling, but not with a crowd around."

"Normally I wouldn't do this. Private beaches are hard to find, and I don't want to take advantage of anyone, but I do know one person. I'll have to contact them and get back to you. Anything else?"

Dak noted the genderless "them," but said nothing. "Just one more thing. Could you call Laurel and see if she needs to talk to someone about this trip? She's never been out of the country, I don't think. Not my usual sort of trip planning with a client. She probably doesn't know enough about it to know what to ask about. I want her feel as relaxed as possible."

"Of course you do." Rachel's voice had a tinge of sarcasm that quickly softened. "Of course I'll call her."

~

Rachel called and suggested she drop by Laurel's on Saturday afternoon rather than talk on the phone. Even the face-to-face setting did little to crack Laurel's resolve to maintain a confident facade. "No...why should I feel anxious about such a trip? You do it all the time. I can't wait to go."

Rachel wasn't sure if Laurel meant the trips outside the country or trips with Dak. "Yes, but that doesn't mean I knew as much as I would have liked to in the beginning. I brought some of the photos I took on my first trip to Bali. You've seen more recent ones, but I thought I'd show you the kinds of things that caught my eye way back then—when it was new to me."

The photos were good conversation starters, but Laurel's questions about them never led to any discussion of insecurities she might have. The closest she came was to ask about packing tips.

"I suggest you don't do much of that, but bring a large suitcase. You'll probably want to buy things there, including cool clothing."

As Laurel thanked Rachel for coming, she added, "This is going to be a true milestone for me. I have to do this."

~

Dak explained to Laurel that he must schedule the trip for a particular time and would probably need to have her return home from there without him, but that wasn't a certainty yet. The return flight would be lengthy but as direct as possible. "It will be long and tiring," he warned her. Laurel had some hesitation. She had not planned on doing any of this alone…but she agreed.

Laurel had nearly finished her packing, which had turned out to be much easier than she had expected, thanks to Rachel's seasoned advice. Laurel would only pack one or two spare sets of earrings and little else in the way of jewelry—she planned to shop for some once there.

Jewelry, she thought as she looked at her wedding ring. *Is that what this ring has become? Just jewelry?* It no longer represented the marriage she had, but it did represent the good things in that partnership. *Gone, but still to be cherished,* she decided. She slipped it off and put it in the wall safe.

~

Dak was in the store's parking lot. "Hi. Thought I'd give you an update. This current client…she's toying with the idea of expanding her business. She's paying me full price for my services with no questions asked. No, not yet. I don't want to scare her off…I will. Thanks for taking care of everything there for me…I don't know. I'm on my way to Bali with her. Any news from France? Fiji? You know how I feel about that. It's not going to work…Dubai has the resources and, in some ways, so do the Maldives. Sure. Bye."

~

Laurel and Dak were sitting in the coffee shop, waiting for the boarding call for the connecting fight. It would be a long wait. Laurel had chosen a table off in a corner. It was a choice Dak had noticed. They settled in, arranging their belongings safely around their feet.

"Dak?" she said, looking into her empty hands.

"Yes?"

"I want to learn about something, but I don't know how to ask without sounding like I'm prying."

"Try this. Talk about yourself. Try using 'I' words instead of 'you.' Tell me what you need or want to know."

Laurel took a minute or two before speaking again. "I want to know how I can know more…and why I don't already know more. Conversations with you have already taught me so much about how women respond to touch…and so much more. I suppose I'm asking how you learned so much and I didn't. Hypothetically, how do some people know and learn more than others? How can I learn, too? Oh, I don't know! The more I thought about how to ask you, the more befuddled..." Laurel never specifically mentioned the word "sex."

Giving himself a way to get a few minutes to think, he diplomatically answered, "Let me get some tea first. Would you like something too?"

Laurel's first thought was a stiff drink. Her second thought was one of staying alert and focused. "Latte?" Even her order sounded unsure.

Dak returned with his hands full. He brought the latte and a small bag of cashews. He put those on the table along with napkins, coffee stirrers, two biscotti, and the company credit card.

Laurel eyed it and thought to herself, *Don't worry. I know you're still on the clock.*

Dak sat down and rearranged the items on the table, sliding Laurel's latte towards her and pulling his own toward him. They each got a napkin and a biscotti; cashews delineated the space between them. The credit card went back into Dak's wallet.

He exhaled audibly. "You want to know why you don't know more and how you can learn more. The two questions and answers are very tied together. Sex is as much cultural as it is physical and mental. Maybe more. People can recite the morality surrounding sex in their own culture, but they can rarely be clear when asked to specify their own personal morality and why they draw the lines at certain behaviors.

"Before anyone is open to learning new methods and techniques about sex, they must first be clear on their own morality of sex. They must be clear as to how open they are willing to be.

"For instance, is it wrong to have a nude photo of yourself hanging on the wall? What about a stylized nude oil painting or watercolor of yourself? Of someone else? By someone famous? And a photo of a nude in a gallery? You wear a bathing suit in public places, but not *all* public places.

"Why are cultural lines draw where they are? Taboos and mores are always cultural constructs. Living in, and going to, other places helps us to see how other societies function successfully with completely different values—if we are open enough.

"People within a culture have different values as well. We might consider sexual activities very private. Yet, some people consider the most private sexual act—masturbation—less acceptable than an orgasm brought on by someone else. There are many cultural contradictions.

"People can't get what they want unless they ask for it. But first, they have to discover what it is that they want. And to discover that, they must be willing to explore new things. The more you explore, the more you will learn. Not only about the pleasure of sex, but about yourself and others. And, going back to the beginning, people can't explore unless they know their own standards of what they are willing to participate in."

Laurel reached for one of the cookies. The sound of the wrapper on the biscotti was deafening. Neither of them spoke.

Dak watched as Laurel tossed his words in her head until he was sure she would remember them, or at least the ideas they held.

"So, Laurel, here we are on our way to a country that might give you a way to boost your business, but it's a country with a rich culture, too. Do you know much about it?"

"Actually, I do know a little. Megan has talked about Rachel's trips. And, when Mark was alive, I had been going to meetings that were held by a local environmental group. One time there was a presentation about Bali"

"Are you still going to this group?"

"No. I haven't been in a long time."

"Why not?"

"When I started out, I thought it would be local interest things. You know, like recycling the trash from the store. But it wasn't long before I learned how much it's all connected. The 'butterfly effect' of garbage, I guess." She was smiling again as she looked up at Dak.

"I know about the butterfly effect, but what do you mean by the 'butterfly effect of garbage,' and how does that figure in this trip?" he urged her on.

"Well, I guess the term originally came from some theory about all of existence being so intertwined and interconnected that the flapping of a butterfly's wings might ultimately cause a storm somewhere else in the world. That still seems beyond my grasp, but with this environmental group, it got very easy, very quickly, to see how a bit of trash carelessly sucked into the ocean can end up in a floating island of plastic and other junk—and kill wildlife in the process. And when wildlife dies, it affects us, too. You've heard about the far reaching effects of a bee die-off?"

Dak was in his element. "Yes, sure. The bees die, the fruits and vegetables don't get pollinated, there's a food shortage, farms close down, people are out of work, food prices soar, people riot, and the economy is ruined. But you sound like it interested you. Why did you stop going to the meetings?"

"I was dealing with enough depressing things, and it only got worse when Mark died. The more I understood about the group and its goals, the more helpless I felt and the more futile it seemed. Then Mat came along, talking about his uncle's fair trade business. There he is, one man, not doing much as far as the global view goes, but still changing lives for the better in important ways. So here I am, trying to do something good for the company that will, in turn, be good for all my employees while helping some carpenters I will never meet in places I'll probably never see. Taken one person, one purchase, at a time, I'm not so overwhelmed. I'm even beginning to feel a smidgen positive about the whole environmental scene again."

"And hopeful?"

"Maybe. Yes. But on that small scale approach."

"And less depressed?"

"Hm. Yes, but it seems to take an awful lot of hope and a lot of positive goals to displace a tiny amount of sadness."

"But there *is* progress?"

"Yes. There *is*. I almost forgot to count that."

Dak's mind was racing. "Well," he said cheerfully, "we'll just have to find ways to give you, and the company, goals that will protect and nurture the world's bees and butterflies!"

Laurel laughed, but she knew there was seriousness in his statement, too.

They rose, picked up their trash, and put it in the bin on their way back to the gate. "We still have a few minutes before boarding. I'm going to make a stop in the men's room," he said to Laurel.

"I'll make a stop too. I'll see you at the gate."

As Dak rounded the corner of the wall blocking the view into the restroom, he pulled out his cell phone. "It's me. I'm about to board with my client. This might be the one…the widow who inherited her husband's company. She's running it now, but it's not going to be enough to make her feel fulfilled. Sure. I'll talk to you again when I get a better feel for how to go about this." He hung up without another word.

~

Dak had given Laurel the window seat so she could watch the sea become the landing strip in Bali. She had seen hundreds of pictures of this island. Its beaches were on every calendar labeled "Paradise," and

Megan had shown her pictures of Rachel's trips there. Rachel had told Laurel that this airport saw nearly 20 million passengers a year. She went on to explain that Bali may have once been paradise, but it was now a tourist trap for those who let it be. For others, those who were willing to take the effort and befriend those in the know, there were still areas free of man's concrete and commercialism.

Still, before they ever touched down, Laurel knew she wasn't really prepared for the real Bali. The Ngurah Rai International Airport was visible out the window. It was as busy and bustling as any international landing point, but the architecture looked like a cross between a sprawling modern terminal and a large, spreading temple. There was traffic on the busy roads and planes parked on the tarmac, along with undulating roof lines and temple-like towers.

As they flew in closer, Laurel could see the runway spanned a narrow strip of land that left little room for error. A miscalculated landing or takeoff meant a plane would wind up in the water.

Dak, with suggestions from Rachel, had arranged for a hotel not far from the airport. He had contemplated a small two-bedroom villa that could have been less money but decided it would not afford the level of privacy from each other that they both needed. Adjoining rooms with doors between were a better option.

It had been a long trip. Dak's first task was to get them settled in. Through the open door, he explained they would be keeping to local times regardless of how much their bodies were insistent that it was time to be sleeping. A walk down to the open-walled cafe would help, he suggested.

Dak asked the host for a secluded table. He pulled out a chair for Laurel, positioning her so she would face the view and not all the people. After a few minutes of small talk, he said to her, "I want to talk to you about something. You've been without a relationship for how long now?"

"Before Mark died, he had already begun to cut himself off from me. He knew he was in bad health and did everything he could to prepare me for it. But I didn't know about that at the time."

"Sounds like you were feeling isolated from him even while he was alive."

"There you go, sounding like a shrink again! But, yes. I did. Now I understand why he acted that way, but I still don't think it was right. He excluded me and prevented me from having—and appreciating—that last year with him."

"Do you think you'll have another relationship?"

Laurel knew this wasn't a come-on. Dak had always made it quite clear they would maintain a professional relationship.

"I would like to, but it's unlikely."

"Why is that?"

"Well, I do spend a lot of time at the store and doing store business."

"That's also an opportunity to meet others. There are contractors, suppliers, businessmen in the community."

"Yes, I suppose."

"Then what is it?"

"How do I explain this? I often get…well, stuck. When I want to start something new, something I haven't done before, or haven't done in a long time, I have to get past the inertia—over the hump. Or something. I just can't make that first move to do whatever it is. If I can get past that first time, then I'm usually fine.

"I'll never forget the first time I went on a roller coaster. It was huge! I was 16 or 17 and was with about six others I knew from school. I wanted to go on it, I knew I'd love it, and everyone else was there to do it too. But I was frozen standing on the platform. Some of them thought I was kidding around. One boy finally just pushed me in, hopped in next to me, and clamped down the safety bar. I was so angry at him! But after the first drop, I was glad he did it."

"Were you still angry with him?"

"I was, and I still am! And I'm still glad he did it! That doesn't make sense, I know."

"In a way, I understand it. Let me ask you—do you swim?"

"Well, yes and no. I know how to but almost never do. Living near the Atlantic, my parents thought I should learn, but the cold, dark water never seemed very inviting. The lakes and ponds with their muddy bottoms and murky waters were even more frightening."

"Perfect! If you don't have a bathing suit, get one. I'll meet you at the hotel pool in three hours. In your suit. And what size shoe do you wear?"

"Um, eight, but—"

"No questions right now. I'll explain later."

Laurel had to shop for a suit. There was the hotel shop and then some surrounding tourist-friendly stores nearby. All were full of skimpy two-piece suits designed more for showing off and tanning twenty-year-old bodies than actually doing any swimming.

When, in one of the larger shops, a clerk asked if she could help, Laurel blurted out, "Do you have anything for doing laps or real swimming?"

The clerk said, "Oh, yes. Our sports section might have what you're looking for."

Laurel was led to a back corner that had very practical one-piece tank suits. This was more like it, but it had been some time since she had been in any water beyond her own bathtub, and she was at the edge of being too self-conscious about her body. She tried on one of the plain ones but felt it was too revealing in a wet T-shirt sort of way and not very flattering.

She continued searching and found a simple black one that had a built-in bra and a single small inset band of bright blue that formed the strap on the left shoulder, then curved down to the edge of the suit at the right hip. It would work if they had her size.

After pulling it on, Laurel pushed open the swinging doors on the dressing room and beckoned the sales lady. "Do you have this in one size larger?

"I'm sure we do. I'll get it for you." And eyeing the fit of the one Laurel was wearing, she added, "And the hotel has a day spa where you can get a bikini wax."

Laurel thanked her and blushed. She had shaved her "bikini area" once, but it left an itchy stubble that turned a rashy red when she got into the stinging salt water. She had never had a bikini wax, but she would have to do something to look presentable in public.

When she checked out, the clerk asked if she needed a hat or sunscreen. The pool was outside, but there were umbrellas for shade. The lotion would help against the reflected sunlight. Laurel found a bottle of waterproof lotion that was only mildly scented and added that to her tab.

Not knowing what to expect, and not wanting to prolong the anticipation of what the experience might bring, Laurel went immediately to the spa and asked about the waxing service. It was *not* pleasant. She was as self-conscious as she was unfamiliar with the ordeal, and the numbing solution didn't seem to work. She wasted no time in heading back to her room as soon as she could.

She gingerly undressed to take a look at her newly naked body. She expected it to feel exposed and vulnerable. Surprisingly, it didn't at all. She looked forward to getting into her new suit with confident abandon. She wondered why. Then it struck her: What she had always felt before wasn't an urge to hide or cover her pubic area as she had always thought—it was the need to cover the hairiness. Liberated from that stigma, she was almost as willing to "bare all" as she was willing to expose smoothly shaven armpits. Now it was just more skin like that on her arms and face after a shower—fresh and clean.

She was at the pool fifteen minutes early, chose a sheltered lounge chair, and ordered what she called one of "those frou-frou tourist drinks" complete with a live flower and a little paper parasol. "Where is everybody?" she said to the waiter.

"Those who swim are in the sea or sleeping because they are already finished for the day. It's a good time to use the pool. No crowd."

Dak saw her, eyed the drink, and said, "Have you been waiting long?" He seemed relieved to find she had only one drink. He noted the well-chosen suit but drew no attention to it. The one-piece design and high cut at the hip told him she was concerned about how her body looked but didn't try to over-hide, either.

He was carrying a duffle bag. "I've brought us some masks, snorkels, flippers, and vests."

"Why? I thought we were staying here at the pool."

"Because I want to show you something, but you'll need to be comfortable with a mask to see it. We don't have to go into any deep water, and the pool is a perfect place to practice. One of these should fit. They're soft silicone and clear. That lets light in and gives a sense of peripheral vision. Besides being secure and comfortable, it minimizes any sense of claustrophobia."

Dak showed her how to check for fit without the straps and explained how to clear the snorkel if the valve didn't work well. He had a bottle of Spit to keep the glass from fogging.

"It's a normal reaction to have a sort of startle reflex when your face hits the water, so don't be surprised if that happens. Just put your face in slowly. You'll get used to it in no time."

He explained that the buoyancy vest was only for confidence and she was to learn how to use it if she felt she wanted to. They practiced in three feet of water and quickly graduated to four and a half feet after checking her comfort level.

"Now for the fins. The back strap is adjustable, but knowing your shoe size helped me to pick the right ones."

He showed her how to kick gently and loosely from the hips rather than from the knees. Once Laurel mastered that, they practiced swimming using no hands.

"Pretend you're a mermaid; or better yet, a dolphin. Let your body flow in the direction you want to go."

After Laurel became accustomed to getting the snorkel under water and clearing it when needed, Dak showed her how to bend at the waist until her head was straight down and then kick her feet straight up so the weight of them would force her body downward. After the third attempt, Laurel was making perfect surface dives.

Through this, Dak didn't use fins but circled around her underwater as supple as a sea otter. He could see she was rapidly gaining confidence, but he still asked about her comfort level with every new maneuver.

"Time for a break. I'm curious. I know you said you could already swim but didn't feel secure in the Atlantic or the ponds and lakes near you. Yet here in the pool, you've showed no signs of discomfort at all. What makes the difference for you?"

"It's a pool! What is there not to like about the water in a pool?"

"All right. Start from there. Why is pool water easy to be in?"

"Well, let me think. It's the opposite of everything I said I didn't like back there. Here, the water is warm. The visibility is limitless. And the cement bottom means nothing is lurking in the mud to grab me by my feet!"

"So if there was water like that in a natural setting, you'd be fine?"

"I assume so, but that isn't anything I've ever experienced."

"Tomorrow we'll go to a place I know. The water is no more than four feet deep at high tide for quite a stretch…and it's body-warm with unlimited visibility. The sandy bottom has some coral, but you can maneuver around it near the shore and then, farther out, your feet will be floating. Sound good?"

"Sounds very good! I can't wait. But we'll come in if I decide I don't like it, right?"

"Absolutely!"

The next day, Dak drove the rental car to a beach that was part of the property of someone Rachel knew. The gear was unloaded, and Laurel started to apply her sunscreen.

"Here, let me help with the back of your shoulders. You'll be standing up or floating stomach-down, so you'll have to be particularly careful with those areas. I'll do the back of your legs, too."

There was only that split second of warning that he would be touching her as he squatted to reach her calves. He applied the lotion quickly and efficiently. Her thighs haven't been touched in a long time, but he moved right along without the slightest hint of anything more than helpfulness.

"Come over here and wash it off your hands. Use the sand to scrub them clean," he said as he washed his hands more carefully than Laurel thought was needed, even between his fingers and around his nails. She followed his example.

"Why are we being so careful about cleaning it off our hands?"

"It's not good for anything you touch. Go ahead and put on the flippers. Walk in backwards if they're too awkward. Now get the mask ready and around your neck. We'll have a quick review before we go much farther."

Dak and Laurel practiced with the equipment in three feet of water. Laurel had remembered nearly all he had told her the day before. With Dak checking on her, then taking her hand, they floated out to three and a half feet, then four. Laurel had been concentrating on proper use of the flippers and getting proficient at clearing her mask of the smallest leaks.

"Stop for a minute and just look around."

It was her very first look at live coral with its colonies of small, colorful fish. Laurel nearly leapt out of the water with excitement. Completely forgetting any self-consciousness about her body or her awkwardness with the equipment, she was bobbing up and down, trying to see this new world and ask a flood of questions at the same time.

"What are those tiny little purple fish? And are those white things flowers?!"

"No, they're not flowers. They're soft corals. Look again. Watch until you see them react to the fish—or your touch. But don't touch anything unless you check with me first. There are some things, even small things, that aren't so safe—for you or for them."

Laurel had never heard of soft coral or of fish that could change gender or of the names of all the creatures she asked Dak about. She had heard his warning about not touching anything for the sake of her own safety, but in her excitement, it didn't faze her in the least.

Further on, Laurel saw an astounding variety of fish, corals, nudibranchs, crabs, shrimp, sponges, and other creatures. She was reluctant to lift her head, but she wanted Dak to tell her about every one of them.

Then, when over a densely populated area, he brought her up and said, "Go down again, hold your breath or breathe softly, be very still, and just listen."

She expected a sort of hear-the-ocean-in-a-seashell sound…maybe with distant small wave sounds. Instead, she heard a variety of distinct clicks and squeaky noises. The last of Laurel's reserve shattered. "Oh my God! They're talking to each other!"

"Isn't it a miracle? I never get tired of listening to them. Don't you wonder what they say to each other? I don't think anyone has ever done a study on shallow ocean sounds. But I hear the University of Rhode Island has some recordings—some old ones made by a woman named Marie Fish."

"What? Marie *Fish*? You had me believing you for a minute."

"No, really, it's true! She and someone else made the recordings before I was born! I think they were discovered a few years ago and then put on CD. But it gets even better. Some British researchers found some fish communicate by passing wind."

"I know a couple of people who are divers. I've watched divers on science programs. I never heard any mention of fish making sounds to each other. Is it that they don't know about it? But how is that possible?"

"To know there is sound, to know there is communication, you have to listen. If it never occurs to you that another species might be communicating, then you won't ever be listening for it," Dak told her.

Laurel's excitement continued to mount. "It really is an alien world under there! I can't believe how little I know about it. Especially considering the earth is covered in more sea than land. Is there any school anywhere that teaches children about where they live?! Mine didn't!"

Now in mid-chest deep water, Laurel had long since forgotten any misgivings about being in limitless expanses of ocean. She hadn't even mentioned sharks.

"Well, there are a few. Ah—here we are. These are called cleaner wrasse. Watch what I do."

Laurel bent forward, putting her masked face in the water once more. She watched while Dak slowly extended his hand to them. They began pecking and poking but found little to forage on. Laurel didn't have to be told what to do; she couldn't wait to see if they would investigate her hand. The bright blue and black striped creatures readily switched to Laurel's fingers, hoping for a better food source.

"Take off a flipper and offer them a foot. They'll find more to graze on. Hold on to me to steady yourself while you watch them. It's a bit awkward, but it will be worth it."

Dak was right. She withdrew her hand to remove the flipper before extending her foot. They swam in and went to work. This time they found a bonanza of tissue at her heel and where her thong sandals had rubbed a thin callous between her big toe and her second toe. But in these sensitive areas, their gentle nibbles tickled so much, Laurel had to come up so she wouldn't choke from laughing under water.

She was full of joyous energy. "I could stay here all day! I've missed all this for so many years, I want to see it all!"

"I'm sure you do! But you're weightless in the water; when you get out, you'll be shocked at how heavy your body will feel and how tired you really are. You'll be dehydrated, too. We can come back again…it wouldn't be wise to push your body too much."

He was right. Laurel could barely carry her own weight as she emerged back onto the shore. They loaded the car and headed back. She was unusually quiet, lost deep in thought. Being on dry land seemed to have dried up her joy of being in the water.

"What did you think of it?" Dak finally asked.

"I don't know if I felt like a child being shown an amusement park for the very first time or Captain of the Intrepid landing on an alien planet. It was beyond words.

"You must have been doing this for a long time. You knew all their names."

Dak nodded. "It's important that we—that *people*—especially children—know their names. Not just the names of the fish and the corals, but the trees, clouds, birds, insects, and rocks—all of it."

Laurel noticed he had avoided the question about himself.

"We weren't taught much of any of it in school."

"No. That's a problem."

"A problem?"

"It's part of the disconnect that got humans in the fix we now find ourselves in."

"I'm not sure what you mean."

"Let's say there's a stranger on the street. His clothes are old, and he looks like he could use some money. But he doesn't ask for any—what do people do?"

"They keep walking."

"Exactly. But what if they know the person? What if they depend on him to drive their children's bus to school or plow the snow from their street or stock the groceries on the shelves in the store where they shop? Or what if they only know his name?"

"Then he wouldn't be a stranger. They would be much more likely to stop and see what the problem was and how they could help."

"Of course. And that is what we must understand and teach our children. It might sound like a radical tree-hugger idea, but we are all neighbors on the same planet. What we do affects us all. And if we know the names of our neighbors, including the leafy ones that filter our air and the rocky ones that provide the metals we build our machines with, and all the others, we are more likely to try to live without harming them and maybe even protect them. In the end, we might just save the planet and ourselves in the process. Later, I'll show you what I mean. Words don't make it very clear.

"So you got over the hump of getting into the ocean?"

"Yes. But I wasn't forced and don't feel any anger this time—only excited and appreciative." It was a quick change of subject. He often did that. But Laurel carefully filed his words away.

"You were pulled on by your own positive feelings before your mind could talk you out of it."

"And by trust," Laurel added. "I trusted you. You obviously knew what you were doing, and I felt safe with you."

"Well, you can trust me when I tell you, you're going to be exhausted. Pulling yourself through water takes a lot of energy. Let's get back to our rooms, rinse off the salt, and then we can talk. Look in that box. There's some fruit and sandwiches we can have as we drive back. Swimming always makes me hungry.

"When we get back, you'll find a small package I left just inside your door. After you shower, just slip it on."

"What is it?"

"It's a loose caftan. The design is very simple: it's about three and a half yards of material, folded in half, then a neck opening is cut out at the fold. The sides are sewn up about six inches from the sides, leaving a space at the top for arms.

"It's such a simple design, but I think it works to show off the batik print. One size fits all but drapes nicely so it doesn't look like a tent. It would be a good thing to sell. No stocking different sizes; it wouldn't break in shipping. And it covers everything, so you can slip into it without any constricting underwear.

"You try yours on, and I'll put on a batik wrap for men I want you to see, too. I want you to look at the artwork in both pieces. Leave your door ajar when you're ready for company."

Once back at the hotel, Laurel found the package where Dak had left it earlier. They showered and changed, Dak into his sarong and Laurel into the caftan. Her hair still wet, she opened the door and found Dak was already waiting.

"I know. I look like a drowned rat. You were right. I'm too tired to do the blow dry routine."

"But you were even wetter earlier today!"

"See? I'm so tired, I can't think straight."

"So what do you think of that material? And the batik work? Hold your arms out so it will unfold, and turn around slowly so I can see."

Laurel did as she was told, saying, "I love this material. It does drape nicely, and I like these vibrant, rich colors."

But Dak wasn't listening; he was watching. As she turned, he caught a glimpse into the open arm of the garment. She was wearing nothing underneath it.

"Let me show you this sarong, too." He unwrapped the material and held it out for her to see without exposing his body. He was talking about the batiking process as Laurel watched how easily he re-wrapped the cloth and tucked it securely. "Do you think this would make complementary drapes and pillow coverings for the furniture you might buy from here?"

"That's a good idea," Laurel answered. "And, as you said, cloth is an easy thing to ship for import. Mmm…I have to sit down. I must have used some muscles today that weren't used to doing any work before."

"Here," Dak said as he patted the bed. "Let me rub your feet. I'll start at your ankles so it won't feel so ticklish."

Laurel got on the bed but was not immediately relaxed. As promised, Dak sat in the chair and began at her ankles. He cupped a hand around the bottom of her foot as he began to work downward with his other hand. Laurel visibly began to relax. Dak then rubbed the tops of both feet at once, gently with his thumbs, still keeping pressure on the bottom of her foot with his other four fingers. Without a hint of a tickle, Laurel became more and more relaxed.

Dak moved painstakingly slowly. Laurel began to doze. By the time he was working on her toes, she had fallen into a deep sleep devoid of sense of time or place. Dak's pace did not change. He slid a finger between each of her toes.

He methodically worked his way back up her foot and moved farther, sliding up the caftan's soft material as he went. With the touch of a warm summer breeze on her skin, his fingers caressed her hips, her ribs, and moved towards her breasts. His hand moved across her chest towards her nipple then inched downward to her inner thighs. Persistent. Patient.

Laurel began to rise from the depths of her unconsciousness. She was completely aroused. Even with her eyes closed, she could tell the day's light was nearly gone. She was awake and not awake; dreaming, and dreamily aware. The burning longing and silken warm fluid on her thigh told her she was beyond making any decision. Her body had already chosen. Her hand and a low moan both rose to tell him she was no longer asleep.

"Now," he breathed into her hair. It was neither a question nor a command. Just a simple statement.

A slight opening of her legs, the lifting of a knee, and a deeper, prolonged moan was her affirming reply.

She expected to feel his weight on her but only felt two fingers slide gently inside her. A gentle rotation gave way to an upward flicking motion. He began to increase the speed and pressure on her G-spot until she dissolved into pure sensation followed by a clenching orgasm. He slowly pulled the caftan down to her ankles and held her until her breathing subsided to an easy rhythm.

Dak walked across the room in his bare feet, sarong still firmly around his hips. He took a drink from the hotel room fridge and sat on the bed. His arm around her back, he helped her sit up and handed her the glass.

"What's this?"

"Coconut water fresh from a real coconut. Not processed and canned. There's still some pulp in it—not filtered. I had some delivered to the refrigerators in both our rooms. Magical stuff."

"This is definitely not like any I've had before… "

"Finish that, and then I'll go."

They each sat in their own silence. Then, taking the empty glass from her hand, Dak nearly whispered, as if she was already asleep again, "I'll meet you at 8:00 for breakfast, and we can plan what we need to do for the day. Go back to sleep. I'll make sure the doors are locked." He pulled the cover over her. She was already drifting away. He watched her even breaths for several minutes. With a slow and tender touch, he kissed her on the forehead and left.

Hours later, Laurel sat bolt upright in the dark, inexplicably off-kilter. It wasn't what had happened, but what had *not* happened. He had made no effort to accommodate his own needs. And he never kissed her. What did it mean? Before she could think any further, she lay back down and fell into sleep once more.

~

At five minutes before 8:00, Dak tapped on the door between their rooms. Laurel called back to him, "I'm ready; come on in."

During breakfast, Laurel took out her notebook to plan the day. Dak already had activities in place without committing them to an airtight schedule. Thanks to Rachel's connections and working with Dak on the goals for the trip, Laurel would see textiles, carvings, paintings, lamps, garden umbrellas, bamboo furniture, recycled teak, and carved frames—not at stores or with wholesalers, but as the craftsmen and women were working on them.

Neither mentioned the previous night. Laurel was grateful. She needed time to let it sit on the back burner by itself. She needed time to decide what her own reactions and feelings were. She felt at ease with Dak's attitude. It happened, it was a natural reaction, and what was there to discuss? At least that's what she thought he felt. She might ask him about it later. Or maybe not.

Breakfast over, they lingered over the last of her coffee and his tea.

"You know, before I met you—even *when* I met you—I was against hiring you. Not because of any particular lack of qualifications, but because of your...well, let's just say, your job description. I didn't object on moral grounds, but I objected for myself. I wasn't going to be the grieving widow so desperate that I had to hire some gigolo. It wasn't long before I had to admit, Megan and Rachel were right. You were trustworthy and very capable. And I became curious about you. But I suppose that's not unusual for your clients."

"No, it's not."

"Even now, I couldn't begin to guess your ethnic background, though I keep wondering. You have an American passport, and your English definitely has an American accent. But every now and then, you use a word in a way that most Americans don't."

"Such as?" Dak was still avoiding Laurel's implied questions and turned the focus back on her.

"I don't know...let me think. The other day, you said a cookie was brittle instead of crisp. I hadn't heard you say that before, so that might not be the best example, but there have been others. Once you referred to having too much hair spray as making hair 'crunchy.' It's not a 'wrong' word; it's just an unusual use for it. And after watching you swim, I'm convinced you were born in the sea!"

Dak laughed, "Oh no. My secret's out. No, really, it's true. Have you ever heard of water births and tiny infants instinctually holding their breaths and swimming? Well, my mother did. Before I could sit up, I was floating over her back, clinging to her hair with my fists. Years later, when I was at university, I read a couple of old books by Elaine Morgan that I had seen on my mother's book shelf. Then it all made sense to me. Or at least, I could see why some of us might be genetically drawn to the sea. Sounds far-fetched, I know. But no more time to talk about this now. We have a lot to do today!"

Elaine Morgan…Elaine Morgan, Laurel repeated in her head. She wanted to remember the name so that she could look it up later. In the last two days, Dak had just given her more information about himself than he had the entire previous time she had known him. She had Googled "Dak" once and found several references—none of which seemed to apply to him in any way. She had no better results looking up his full name, Dak Gordon. Now she knew he had gone to a university. She had noted he referred to it as "university," leaving out the "a" or "the." And she knew he had strong ideas about the balance of ecology. But where did he learn to excite a woman so intensely while she slept so soundly?

Remembering Laurel had been reluctant to ever use the word "sex," he asked with no direct reference to the lovemaking, "Do you think you are more ready to move forward in your private life now?"

"Emphasis on 'private'? More ready. Yes. Completely ready? I'm not sure. Not quite. You were the director of that scene in my room, so I didn't have to 'perform' in any sense. My body responded, but I didn't have to respond to another person. I'm not over that 'first time' reluctance yet."

"I think I know a way to help with that. But only with your agreement, of course."

"I have no doubt. Yes. I wouldn't object to your 'help.' But other things—unexpected things—have changed for me, too. To throw myself into the company the way it's been now seems so...what? Confining! The world—*my* world—is so much bigger, more inclusive. So much more complicated. Intertwined and interconnected. And I can't imagine how the company can even survive in its present isolation anymore. Besides that, it's too late for me now. I'd die of boredom.

"Rachel has made it all work for her. She has a thriving business, she travels, and now that I know how some of it works, it looks like she is going the fair trade route. Why can't I do that with the furniture business?"

"I thought that's what we are doing."

"Well, yes, but I mean *more* than a one-trip fling for some accessories."

"Keep that in mind during this trip. You might see things that will give you some ideas," Dak went on. "Yesterday, when we were in the water, you said something about schools not teaching children about the planet they live on. Remember?"

"Of course."

"Would you like to see a school that does?"

"And where are we going to find that?! Some fantasy land somewhere?"

"Not at all. It's a school I went to for two years while my parents were here on Bali. It's not far from here, but I think we should block out the full morning schedule to see it. It's literally a school without walls."

"What's the name of it?"

"The Green School."

"No, really; what is it?"

"It really is the Green School, and it's really built from bamboo and fresh air."

"Is it fairly well known, or is just a tiny little place in the jungle?"

"Well, for the 2014 high school graduation, the keynote speaker was Jane Goodall. And in September of the same year, the Secretary

General of the United Nations came for a visit."

"Oh, God. Along with everything else I don't know, I now feel absolutely illiterate."

Dak answered before he could think about it. "No. *No*! That's not why you're becoming a part of all this. It's not to show you how little you know or how poorly educated you were. In so many ways, this environmental issue, all the knowledge about nature and climate change, all of it is just a slim slice of our lives. It happens to be a slice you hadn't been educated about, but think how narrow *my* world has become. I don't read novels, I don't read magazines, and I don't participate in sports. I can't have a wife or partner. I don't write essays or letters. My emotional health is barely a passing thought. Everything I do is always, somehow, related to this one cause.

"I look at your life with such admiration. You are able to, or able to learn how to, move from place to place, life to life, re-identifying and re-inventing yourself with every turn and trauma. And how many people are able to separate emotions from sex in a way to be able to ask questions to learn the techniques? You have broadened my world far more than I have enlarged yours."

"But..." Laurel stumbled.

"No. Please. Just think about that. Let it sink in. And if it makes you feel any better, think about visiting the Green School as my showing you about what some of my childhood was about rather than some sort of educational field trip."

"What can I say? Let me grab my bag, and I'll be ready to go." Laurel was on her feet and on the move—as if she was afraid, given a moment of stillness, Dak would realize his slip in secrecy, his revelations about his personal life, and somehow take it all back. It was the first time, and would be the last time, she heard such emotional self-disclosure from him.

"I'll just make a phone call to let them know we're on our way."

~

The man was wearing sandals and a sarong. "Dak! So good to see you again!"

"It's good to be here. Sorry about the short notice."

"A lesson in 'going with the flow'! And who's this?"

"Bob, I'd like you to meet Laurel—she didn't know such a school existed, so I wanted to show her it was real."

"Oh, we're real, all right. Unfortunately, I have to be in a teacher-parent meeting in a few minutes, but Dak knows his way around at least as well as I do, so make yourself at home and poke around anywhere…which isn't hard, since everything is open."

"So I've heard. I appreciate your welcome."

Dak and Laurel took their time strolling the grounds of the school. They passed some children in seated meditation while others squealed in a mud puddle. Older ones were moving across the landscape in small groups. Words about a math problem drifted down from a classroom. For the first time, Dak didn't take a factual teaching stance. Instead, he led her through memories evoked by what they saw and heard.

"But Dak, you went to this school before your high school epiphany about environmental issues. How does this fit in?"

"Yes, it was long before. But it was like so many things children are exposed to. They see and hear it, but they don't understand the full impact or the true meaning. Yet something in them knows it's important enough to remember. Only later, perhaps as a young adult, do they understand what it was all about. Like walking in on your parents during a moment more intimate than you've seen before at age 6. You have no idea what they're doing, but you never forget what you saw.

"I did know I felt more at home here, in places with no walls. It was one of the happiest of my childhood experiences. Sadly, as adults, walls are constructed to the point where we cease to notice them."

Laurel was bubbling with questions. "I can see how it could help with a foundation in your psyche, but what about all these other children, year after year? On one hand, I want to ask how they take this into the world, what difference does one school make? And on the other hand, it seems so monumental, so world changing. After going to school here, how could they ever live in a concrete city? And their parents—they're the ones who have enough awareness to send their children here. Where are they? Or who are they?"

"Too many questions! For now, instead of intellectualizing, try to be childlike. Just take in all new the experiences with an open mind, without steering your perceptions with logical answers or someone else's thoughts and ideas."

Dak kept his promise. It was no academic tour. He told her about the memories of his childhood here, before his walls were built… while he could still allow himself the full range of emotions.

Laurel joined him in those memories. They took off their shoes and splashed in the stream, clapped to the sounds of the music coming from a space with an uplifting roof of gentle curves, and shared swings with energetic youngsters.

Laurel slipped back into adulthood only once. Completely enchanted by the bamboo used for everything from support structures to eating utensils to places to sit and rest, she pulled her notebook from her bag and hastily wrote a note to herself to research and order sustainable bamboo furniture.

~

In the afternoon, Dak and Laurel went to the craftsmen's places and made arrangements for purchases of several lines of products. These people were not under contract with anyone but locals that Rachel had befriended. As she had promised, there was no outlet store and no middleman. This meant better profits for the craftspeople and a better deal for Laurel.

At the very first stop, Dak suggested they get photos of the weavers, along with their names and permission to use their photos. They readily agreed, hoping it might lead to more business for them.

But Laurel was puzzled. "Why the photos, and why the names and formal permission?"

"Let me get my laptop out from the car, and I'll show you some photos." Dak and Laurel sat in the shade of an overhanging tree, thick vines providing cooling shade on a flat rock below. Dak opened his laptop and showed her a photo.

"What do you see?"

"An old dilapidated building about to fall down on a beach."

"Okay. If someone asked you to spend money to save this area, what would you say?"

"No! Of course not. What's there to save, and why would anyone want to save it?"

"Now let me add some information. This was someone's home in Alaska. The town is being washed away by the Ninglick River because of climate change. This shot was taken back in 2013, so by now, the entire town could be gone, making these people America's first climate refugees.

"Now look at this article. In March of 2012, this teenaged boy was trying to draw attention to the fact his home was about to be washed away by another river in Alaska. He is trying to sue the state because they've done nothing about the climate change caused by global pollution.

"Now, are you more likely to give money to support this boy than you were after seeing that first photo?"

"Well, yes! The problem has a face—a real person. A child—children—are being affected in my own country."

"Now, apply those same principles to the sale of products."

"Let me think a minute... Of course. If we can make the products personal, someone will buy these textiles at my store, the fair trade system will help these people, this one woman, this mother. They can contribute to her welfare without giving away money. All they have to do is to choose this product over the nameless, faceless ones.

"And how did you learn these marketing skills?"

She laughed and nudged him playfully in the arm, but both knew she was genuinely curious.

With each stop, Laurel conversed with the women, and Dak chatted with the men. Laurel began asking the women about having their pictures taken and permission to use the photos while Dak pulled out his camera. The pattern continued throughout the day.

"You know I'm anxious to see what you've taken."

"I'll show you. When we get back to the hotel, you can relax. I'll have them ready to show you after dinner."

Dak was anxious to see them as well. He downloaded them onto his laptop, cropped and adjusted them. Some he discarded altogether. Others, he laboriously fussed over, getting every detail to his liking. He had only a few minutes before he was to meet Laurel for dinner. Just time enough. He pulled his cell phone from his pocket.

"Hi. She's the one; her name is Laurel Bradford. Well, yes, but her potential for this other thing is undeniable. I think so…will you be able to help with that? By doing what you do best! I'll talk to her about it when the time is right...I know there isn't much time. I'll do it in the next 24 hours. I'll call again with details for you...and tell Tibu I'll be there soon. Bye."

~

Dak tapped on the door between them. "Laurel, would you be willing to let me come to your room after dinner?"

"Sure. More about business tactics?"

"No. We can talk about that over dinner. What I had in mind was another step toward getting over that 'first time' feeling."

"Oh! Well...maybe. What did you have in mind?"

"To begin with, a warm soak in the tub with a glass of wine. Then we'll see how it goes. You can stop at any time, and I'll go back to my own room."

"Hmm. That first experience must have helped me to get over something, because if you had made this same offer before that, I would have said no without hesitation."

"Is that a yes?"

"It's a maybe yes. As long as I know I can stop whenever I like. *A* glass of wine, right? Not a bottle?"

"A glass or two, but no more. If you are tipsy, you can tell yourself that was the reason for your participation and it didn't count. Then you wouldn't feel any progress. Your body probably wouldn't respond very well, either."

"You're really good at your job, aren't you?! We'll see how it goes. No promises."

"And no pressure."

"Bring the photos with you so I can see them at dinner?"

"I'll bring them on my laptop, but we'll wait for desert or after dinner coffee, if that's all right with you."

~

Dak never talked much over a meal. When he did, it was about the finer points of the food. Laurel respected that and waited for the final cups of tea and coffee to arrive.

"I want to see those photos you took today."

Dak opened his laptop that already had the photos on screen. "Here. These are from our first stop."

Laurel was stunned. "These aren't snapshots, they're works of art. I had no idea," she fumbled.

"They must be powerful to be effective—to do the job."

"You've been keeping all sorts of secrets," she said, her eyes still glued to the screen. "This has nothing to do with client confidentiality. Why have you kept this talent so buried?"

"My secrecy must seem over the top to you, and my reason will seem melodramatic if I say it's a matter of life and death, but, in fact, it is."

"Please don't tell me you're running from some illegal mob or government."

"No, nothing like that. I'm sure you wouldn't want it public knowledge that you've used the services of a professional gigolo, as you called me. So at least on some level, you understand the need for confidentiality for your own reputation. But this goes far beyond my own sense of public reputation."

"Now you're going to have to explain. We're going to have to trust each other."

"Yes, we are. We do.

"First of all, I have two careers. Besides the one you are familiar with, in more recent years I also became an environmental photographer. I specialize in climate change impact on all living species. It pays very well. And, even though I use a pseudonym, if my escort service was to be exposed, I would be blacklisted as a photographer. I'd never be able to work again as an escort, either—which also pays well. If I plan properly, I can sometimes be doing both at once, in effect doubling my income.

"The funds I earn are essential. I hope they will be life-saving on a fairly large scale. Not only life-saving but culture-saving. Or at least help toward that goal."

"I still don't understand."

"Let me go back further. Legally, I'm an American. I was born in Hawaii; most of my schooling was there, and I have an American passport. But I am I-Kiribati."

"Wait. I consider myself well educated, but that's a new country for me. Where is 'Ikiribas'?"

"The country is spelled K-I-R-I-B-A-T-I but pronounced 'Kiribas.' We call ourselves 'I-Kiribati.' And, if I don't succeed, you won't have to bother to look it up because the entire nation will disappear off the face of the earth, along with the Maldives, the Seychelles, parts of Alaska—but I could go on and on about other places.

"Kiribati is a group of—at last count—over 30 atolls and one 'real' island, in the Pacific Ocean between Hawaii and Australia. Really in the middle of nowhere. I spent a few years and every summer back home there with my grandparents and other family members. That was my 'mother culture.' I learned photography, drawing, and even some cooking from an early age. It was an easy flow for me of ancient and modern, Pacific and American cultures in Kiribati with neither more important than the other."

"But the photography? How does that fit in?" Laurel asked.

"It was my grandmother that started me on the photography, even though she didn't own a camera. It was supposed to keep me grounded in both worlds—my parents were quick to agree—but instead, it eventually turned my world upside down. My grandmother made sure I had albums of my photos of Kiribati in Hawaii, and my mother made sure I had albums of my photos of Hawaii in Kiribati. Letters and pictures going back and forth from wherever I was continued to be 'homework' to make sure there was always a seamless connection.

"One year, I was in high school in Hawaii and had a library full of albums by then, all dated and shelved in order. My mother said when she retired she would compile them all in some sort of compact computer form, but that time hadn't come yet. Never has.

"Anyway, I remember it was a Sunday. I took one of the oldest ones down and saw some shots of storm surges splashing on a familiar coastline in Kiribati. It was always an exciting topic for a kid to take photos of. I remembered doing it many times. I was probably no more than four years old when I took these particular ones. They were a bit blurry and crooked, but I had such fun taking them.

"I skipped ahead several years and looked for a similar shot to see how my skills had improved. What I saw wasn't just better pictures. There seemed to be a higher base line of water and a higher surge of waves in those next photos. I thought it was probably a bigger storm. So I began pulling them all down—all the storm pictures I could find. Then all the coastline pictures of the same area. Then all the low-lying areas in general. Was the sea rising? I couldn't positively say it did. It certainly looked like it."

"What was it?" Laurel asked like a child in the middle of hearing a fairy tale.

"I didn't know at that point. There was something that wasn't right. I was sure of that much. Breadfruit trees didn't look as healthy or as plentiful. Coconut palms weren't doing as well either. I was due for a trip back for summer vacation in less than five weeks, so I got busy making copies of a series of photos. I had to make careful choices because I didn't have much time; I had finals to study for.

"As soon as I settled in back in Kiribati, I showed the copies of the photos to my grandmother. She knew right away. She said, 'Dak, you think this is a poor coconut harvest. It is not. It is an open Pandora's box.'

"'When did it open?' I asked her while I tried to remember the story.

"She said, 'Oh, there was a crack in the lid a long, long time ago. Then the lift began with the Industrial Revolution. But it was ignorance and greed that propped it open to stay.' That's my grandmother!

"I asked her what would happen to us. She looked me straight in the eye and said, 'We will disappear.'

"I was staring at her, still trying to figure out what she was talking about, and what to ask her next, when she added, 'Unless you save us.'

"And there it was. I was a teenager given the mission to save a nation. But first, I had to figure out what I was saving us from. My grandmother rarely answers questions directly. But I had the whole summer to piece it together. It all had to do with climate change. And don't call it global warming; that confuses the issue for too many who don't understand how 'warming' can cause blizzards. In any case, our nation was—is!—drowning. Thanks to climate change, our entire nation will be submerged in my lifetime. And probably in my grandmother's. Her home will certainly be uninhabitable in her time. Salt water is creeping in, population is soaring, food sources are failing. It's a deadly course of death and destruction."

"What are you going to do? How will she survive?" Laurel was completely caught up in the story now.

"I didn't know yet. So I took environmental studies, photography, art, and business university courses and headed out into the world. Partly because she put me on that path, and partly because I became driven."

Laurel didn't want to interrupt his flow any more than she already had, but she had to in order to fully comprehend what he was trying to tell her. “This doesn’t make sense. You’re trying to make all the money you can to save your country from being swallowed under rising seas due to climate change? How is that possible with any amount of money?!”

“It isn’t, in the usual sense. But we have to redefine—or simply define—what makes a nation a nation; what makes a culture a culture. What has been tried to save them already, what is working and what hasn’t, or won’t, and what will.”

“I’m beginning to see where you’re going with some of this,” Laurel answered. “I’ve always thought of a nation as a place on a map. But if that place is eradicated, and the people still exist, does the nation still exist? And if the answer is no, then what about the people? You can’t say they don’t exist. But if you plop them down somewhere else, what happens to their culture, their heritage and history, their self-identity? How can they successfully assimilate into another culture? Would they even want to if they knew how to?”

“This is going to be easier than I thought,” Dak smiled. “You’ve already got a solid base of understanding going.”

“If that’s the case, do you mind if I ask some personal questions to fill in some of the blanks in what you’ve already told me?”

“Might as well!”

“I gather Kiribati is not a huge place. Well, maybe it covers mileage considering the number of islands and ocean around them, but the population and resources must be limited. And you did say your schooling was mostly in Hawaii. But it’s your grandmother that you refer to when you talk about learning new things as a child. Did she teach you photography?”

Dak smiled broadly. “Yes and no. She taught me photography like she taught me so many other things she didn’t know about. She taught me how to learn. How to ask. How to find out. I was about ten and already had an extensive collection of photos. Most of those ‘homework’ assignments of hers involved photos of family members, neighbors doing various occupations, flora and fauna of the islands, weather phenomena, and so on. Then I had to write an explanation of the content in a letter back to the rest of the family. She was quick to point out the ones that were also esthetically pleasing and had me draw those or use them as the basis for some other art project.

"But I liked the photography better than drawing and asked her how to make the photos better art. She said to me, 'What is a photo?'

"I said, 'A picture!'

"She said, 'Where are there lots of *good* pictures—artistic pictures?'

"I had to think about this, and knowing this routine from many times before, I knew she wanted more than a single answer. But she was patient. I always stalled with a long 'Ahhhhhhhh' while I thought and then started my slow answers. 'The museum in Hawaii has paintings, and Auntie has pictures on her walls, and the school library has some art books, and you saved some of my best pictures.'

"'Good,' she said. 'Go to the school library. Find the art books. Find the old pictures that are still considered good art. Figure out why they are good.'

"That was it. Again, it was up to me. Pictures are pictures, whether photos or paintings. What makes one good is going to apply, at least to some extent, to all."

"What did the 10-year-old you find out?"

"The 10-year-old me didn't know what it was I had found, but I did know I had found *something*. To this day I wonder how much Tibu knew when she sent me to the school library. Did she know what was there for me to find out?

"Anyway, because we've never been a military power but have been in a strategic position, Kiribati has been under control of the British and the Japanese and has been influenced by other cultures as well, including Americans, and others, who came as missionaries, merchants, and fishermen who brought in the Bahai faith, Christianity, and Islam, as well as their own interests and cultures. So you can find all sorts of things in bookstores, libraries, and people's shelves.

"When I asked the librarian for art books, I wasn't into reading the tedious text. I wanted to look at the pictures. I could tell which ones were older by the settings and costumes. I didn't know what I was looking for, but I kept looking. I knew immediately when I found it. It was a single book *full* of wonderful paintings. I checked it out, ran all the way back, and dropped it breathless in her lap. 'I found it!'

"'Ah. Dutch and Flemish Masters,' she said as she turned to the table of contents. 'Utrecht, Rembrandt, Frans Hals, Jan van Goyen, van Eyck, Vermeer...why these?' She sounded a bit puzzled by my choice at that point.

"'Ahhhhh... Because they're *magic*!' I told her.

"'Yes. They *are* magic,' she said as she had held up Rembrandt's *The Night Watch*. 'How is this one magic?'

"I stalled. 'Ahhhh...it tells secrets without words!' I knew I was on a roll even if I didn't know what it was I had found.

"'Yes; what does it tell you?' she persisted.

"I took a stab. 'It says this man here with the big white collar and the red cloth across his chest is very important. He's even more important than the man next to him in the shiny yellow suit because that man is looking at the one with the white collar. But that little girl is important too, but I don't know why.'

"Then she asked how I knew the man was so important. I knew he was, but I had to look very hard to figure it out. Tibu didn't care if I took all day. She sat with her eyes nearly closed, back upright, and a half smile on her face.

"'*Everything points to him*!' I startled her so badly I think she nearly had a heart attack. I showed her all the lines of the spears, arms, rifles, legs, and banner poles.

"'So,' she said, 'even without your knowing it, lines pointed your eyes to him. Remember that. But no lines pointed to the little girl. What is there about her and the man that shows you they are important?'

"It was the use of light, of course. She said, 'Without light, there is no life. Lines carry the eyes, and light gives life.' We spent weeks talking about the paintings in that book, taking pictures and applying the principles, most times without my even knowing that's what I was doing.

"I learned the most dramatic light was at dawn and sunset or from a single small source in a dark setting. The brightest light was at noon, but it was a flat light, without depth. A sky heavy with gray clouds at noon gave enough light but was also darkly ominous, full of fear or sadness. Light didn't just give life; it gave life full of emotion."

Laurel was hanging on every word, enthralled. "But what about color? How can you have dramatic and emotional pictures without color?"

"Are you familiar with Ansel Adams?"

"Yes, of course," Laurel told him.

"His photos are black and whites and unsurpassed, some say, for drama, emotion and beauty. Of course color can play a part too—as well as contrast, scale, and pattern. But all that can be considered a separate dimension—another discussion—for the moment.

"So, back to those early days. I learned to walk around leaning on coconut trees until they pointed or flowed in directions that accented my subjects and drew the eyes. For people and animals, I learned if nothing else was in focus, make sure the eyes were. I learned about how to convey messages and feelings in topics, too.

"Sometimes I would spread my latest pictures out for my grandmother. She would look at the all of them slowly and carefully. Then she would ask me, using my own words from that first discovery of mine, which ones were magic and why. That summer was life-changing. Or, more accurately, life-directing.

"After I went back to Hawaii that fall, my grandmother wrote my parents and told them to get a camera for me that I could use under water. No explanation, no homework assignment, no waiting for a special occasion."

"Why did she do that?" Laurel interrupted.

"I can only tell you what happened when I took it swimming. By then I was eleven and had gotten very good at free diving—that is, just holding my breath and diving down to explore the bottom with nothing more than goggles."

"Please tell me your parents were nearby!"

"Someone was always near enough and watchful, but I was also left to test my own limits, too. But anyway, I was anxious to take photos of things big and deep. It didn't take long for me to discover that what I ended up with were very dark blue images of unrecognizable shapes."

"Was it the camera?"

"Not at all. It was...well, science. To my eyes, things under water were appearing about 25% larger. My eyes were also adjusting somewhat for the lack of light as the water increased in depth. And in that darkness, there was much less to see. Where there is light, there is life. I quickly learned my best photos were going to be in the shallowest water of the smallest things, in the most light. Things I could look most carefully at, the things that could magically carry messages in my photos of them.

"Later, in business courses, we called it 'attention to detail,' which ties in with the butterfly effect and the concept of keeping the big picture in mind. Oh, and that summer? I also learned to wear a long sleeved shirt in the water so my back, shoulders, and arms didn't burn raw."

Laurel jumped in. "I want to hear more, but if the final goal is saving a nation, I want to hear how you're going to do that with money. And I want to hear why you're not completely overwhelmed by that sense of responsibility."

"I'd love to tell you about it. But this could take a while. Do you want to wait for tomorrow?"

"That would make sense, but no. How are you holding up?"

"I'm okay. The 'big picture' is very big, but I can help give you a beginning. First of all, it is very easy to get overwhelmed. It happens to me all the time. I've had to find a way, a path to retread, to retrace and go back on, and to keep myself focused. For me, it's become a basic priority list. And what works for the first things on that list will usually also work, in one way or another, and in a larger scale, for the entire 'big picture.' Which, ultimately, in this case, would not only be the survival of a nation, but the planet. How's that for overwhelming?"

"Not just overwhelming…it sounds crushing!"

"The other factor in not being overwhelmed is remembering that I'm not alone. More and more are trying to do what I'm doing. In different ways and different places, but this is the age of easy communication. Of course, what we're all up against is substantial, too."

Laurel kept pace with Dak. "The others that strive to accomplish similar goals—I can understand that. And communication with them. The Internet can make that easy. TED talks alone have certainly opened my world. But personal priorities that work, ultimately for the whole planet? You'll have to help me out with that one."

"Maybe it would be easier if you started off thinking of the butterfly effect. Or maybe it would be easier for me to explain if *I* kept that in mind. So if my first priority was the happiness and welfare of my own extended family and I knew the immediate danger to them was being caused by climate change, would there be anything I could do to help eliminate climate change that would not also help the planet as a whole?" he asked Laurel.

"No, but you're leaving out a lot of steps in the process there. And maybe yes. You would be up against some strong opposition from businesses that are very profitable and do a large portion of the polluting and destruction."

Dak agreed. "Of course. I would be going against businesses, but it would still be helping the planet. I know that was a gross generalization, but still an accurate one. And it's a fairly good segue back to that big picture discussion. Although, if we include the whole planet, talking about a single small nation suddenly doesn't seem so big anymore. See, it's already getting more manageable. Size is relative.

"That tiny nation is a gem of another question. How would you define a nation, leaving out anything to do with physical territory? That concept isn't new. Think of all the nations that lost their territory to others and then regained it later, with their sense of national identity still intact."

"Like?"

"Like the Soviet Union nations that are once again independent countries and the Native American nations that have regained their identities."

Once Dak said it, it seemed obvious to Laurel. "Oh, of course! A nation has to share a basic culture, a language, a religion—no, wait… now I'm thinking of the U.S. We have Americans of every ethnic background, color, religion. Damn, I'm in trouble already."

"Maybe that's the point. You can't do it—or *shouldn't* do it. It's the people themselves who decide if they belong together as a group, whether or not they define it. Like any family, they can have dysfunctional relationships and argue amongst themselves, but in the end, they define themselves as a unit. Or they choose not to and leave. And that can be an acceptable choice, too.

"So, we have our group of I-Kiribati—a large group if not all 100,000—that want to maintain their national identity and culture. Or, psychologically, will need to for their own mental stability."

"Has anyone come up with any ideas yet?"

Dak was quick to respond. "Absolutely. Many people are very concerned about this. And climate change doesn't happen at a set and steady rate worldwide, so we have already seen severe effects in other places. That has already prompted many into action.

"The Maldives average about four feet above sea level, so as storm surges become worse, that entire nation—all of its islands—could be under water very soon, too. The Seychelles are losing beaches already. Palau, Micronesia, Venice, and Bangladesh are affected. You already know about Alaska. Kiribati is hardly alone.

"At first, before the full impact of the problem was understood, the solutions in Kiribati were simple seawalls and manmade mangrove forests. Those are still being used, but it's now clear that those are not enough.

"Buying land on one of the islands in Fiji and then moving a small part of the population there is under consideration. Then, a small portion of the population would be separated from the rest by about 1,300 miles and would be refugees in a different culture. They would have to have, or learn, skills that would make them independent there—not a burden on that government—without taking jobs away from the native population.

"Whether some of the I-Kiribati move to Fiji or to those countries held responsible for climate change, it is a solution I strongly object to. First, every person from Kiribati would have to be trained to be skilled. And not just skilled, but trained in a profession that the host nation needs, not necessarily a profession of their choice. They would also have to learn a new language and culture. All this makes success unlikely. But more important, with the population scattered across the globe, families would be torn apart, and the nation, and its culture, would become completely extinct. Extinct. Like the dodo.

"Some of the endangered island nations' leaders are turning to the very cause of the problems. The extensive use of fossil fuels—as far back as the Industrial Revolution—started one of these profitable and dangerous trends. But have you ever really looked at the drilling rigs used in oceans? Here. Here's a photo of one made by an Italian firm that's for severe weather climates. It will take 35-meter waves. Something like this could be converted into a stable manmade island that could house 5,000 people and become a tourist attraction while calling attention to the ecological situation as well."

"Are you thinking of doing that? It would be expensive but possible, wouldn't it?"

"It would be possible, but no. For me, for my family, for my nation, I would not support this. And before you ask, I'll tell you why not. For an island to be habitable, it must be a very complex and self-sustaining eco-structure. There must be a way to procure water without dumping salt or sewage into the sea, there must be a way to produce clean and sustainable energy, there must be a source for a complete and balanced diet, room to provide medical needs, educational needs, esthetic needs, and mental health needs, and governing systems, to name a very few. Those structures aren't that developed at this point.

"And people don't do well in square concrete and metal boxes, even if all other needs are met. With extensive conversion planning, it might work, but there are already other interesting plans. Here's a round home for a family of six that is supposed to be incorporated into a community of water-based pods that all have parts of their structures under water. They can be docked or connected together or free of one another.

"Then here are some designs by the Dutch. I believe about 20% of the Netherlands is already underwater, so you would expect them to be in the forefront. People are already buying and living in these.

"This is a beauty by a German company—at an astronomical price. It's a five-story structure with parts underwater.

"This is the site for the Seasteading Institute out of California. Their approach is to build a floating city that is completely independent. It's very intriguing. It addresses the political climate and security more than most others.

"I would have to do more research to see if any of these are truly completely ecologically independent. For example, have they, or could they, take into account the pollinators for our native plants? As they are originally designed, they, of course, don't take our culture into account, but it is probably adaptable."

Dak had hardly taken a breath. "And this one—it's huge; it would hold half our nation. You can imagine the cost! Billions! It's by a French-based Belgian designer. These designs seem quite ecologically sensitive. But I find them the most beautiful, too. Full of curves and trees. You don't find lots of straight lines in nature, and the basic designs in this are not straight.

"Many are designed to be free floating. I have no idea what the psychological impact of 'drifting rudderless,' so to speak, would be. Emotionally, many I-Kiribati are already there."

Laurel was quick to note, "No matter how good you are at both jobs, you could never buy any of these!"

"No. Of course not. Not by myself."

"How much time do you have to find a solution?"

"For Kiribati, time has already run out. And it's not just me that thinks so. Way back in 2008, when President Tong was in New Zealand for a United Nations Environment Day, he told them, 'We may already be at the point of no return.' Right now, wells have salt seeping in. Storm surges are higher. Vegetation is dying, fishing is being ruined. We, and the rest of the island nations, should be evacuating this very day. We should already be gone.

"But I think I know a better way to answer all your questions. We'll talk about that more tomorrow. Time to get out of this restaurant! One quick stop at my room, and I'll be at your door in less than five minutes."

~

Laurel's head was swimming—not only from the information Dak had shared with her, but also from the fact that he shared it with her at all.

Dak knocked before entering her room, a piece of folded cloth in his hand. Laurel recognized it as his sarong, but it was bulky and appeared to be wrapped around something else. He was also carrying a magazine and a bottle of wine. Once in the room, he placed the bundle on the table just inside the door but brought the magazine and wine with him. He began in a way that was unexpected by Laurel. He took his time with no mention of what was in store.

"Remember our discussion of the climate refugees and other places in danger? I have a publication here with me called '100 Places to Explore Before They Disappear.' That must be the byline of the new disaster tourism business. Anyway, let me show you some of the photos. Look at the island in this cover shot. I love how you can see below the water's surface all around it. Such an effective statement."

"The colors are gorgeous. Where is this?"

"It's the Maldives. Here's a complete opposite."

Dak flipped to a double-paged photo of Sagarnatha National Park in Nepal. "What a photo this is. That cold, snowy mountain in a nest of purple clouds below against a sky on fire. Amazing shot. And on this very next page is this desert in Saudi Arabia. A monochromatic portrait of line and texture. Why don't you flip through and look at the rest while I get the bath ready." He knew keeping her mind busy would kept her from thinking too much about what he might have planned for her.

Dak poured a glass of wine for Laurel and one for himself. She had already dutifully engrossed herself in the pictures when he wordlessly handed her the glass. He took his own glass with him and ran the water in the tub until it was warm. Sealing off the drain, he added a squeeze from one of the bottles left by the hotel. A thin, fragile layer of bubbles frothed and rose with the water until the tub was full. Dak turned off the taps and looked upward. The row of lights over the sink glared harshly. He reached up and loosened all but a single small bulb.

Leaving his wine there, Dak returned to the bedroom, picked up Laurel's glass, and said to her, "Come get in the tub while I do a few things in here. I'll only be a couple of minutes." Dak led her in and put her glass on the edge of the tub. He walked out, leaving the door slightly ajar.

Laurel's eyes were not yet accustomed to the level of light. It seemed almost too dark as she folded her clothes, tucking her underwear out of sight, between the layers. She slid under the frothy foam. *Did he really having something to do, or was he diplomatically respecting my privacy?* she wondered. *Or both?*

Dak knocked softly on the door. "In the tub?"

"Yes. It's lovely," she said, glass in hand and trying to sound casually composed. Laurel glanced down and noted with gratitude that her forty-something breasts looked youthfully buoyant in the deep water.

Dak was barefoot and wearing one of his sarongs. He sat on a stool next to the tub. Slowly swirling the water, he tested the temperature. "I'm going to add a bit more hot water." Re-testing, he took the slippery bar of soap and put a bit on his hands, gently rubbing her back. Then her arms. Bubbles were rapidly disappearing while the soap was making the water milky. He moved to her legs, lifting and soaping one and then the other. Dak cupped his hand to rinse her back and arms, his left hand on her shoulder. She remembered that gesture from somewhere, but right now she couldn't—didn't want to—think.

Dak swirled the cleansing water around her legs and poured the warmth over her chest. Laurel sighed heavily, relaxing in spite of herself. He parted her legs and swirled the warmth between them. After a few moments of stillness, he stood, holding a large bath towel in one hand for her. He extended his other hand to steady her as she stepped out.

The air was warm and steamy. Dak toweled Laurel dry and wrapped a larger dry bath towel around her, tucked in the end, and walked her toward the bed. He had already drawn the drapes, leaving the room a shade darker than the bathroom. He sat beside her as she stretched out.

"I want to offer you a way to be responsive but without feeling a need to be responsible for reciprocating."

"I'm listening."

"What I have is a pair of towel strips made into large loops. If I hang them over the headboard, you can rest your wrists on the loops as you hold the material with your hand. It can give you the sensation of having your hand movement restricted but the confidence of knowing you can take them out of the loops at any time."

Without waiting for a response, Dak lifted the loops from the floor next to the bed and positioned them on each side of the headboard. "Now close your eyes and take four slow, deep breaths, relaxing more with each one. Keep your eyes closed from now on if you can. That's it…one more deep breath. Good. I'm going to massage a bit of coconut oil into your skin. You won't smell this kind. Just feel it."

Dak squeezed a small amount of the white, pearly translucence into his palm. It liquefied so quickly, the fluid fell in drops on Laurel's skin. He began to smooth it onto her shoulders, coaxing it down to her arms and hands. He meticulously massaged each finger on her left hand with patient gentleness. Raising her surrendering hand, he placed it in a loop, closing her fingers around the material. As he stroked her right hand, he murmured to her, "Relax every muscle. Let your eyelids be heavy; too heavy to open."

Dak untucked the large bath towel and, exposing only one side, laid it on the bed next to Laurel's body. He smoothed the fluid down her ribs on one side. He opened the rest of the towel. Now fully exposed in the dim light, Dak's fingertips began again just above her collarbones. Gliding even more slowly, he worked down the front of her chest, at first avoiding her breasts, moving across her belly. There was an involuntary ripple of Laurel's abdominal muscles that calmed as Dak continued, never allowing her skin to lose contact with his.

His warm, slippery touch caressed the flesh of her breasts before moving to her now erect nipples. Laurel's fingers tightened around the towel strips as she heard a low moan coming from deep in her own throat. Her hips began to rock almost imperceptibly as her heels searched randomly across the sheets for a nonexistent foothold.

With more speed, he moved his palms over her body, down her thighs. Sliding his hands further, he lifted her knees and placed his body between her raised feet. With a quick sliding motion downward and then up, he easily found his goal and thrust his engorged penis into her. Laurel sensed his body tightening as his movements intensified.

With barely a breath between his orgasm and withdrawal, Laurel immediately felt his touch on her clitoris. His fingers glided with a slowed and nearly imperceptible pressure. Instead of dropping her arousal, it sent convulsions of desire through every cell in her body. Her orgasm was far more powerful than any she had ever had before.

Dak moved up beside Laurel. Her head fell onto his chest, and her breathing subsided to an easy, relaxed level.

"Could I ask you something? Something about just now."

"Of course," he answered.

"How did you know? How did you know I needed more? It was easy to fake an orgasm with my husband. He never knew."

"Maybe he did know but let you take the lead—let you make the decision. Maybe he was waiting until you felt you wanted to discuss it with him."

"Maybe. I never considered that. But how did you know?"

Dak resumed the academic approach that worked for Laurel. "There are a half-dozen ways. One of the first signs of orgasm is a strong rhythmic contraction of the vaginal muscles. A woman can learn to do that voluntarily. Sometimes to enhance her own experience, sometimes to squeeze her partner's penis or tighten the passage to enhance his experience. And some use it to fake an orgasm. Look up Kegel exercises on the Internet."

"I will! You always—or nearly *always*—sound so clinical and non-personal. It actually makes it easier for me to talk to you about these things. If you had ever used some icky fake flattery or said the wrong thing—what I would expect from a cheap man-for-hire—that would have been the end for me."

He had judged his approach with her accurately. It was a style of interaction that served *him* well, too. "Silence over insincerity?"

"In a nutshell, yes. But I still want to know, do many women fake orgasms?"

"Even one is too many. Communication and know-how—finding *out* how—can fix most of the problems. Attitudes, stress, personal beliefs all have an influence."

"How else can you tell?"

"Well, it's not exactly an exact science! I need to know the woman well and know how her body reacts to an orgasm. Then I'll know what to look for. But there are some general signs. Along with those rhythmic vaginal contractions, there are also contractions of the uterus, anal area, and feet. Do you curl your toes?"

"Sometimes. All the time? I'm not sure."

"Some women have involuntary muscle reaction in their hands, too. All the body parts that became engorged, swollen, and different in color will quickly go back to normal. Before climaxing, the vagina opens but then collapses. Is that clinical enough for you?"

"You're doing fine! Anything else?"

"Believe it or not, the best indication is the emotional reaction. It's actually triggered by a hormone release. Afterwards, women are not likely to be restless or say, 'Thanks, I have to go now' and jump up to leave.

"Let me ask you," Dak said, leading her in to being more open. "Would you always want your partner to know if you were faking it?"

Laurel hesitated before answering. "Maybe what I'd prefer would be a partner that I would never feel I needed to fake anything with. Oh. That puts you at the top of the list, doesn't it? Actually, if I think back, it's a list of only one person."

"Now that you know more, you can share that with anyone you're with from now on. The quality of communication is in your hands. Your list can be endless!"

"That is, if I ever find someone who meets my new and higher standards."

~

Dak went to his room and made some calls. He wanted to be sure everything could be arranged before he talked to Laurel tomorrow. Yes, Megan could continue taking over the business while Laurel would be away. Rosa was happy at the house. And she and Gus were getting along fine with Greta.

Now for Lila. Dak told her about his plans. Could she be ready to help get Laurel ready? She could. Everything was in place.

~

As soon as Lila hung up, she sprinted to share the news. "Tibu! Tibu! He's coming and he's bringing her with him!"

"Slow down, Lila. What did he say?"

"He just needs to ask her if she'll come. He said he would be here either way. But if she does come, he'll bring her here so you can meet her. He's never brought anyone here before. Why this one? Don't you wonder, Tibu?"

"You're doing enough of that for both of us."

Lila took the hint and calmed her behavior, but not the questions ricocheting in her mind.

~

Laurel knocked on Dak's door. "You ready for breakfast?"

"I am. Come in. We can walk to the restaurant together."

"Good, because I'm starved," she said as she was already moving out the door.

"Me too. Did you sleep well?" Dak asked.

"I did."

As they were about to enter the dining area, Laurel began again. "Don't we need to see if there are any loose ends to tie up here before we leave the country?" she asked as they sat at an empty table near the sunny window. She was suddenly distracted by the view. She gazed at the lush vegetation and blue waters beyond. "Maybe I don't want to leave at all," she said, to herself more than to Dak.

Dak understood the depth of that one comment. He paused to see if she would say more. "You want to stay?" was all he said.

She was still looking beyond the window. "I feel as though I've let myself be picked up and swept from place to place, so busy paying attention to what I was seeing and experiencing in the moment that only now have I stopped to see how far I've come, in so many ways. It's mind-boggling. I need to stop, catch my breath; let in sink in. So much in such a small space of time. I need to get a better hold of all of this before going back to New England and my life there. I don't want this all just to disappear into my past.

"Then maybe this is a good time to bring something up. I want to show you something I've never told any client about, never mind *shown* them. In order to see it, it will add extra days to the trip. I will pay for any extra costs as my gift to you. You could even call it an investment on my part if a 'gift' sounds too personal. I've been able to reach Megan, Gus and Rosa and they have all agreed to take care of everything there. The choice, of course, is still yours."

"My curiosity is certainly piqued. But you've done too much to make sure it would work without saying anything to me! It feels so much like that last year with Mark, making decisions for my life without my knowledge. You really went behind my back, even with my staff. It feels manipulative and less than honest."

Dak was shocked at his own faux pas. His excitement gone, he could barely make eye contact. "You're absolutely right. I'm so sorry. I shouldn't have handled it that way. I only wanted to make sure it was at least possible for you so a decision would be easier. But that's not a valid excuse. I apologize. You do have a choice with this."

Not yet in a forgiving mood, Laurel's voice was still tense. "I understand. Maybe I'm just being too sensitive. May I ask what it is that you want to show me?"

"I want to show you Kiribati."

Laurel's breath caught in her throat. She answered cautiously, and not without some suspicion. "I truly don't know what to say…why did you call it an investment? Do you want me to invest money in some project?"

"No. I want more than that. I want some of your time and your ideas. I can't do this alone. We have different ways of viewing situations and problem solving without it causing friction between us. If you see Kiribati, and see what I'm working with and trying to do, I think it would make for some very productive brain-storming. I'm often in the Boston area, so we could confer on developments and ideas when I'm there.

"But I'm not asking for a commitment now. I'm just asking you to go and look at the place and talk to me about what you see. If nothing else, it will give you a little more time before you have to return to work."

"It's quite an offer, but I feel like I need more information. Would we see any of your friends and family while we're there?"

"Yes, some. Would that be a problem?"

"I don't know. Would it? Who would you tell them who I am? And where would we stay?"

"The first night, we'd stay at a hotel. From there, we'll take day trips and stay at other hotels—some simple…almost primitive. It will be informative, but fun, too. It will be a week in total; there aren't many flights in and out.

"Then, at the end, there is going to be a meeting of people concerned about climate change worldwide. That's where it all comes together.

"This meeting is important, and the people who attend also need to keep their participation completely confidential—but you're used to that by now. I'd like you to attend with me, but if you choose not to, you'd still have to wait until the next flight is scheduled before you can return without me."

Still stunned, Laurel was softening. "I am intrigued. Whatever else, it will be a once-in-a-lifetime opportunity. I feel I should take you up on it, if for no other reason than, if I don't, I know I'll always regret it."

"There is one other thing I should tell you before you decide. The meeting will run about three days. It's held in a secluded spot on private property, on the small island of Teraina. That means accommodations are limited. We will probably have to share a room or a small guest house with two beds. If it comes to that, I will provide you will as much privacy as possible. But there will be times when it will be less than ideal."

"Privacy and intimacy. I've already experienced a level of that combination on this trip. I appreciate your candor…and your consideration. I think I'd like to try. You know, that's something I never thought was even possible."

"What, exactly?" Dak asked.

"I don't have a word for it. *Is* there one for this experience? Intimacy with privacy. This isn't exactly casual sex, but it isn't the usual escort and client relationship either, is it? Yet, you are being paid… but, at least initially, not for the sex. I'm not under any delusion of a romantic relationship, either. But if I didn't at least like you and find you physically attractive, I couldn't do this."

Dak did not have an easy answer for this. "It has evolved into something…well, atypical. I am still an employee, so a sort of 'friends with benefits' doesn't fit, either. But, on the other hand, there is an element of friendship. Do you need to define it? Label it?"

"I don't know, Dak. Maybe. This is so new to me on so many levels, I think having a name for it would help in some way. This seems so much easier for you to accept without question or examination. Is it because this is nothing new to you?"

"This are no two relationships, professional or not, that are alike. Having said that, there are aspects of this that are both familiar and unfamiliar. How would you describe this to someone else if you were free to talk about it?"

"There will be questions about the trip. That much won't be difficult—an international business trip with a generous dose of sightseeing and observation of business systems.

"If I could, or needed to, explain the rest? It *is* part professional. The other parts? I would like to call another part of it a type of friendship. But I can't minimize—in fact, I can't emphasize enough—how the sexual part has had a profound effect on me. I don't even know what the effect is yet. I do know it has nothing to do with clinging or possessiveness or the stereotypical 'love affair.' I have to mention that because I now realize I always assumed the more casual the relationship, the more lightweight the sex would be. I somehow thought this kind—this intensity and new experiences—was only possible with an intense, long-term relationship. Now? Honestly, I don't know how I ever came to that assumption."

Dak tried another view. "Maybe it's too soon to define it. It isn't over yet, though we know it will be eventually, and I will still be at the store as a consultant until Megan is back to work. Even then, and afterward, we can't yet predict how much contact we'll continue to have. Nor what kind of contact."

"Are you saying there *will* be some kind of contact?"

"There are reasons for me to be in New England at times. I also think there are business reasons we will be in contact by electronic means if nothing else. Neither of us can predict with any accuracy yet."

"You're right. It is too soon to start dissecting this and slap a label on it. Or to figure out if it even *needs* a label—if *I* need to label it or name it. So tell me more about this meeting."

Dak was glad for the change in subject. "The basics are simple enough. It's a group of powerful people who are passionate about the problems of climate change. They meet to learn the latest facts, events, and statistics and then decide what they will do, how they will work behind the scenes, to better the situation or slow the disaster.

"Since my homeland is soon to be extinct, I've been involved for several years. My photography is the tool I use to support the movement. The locations for the meetings change, but this time it will be near Kiribati.

"But before we talk about this more, wait until you see Kiribati and meet some people there."

"What do you want me to see there? You said this meeting is about climate change; will it help me prepare for that?"

"What I *want* you to see are the very things you *can't* see. I want you to see the Kiribati of my early childhood. I want you to see how it's changing—what the changes have done to our lives. The best I can do is to show you how things are now and tell you about the days before."

Laurel was now thinking beyond the immediate scene. "You know, I've never thought of climate change as something personal. I know about it, I've seen pictures, watched the occasional documentary, read some books. I've even sat in the dark when growing storms knocked out our power while I worried about the roof. But still, I've never felt *I* was *in* it. It wasn't part of my life. I was separated from it from the very things that taught me about it—the screen on my TV, the pages in the books, and the knowledge that tomorrow my power would be up and things would be back to normal."

"Well, if nothing else, I hope you'll see this trip, this place, as something very personal."

~

Laurel had been looking out the window at the vast expanse of water when she heard the announcement that they would be landing shortly at the Bonriki International Airport. There was still nothing but water in sight. Finally, as the plane dipped to touch down, she saw the entire length of the single runway—from watery end to watery end across the narrowness of the island.

She heard Dak explaining, "The Lagoon Breeze has Internet, so depending on services, we might stay there later, but for tonight our hotel will be here on South Tarawa. It's government-run—the Otintaai. It's just west of the airport. Once we get our bags, we'll be there in less than fifteen minutes."

"Of course we will," Laurel said. "Any farther and we'd be in the ocean!"

Laurel took little comfort in Dak's calm demeanor. She reminded herself that both he and the plane had landed here many times. All would be well. Considering the landing strip, she shouldn't have been surprised by the airport. "This is my first open-air airport!" she said.

As Dak had told her, within minutes they were checking into the hotel. The rooms were not lavish by international standards but more than adequate. The air conditioning would make the warm, humid night comfortable. The view of the palms and lagoon was framed by light bamboo-patterned drapes. In any case, Laurel would quickly discover they would be spending very little time inside. There was much to see. And boat rides. There would be lots of boat rides. Air Kiribati and other small air services would provide transportation to more distant atolls.

Dak was careful to give Laurel a well-orchestrated tour. First, he showed her the beautiful white beaches and took her snorkeling in the pristine water, so warm that she could barely feel it as her body glided through. They watched surfers and fishermen while perched on a sailboat, expertly handled by Dak. On Kiritimati, he told her the local and English names for a dozen birds, including the already-endangered Phoenix petrel and the white-throated storm-petrel. On Makin and Butaritari, Laurel was shown swamp taro, banana, and pumpkin gardens. They sipped cool drinks while watching sunsets under rustling palms. And not a word was spoken of climate change.

All along the way, Dak taught Laurel the basic words to use for greetings and simple questions. Laurel was enchanted by the reaction of the local people whenever she practiced her pronunciation. She was always welcomed wherever they went, not because Dak knew them, but because they were guests there.

It didn't take long for Laurel to fall in love with the place and its people. She learned to take offerings to leave at shrines and sit properly during a community meeting in the open air *maneaba*. Dak bought her a traditional *tiibuta*, or blouse, in the same bright colors of the tropical fish that she had learned to call by name.

Laurel was invited to join a celebration *botaki* and sample the local foods. She laughed with the women when they tried to teach her one of the dances while Dak explained the symbolic meanings of the movements. They all laughed even louder when he said she looked more like a chicken than a stately frigate bird. Villagers wove crowns from palm fronds and placed them on her head. And at every stop, she heard a welcoming "*Mauri!*" She was beginning to have a concept of "home" unlike anything she had ever felt before.

Then Dak turned her focus to the sadder side of Kiribati. On the island of Abaiang, they were standing ankle-deep in the sea when he said, "Welcome to the village of Tebunginako…or where it used to be."

"What happened to it?!"

"Stronger storms and higher tides eroded the land. The stumps over there used to be coconut palms, but now they are all dead. The taro and breadfruit are dead too, and there is no land left to grow crops to feed the people. They moved farther inland, but the island is low and narrow. It won't be long before the erosion catches up to them again."

"Where will they go then?"

"That's a critical question for many—for *all* of us, in the end. Tarawa is already over-crowded, the sewage systems and fresh water supplies are already at a breaking point. *Past* the breaking point, really. Poverty is rampant.

"All of the atolls of Kiribati are at various stages of the same problem. And when sea water is washing away land or turning fresh water brackish, the droughts parch what's left. There isn't even a safe way to dispose of our dead anymore."

Dak and Laurel went to Kuria. There she saw more coastal erosion, trash, and litter, and was told of the disappearance of fish, the effects of both storms and droughts, and the lack of safe rubbish disposal. Nonouti proved to have more erosion, more people moving back off the shores, and more ruined taro crops.

It was almost too painful for Laurel to accept. "But it isn't like this everywhere, is it? The island with the birds was so beautiful. There was a good number of tourists there, too."

"Even Kiritimati has serious problems. Septic tanks are already ruining the little fresh water that's there, and over-fishing is a problem in some areas."

"This must sound childlike, but what can you do?"

"Internationally, we are already at the lowest-ranking of creating pollution from fossil fuels, so that's a moot point. We are trying to slow down the destruction while planning for a non-existent future."

Laurel was beginning to see the true impact. "What the hell is wrong with our educational system? It's bad enough that our kids get out of high school without being able to read or write well and without being able to identify half the states in their own country. But this? This is worldwide life and death! And not only are we part of the cause, but we're affected too!

"This is so frustrating! *Embarrassingly* frustrating. I should know all this already. Our schools must start teaching reality. The lower grades spend hours a day learning language skills based on the reading books full of make-believe stories. They could just as easily learn to read and spell by reading about weather and climate change and nature and things they *should* be learning about. The Green School is so far ahead of others."

Dak rarely criticized anything or anyone outright. But now, he could not deny her words. "As a product of Western education, I agree. It falls short in many ways. But I also think you've hit on a solution about the reading material. You know, that's one of the reasons why McDonald's is such a success. Things like Happy Meals are designed to attract kids at a price parents will pay. So when the kids get hooked in early, they will buy McDonald's for life. Those same marketing principles could be applied to ideas and concepts.

"The thing is, we have a lot of educating to do in Kiribati too. Better care and use of our resources and ways to stop contamination of water are all our own responsibility. Do you know anyone in the field of education?"

"I don't think so, but there are related fields; publishers, writers...I'll think about it."

"So are you ready for the rest of it now?"

"More bad news?"

"I hope not! You haven't met Tibu and Lila yet. And there's still the meeting to get ready for."

"I'd feel more self-confident in that high-powered meeting than meeting your family matriarch!"

"She's just my grandmother. You'll enjoy it."

"How should I dress? Is this going to be a dress-up affair?"

"Your choice; barefoot or flip-flops! We've been able to make sure her home is storm-sturdy and ample for her needs, but it's also fairly traditional. She has one structure for cooking, another for sleeping, and an open, raised 'living room' like ones you've already seen. Lila lives there too, but she has a separate small building with walls and doors for her work.

"You'll see it all. And don't be surprised if she makes you help in the kitchen!"

~

"Tibu, this is Laurel. And that's Lila," Dak added, gesturing with his gaze.

"*Alláh-u-Abhá!* Welcome, welcome! Sit there by Lila. Dak has told me much about you! So you've seen our home. Tell me, what did you see?"

"Such welcoming and friendly people! The water, the corals, the birds and fish—so beautiful! And so horrifying, to see how much has already been destroyed. Walls to stop the sea aren't working; water in wells has become salty. Dak says some are catching rainwater, but so much vegetation is being killed. How will you survive?"

"Like this, we can't. We won't. But we have hope. We've survived before when strangers came and brought us destruction. We thought all was lost then, too."

Laurel was already feeling more comfortable with Tibu. "Dak has told me about some of the history here, how bad it was here during the second World War. How did you keep from being swallowed up by all the invaders, the missionaries, and the so-called 'protectors'?"

Dak had warned Laurel about Tibu's style of explanation and discussion. "Some brought buckets of their sand. We ran our hands through them until our fingers were raw and bleeding, but we found a few tiny valuable gems that we kept. Some brought buckets of rice. We thought it was a godsend, but hidden in the grains were pests that multiplied and nearly wiped out everything we had. We threw those away. Some brought diseases, but we grew stronger. Some dropped bombs 'to test them,' they said. Some came to take things. They even took the guano! But that wasn't a problem because they made it legal!" Tibu laughed.

"They took guano? Who did that?"

"The Americans called it The Guano Islands Act. It was a long time ago. Their congress made it legal and took about twenty of our islands. They said no one lived there permanently because there were only palm shacks—like this one. They needed the guano, and we didn't, so wasn't supposed to matter. They still have some of the atolls. Palmyra Atoll has no guano, but it's still in U.S. hands.

"But this thing now…this is different. It comes from too far away to stop. It comes from too far away for those that cause it to see, or care, how it's destroying us—and themselves. It's been growing for too long. This, we can't survive like before. New ways to die mean we have to find new ways to survive.

"But enough of history long gone! What did you see that you had never seen before?"

Laurel visibly relaxed with the easier question. "'All of it' would be one answer. I've never been to any Pacific island before. But what impressed me the most was the people, their frame of mind. They all know what the future will be for them, but they are all cheerful and happy, living in the moment today. That attitude is surviving in them even as their homes are being destroyed."

"What else did you see? Things that aren't so easy to talk about."

"Well, in all honesty, Kiribati is a place of many faces. People will be dying of thirst while drowning in water. I saw sanitation was clearly a problem. Many areas need better toilet facilities. And the litter is getting quite bad in places. I think if there was an easy solution, it would have already been implemented. You have no space for complex landfill systems, and the geological structure and lack of drainage ability makes digging a simple outhouse impossible. These are impacting your survival, too. And on top of everything else, I have some questions about women's rights."

Tibu was pleased with Laurel. "You're an honest woman! Good! How will *you* survive?"

"That's a good question. I'm still learning what it is I—what *all* of us in the U.S.— will be facing: storms, drought, record cold, record heat, failing food sources, desperate people out of control...all of it."

"And more. But enough of that! Stay for dinner. Dak will help cook. Lila too. You too. We'll tell about the good days here before and talk about the good ones that are coming!"

Lila had held back at first but was in her element in the kitchen, skillfully directing Dak and Laurel. Tibu watched. And listened. Once everyone was busy with their assigned tasks, Lila asked Laurel, "You didn't say anything about the poverty. That's something the usual tourists find pretty horrendous. But then, you're not the usual tourist, are you?"

"I guess not. I certainly saw enough of it, but it made me think about the word. It's a word in English that is used in many strange ways with different meanings. Like our word 'love.' You know; we love our family, our spouse, our dog, spinach, the color purple. All very different feelings, but the same word."

"And 'poverty'?" Lila pressed on.

"Well, look at the situation you're talking about. The so-called 'poor' people here who have very few material possessions live hand-to-mouth, and are very cheerful and seemingly happy. Back where I live, high-paid executives and people who have more than enough money and things of all sorts dream of being able to live on a beach with nothing more than a way to fish and gather coconuts!

"So which group is 'poor' and which is rich, in spirit? Rich in love of friends and extended family? Rich in peace of mind and contentment? And which group is always stressed to the max? Poverty is relative. I'm not saying there aren't things they could use—or even need. But I think we have to look at how they feel about their own status, too.

"I mean, look at Dak!"

Dak froze for a moment, staring at Laurel.

"When he lives here, he stays in a 'bedroom' with a thatched roof and no walls! Poor thing!"

Lila doubled over with laughter but quickly became serious. "But there's a sadness you don't see. So many loved ones have left to places very far away for an education, for jobs, for a less threatened life. They're not completely happy being away, and those left behind aren't happy either."

"And, if nothing changes, if the way the problems are addressed doesn't change, it will only get much worse," Dak interjected. The women nodded in agreement.

Laurel was never asked a prying personal question about herself. However, the little family listened eagerly to whatever she shared.

Likewise, Laurel didn't ask why there were only the three of them here together. But after what Lila had said, she remembered Dak's parents were most likely out of the country and assumed others in the family were too.

When it was time to leave, Tibu turned to Laurel. "You must come back in July. The 12th is our Independence Day, and the celebrations are something you need to share with us. I never know when Dak will be here, so come without him! You will not regret it!"

"I will try, but that's only a couple of months away. It would be quite soon for another trip this far away from my obligations back in the States. But I promise, if I can't make it this year, I will be here next year."

"Good. We'll make sure you won't forget!"

~

After dinner, Laurel thought about the impact on not only the personal lives of the I-Kiribati, but also, by extension, all those in the South Pacific. She wondered how diverse the populations were. Was there a solution to the rising waters and vanishing resources that could be one-size-fits-all? Who lived here in this vast ocean area? Did they even have a common language?

Laurel asked Dak about Tibu's greeting. She caught "Allah" and thought it sounded Arabic. "She's not Muslim though, is she?"

"No, she was raised Bahai."

"Oh. I'll have to look that up. I know nothing about it." Laurel went on. "You know, I think you've been minimizing her scope of knowledge. You talk about her wisdom, yet she has a lot of information about a lot of different topics. But she told me she didn't finish high school. How did she learn about so much?"

"You're right; she is knowledgeable. How did she learn so much? I guess you could call it 'educational bibliomancy.' She picks up a book—absolutely *any* book—and reads it from cover to cover. She finds most facts fascinating but, for her, mostly unnecessary. It's how your heart leads you to use those facts that she finds more important.

"And she doesn't talk about it, but I know she's found places where she can explore the Internet. The youngsters are more than happy to show her how to do searches. So, when the time comes, I'm betting she'll know more about how to go about saving this place than I do."

"And speaking of saving us," Laurel said, "fill me in a little more on the meeting. Tell me more about how this group operates. What should I expect of it?"

"I'm sure you already know of so-called secret groups in general, like the Freemasons, Skull and Bones, the Bilderberg Group. I shouldn't compare ours to them, but how we work has similarities. This group is not that big or powerful, but it can be, and has been, very influential. And it must be just as anonymous. If you recognize people—and you will—don't be surprised. Most of all, remember that your presence is just as valuable as theirs. You might not have some of their funds or the political power, but you do have other things to offer. Even if you haven't figured out what those things are. You will."

"Why is it such a hush-hush group? It doesn't sound like there are any illegal activities going on."

Dak replied as briefly as he could. "No. Nothing illegal, but anyone with any power or position must always consider security. Especially these days. And then there are outsiders who are profiting from endeavors that the group would like to stop. That doubles the security concerns."

"It sounds more like a mini-summit meeting. I don't think I have the clothes to go! I didn't bring any business suits or anything very formal! What else will I need?"

"The most important will be for an opening formal dinner. Lila has agreed to help with that. You won't need anything else that you don't already have. It gets much more casual after that dinner. We'll be bringing all our things with us and then going to Hawaii for a layover before leaving from there for Boston."

"Does this group have a name? What does it do? What do I do while we're there?"

“Officially, it has no name because, officially, it doesn’t exist. Amongst ourselves we call it the ‘The Silent Group,’ and members are ‘The Silent Ones.’ More often, we just call it ‘The Group.’ That way, if someone slipped and said something about it, the response would be, ‘What group?’ We never speak publicly about our efforts. We are never tied to any of the movements, projects, or leaders that we promote.”

Laurel was still unsure of herself being there. “It sounds like something so far beyond my realm of knowledge and experience. What depth of understanding do I have? I’m an outsider, basically a tourist here.”

“No outsiders would be allowed in the group. I would not bring an outsider. I told you this trip, getting you here, is an investment. I need your ideas. We all need your ideas. You know far more than you realize. This will be an opportunity for you to see that. But more importantly, raging climate change is part of your world just as much as anyone else’s. It’s just happening faster—or in more obvious ways—for some of us.”

“We both know I’m not educated in these areas. I know so little about this.”

“Sounds like you’re fighting that ‘first time’ problem of yours. Have you ever taken a course about something you thought you knew nothing about?”

“Of course.”

“And during a lecture, sat there nodding your head in affirmation?”

“Well, yes.”

“You were agreeing with what was being said because something in you already knew it to be true. It will be like that for you here, too. And if nothing else, go thinking of the opportunity this is to learn about a completely different approach to business, both domestic and international. Especially during casual conversations, you’ll be learning how much silent influences affect all business and politics.”

“Well, yes, it will be that. I’ve got to stop automatically going inert. ‘Old habits...’ as they say.”

"Good! I'll get you set up with Lila. She'll take care of an outfit for the opening evening."

Now that she was set on going, Laurel was already planning how to approach the experience. "I've been doing research on the Internet whenever I could get a connection, but I see I'm going to have to do a lot more."

~

Laurel was alone with Lila for the first time. "Dak must have told you I do some sewing."

"Is that what you do for a job full-time? Is it enough for you and your grandmother to live on?"

"Sure. Our needs aren't that extensive. You've seen how we live. My biggest profits are from the things I sell at the hotel shops on commission. I put a hell of a mark-up on those. I didn't used to, but I learned that when I sold them too cheaply, no one thought much of them. The higher the price tag, the more people thought of them, and they sold like crazy. I also take on the role of a local designer when I need to.

"But no time for stories about me. We need to get you into a proper costume. I keep pictures for ideas and reference. Look at this one. It's a Bottega Veneta. It was originally almost $2,500. Ridiculous! See how the belt draws the attention away from the face and back to the dress? Egotistical designer. But I guess that's the point when you send a model down a catwalk. Anyway, without the belt, I could whip up something like this for you, but longer and in a different color, in less than an hour."

"Why a different color? This is a beautiful turquoise."

"It is, but it's all wrong for you. The black belt is all wrong, too; the eye goes right there. You want the dress to dramatically draw attention to *you*, who you are, not to itself. The major color of the fabric should be a match to your eyes. Or at least a color that will accentuate your eyes, draw attention to them. That's why your earrings are going to have to be carefully chosen too; color, shape, length, and metal."

"Metal?"

"Gold or silver. As in yellow or gray."

"Funny. Color is so important to your work, but Dak says black and white can carry the real drama."

"I've heard him say that. For him, I think 'drama' means despair, danger. Something like that. He needs some hell-raising joy in his life."

"Did you learn about sewing and color from your grandmother? Dak credits her with much of what he's learned. Maybe more indirectly than directly. When he talks about her, he makes her sounds so wise. And she seemed wise to me, too."

"My grandmother *is* wise. And maybe a little lovably nutty. She's wise because there is so much she doesn't know about, and she *knows* what she doesn't know. Who else can say that? Do you know what it is that you don't know? People today are so caught up in what they *do* know, what they *think* they know, what they *want* to know, what they think they *need* to know. The Information Age. As if information is the most important thing to have. Information, power, and money.

"Maybe they're right. I have the information to know how to sew, to make enough money for us to do all right. Maybe I stopped too soon. I don't have the information or the money to save us. But maybe no one does. Maybe no one can."

"Does Dak think he can?"

"Tibu thinks he can. But I have no I idea what she means by 'saving' us. She speaks her own language. Time's running out in more ways than one. We've got to get this dress done."

"Sorry. I'm in your hands."

"Let's do it! What do we have to work with? Did you pack a strapless bra?"

"Are you kidding? I'm over 40! I don't own a strapless *anything*."

"Well, you could. You just have to know how to pick out the right kind of underwear. Like building a skyscraper. Gotta get the girls up to the top floor. Why do you think they call them 'foundation' garments?"

"I think these girls are afraid of heights by now. It would take a miracle to get them up past the first floor."

"Nonsense. If you don't believe me, tonight lie flat on your back and notice where they land on your chest. Never mind that they might slide off to the side a little too.

"So for now we'll go with some sort of strap thing. I still might need a bra I can tack part of the dress to.

"If I base it on what you might call a *sarong* or *pareo*, I can use a silk or silk-like fabric and put it together in no time. But we have to be careful. It can look like a too-casual sarong made out of a nice fabric, or a tourist trying to go native, or it can look like a designer creation inspired by a sarong, like the picture of the one we started with. But it won't cost any $2,000."

"I can't wait to see it. Sounds like you and Dak are both creative people, but in very different ways."

"Yeah, dress designing isn't his strongest skill."

"That reminds me. I don't want this to sound like a criticism... it isn't meant to be, but Dak doesn't seem to have much of a sense of humor. He isn't overly serious or glum. He just doesn't make jokes or make funny comments very often. Is that the 'real' Dak? Or is it just the business-only Dak?"

"Dak has had to play parts and roles for so long, I wonder if *he* knows who the real Dak is. I guess it is the real Dak—but only *one* of them. Reality is relative. The Dak that you know is just as real as the one I know or the one his grandmother knows. Just a different one.

"And he's a man. Do you know a man who doesn't have some kind of issue with emotions? Or emotional commitment?"

Laurel persisted. "With all he travels, it would be hard for him to settle down somewhere. And he seems to have healthy emotions when it comes to his grandmother. It's obvious he respects and loves her very much."

"Yeah, well, let's see how long he hangs around. He can't be around her unless he's moving and busy—distracted."

"But they seem to get along fine."

"They do. That's not the problem. If I try to talk to him about planning ahead for taking care of her as she ages, he says I'm being negative. If he's around her too long, he can't deny her weaknesses. He can love her from afar, but not up close or too long. It's too traumatizing for him or some such shit.

"Has he told you about his fantasy island to replace Kiribati?" Lila asked.

Quick changes of subject run in the family, Laurel noted to herself. "No…well, he began to say such a thing might be possible."

"He will—eventually. And it'll sound like he thought of everything. But will there be any accommodation for the chronically ill? The disabled? The elderly? No. He can handle the whole country going down the tubes, but not one old lady in his own family. Well, nobody's perfect, I guess. What he does do right is pretty far out, so I have to try to be more understanding, I suppose. Here. Slip off your T-shirt and let me try a few things. Hold this here while I pin it.

"Oh...change of plans. Your shoulders are sunburned. We're going to have to cover those, or else that's all people are going to remember about you."

"Is that going to be a problem?"

"Well, it looks like it's going to be pretty sore! And it'll peel."

"No, I mean about the dress."

"Oh! No, not at all. Maybe it's a good thing. I wouldn't have thought of anything like this, but now you'll be the only one there with it. Look. If I gather this material and then pull it over the top of your shoulder, it opens up over the boney part and stays gathered up above and below. Of course, it doesn't give you much freedom to move that arm, so don't take any offers for a round of tennis. But if you forget and raise your arm, it will either dig in right here or slide up, so you'll have to pull it back down. No, that's not good."

"You do think of everything, don't you?"

"If I didn't, I wouldn't be in business very long. Design is what sells an outfit, but comfort keeps you in it. And keeps you coming back for more.

"Grab that other binder. There's a million ways to drape cloth. Any woman who's ever worn a sarong knows that. I wonder if all these designers knew it when they did these dresses. Here's some I saved from the 2014 Academy Awards. I loved that year's dresses. Look at this bright dress by Ralph Laurel on Lupita Nyong'o. No, sorry—this was at the Golden Globes. Anyway, it couldn't be simpler, plainer, or more elegant. And it was the perfect color for her. That kind of cape thing part reminded some of Gwyneth Paltrow's 2012 dress by Tom Ford. Also very plain, unembellished, but white—that gave Gwyneth's skin more color by contrast. The bodice had a flow, and the cape-like part covered the shoulders. I bet she couldn't lift her arms, either.

"So many stylized, formalized sarongs for the '14 awards...Sandra Bullock at the Oscars, Camila Alves at the S.A.G. Awards and the Oscars, Kerry Washington...though I'm sure the designers wouldn't agree with me.

"It was Jason Wu that pulled off a best-dressed list for Kerry, and she was. . .what? Eight months pregnant? But choice of material is critical.

"And by the way, look at Gwyneth. She's about the same age you are and looks like she isn't wearing a stitch of underwear under that clingy material. Now that's a good foundation garment of some kind. Probably cost as much as the dress. Those are the designers that should get some credit.

"Here's a picture of an old—well, old in the fashion business—Alexander Wang from around 2010. It brings up images of a black sari draping with something like the sleeve I was talking about. At least on one side. I like this asymmetrical look. Looks comfortable and easy to move in, too, but that's mostly because of the material. It gives. What do you think of a take-off on something like that?"

"Great!"

"I'll take a few measurements, make sure I have the material. Earrings. . .I have some here that will work. I keep some on hand to go with some of the material. Why don't you come back here with that bra in about three hours? A black one is best because the material will be on the dark side. That will make sure it has a more formal feel. And don't worry if you're early or late by an hour or so. Regardless of this event, we're still on tropical island time."

"Is there anything I can do to help? Pick up anything?"

"Well, sure. First, this is a chance to get some important people interested in what's going on here and the ideas we have, so you need to do it well, okay?"

"What are you thinking?"

"Before you come back, go for a massage and a facial at the hotel. *Relax* so you'll look glowing and confident. You've got to *feel* the part. You have to *be* the part. Then, after the fitting, and I know exactly how the lines are going to drape on you, I'm going to have you go to a woman I know who will help with your hair. She'll show you how to put it up so it will look a little more formal, but she'll take into account what will look best for your face *and* what will reflect the curves and drapes of the dress, too. She's done this kind of thing for me before. She really knows what she's doing. And she knows how to teach others to do it. And shoes. We'll take care of that, too."

"What about a purse or bag?"

"What can you lock up in your room, and what do you *have* to have with you? Remember where you'll be. Think of it as a party at someone's home."

"The room key, and what else? I wouldn't want to pull out a phone, and reception has been a problem anyway. And my notebook? I suppose I could leave it in the room, but it sounds like I'll want to take some notes. I have a very small one I could use—about two by three inches."

"Great. It's all small and flat. I can sew a small pocket inside a seam somewhere in your dress where it won't show. Since you're not the Queen of England, you don't need to carry a purse at all. Keeping track of it would only distract you from the business of doing whatever it is you'll have to be paying attention to. Pockets are better than purses anyway. You're not going to forget and leave a pocket behind somewhere! And having no purse makes shoe choice a lot easier. Besides, none of the men will be carrying purses. Not that you should try to be like them, but it will make an understated mental impression of independent confidence."

Laurel suddenly remembered, "Speaking of purses and money, what do I owe you for the dress?"

"Owe me? You don't owe me anything. This is costuming for a production. This is window dressing to promote our product…which just happens to be a set of ideas.

"And there's one more thing. You'll know how well we pull this off because someone will ask where you got the dress or who your designer is. Tell them it's *a*—not *by*—Lila Gordon, and she can be reached through the hotel or hotel shop. Might as well see if I can help the cause by getting some more business, too.

"I *will* let you pay Mara. She'll be the one doing your hair and make-up. She'll teach you how to do that, too. She's the Wonder Woman of women."

Laurel remembered this could be her last chance to find out more about Dak and his family. "On the surface, you talk more and laugh more than Dak, but there's just as much about you that I can't put together."

"My choices are completely different from Dak's. Feel free to ask away."

"Is Dak your brother?"

"Sometimes I wonder. We're cousins, but we were raised as siblings whenever we were here at the same time. I've always thought of him as an older big brother, I guess."

"You couldn't have learned all you know about design and business from trial and error. You must have the education to succeed far from here. Yet you stay."

"I did my time away. Dak did some heavy-handed convincing to get me to stay away long enough to finish a degree. I couldn't wait to get back. Sure, I'm still young, but I was away long enough to figure out it wasn't where I wanted to be. Why go thousands of miles away when I can succeed right here? Every culture has its own definitions of words, its own concepts of ideals. You know that. But I suppose this isn't really a cultural thing. It's personal. For me, to 'succeed' is to have a sense of accomplishment, be free of financial burdens, have a creative outlet, and work with the ones I love. I have all of that right here. And I have it without the stresses of trying to live and compete in a big city with its concrete walls and bad weather.

"I know that must sound very simplistic. And it is, for now. But things have started to move very fast lately. Some for the better, some not. For the I-Kiribati, it's a critical time. I'm not sure how my skills will be useful, and I certainly don't know what it is that I will want to be doing for my own happiness, either. But all this will make more sense after the meeting. And if not, there's still me, my sewing, and Tibu."

"That mysterious meeting again."

"It must seem that way to you. I can't imagine what it's like for you to be learning about it for the first time. I've never attended, but I'm no stranger to it, either."

"You take it all rather lightly. Or at least compared to Dak."

"Yeah, but Dak lives out there in that huge, complicated, fucked-up world. I live here. The safety and success of the group is as dependent on Dak as it is on every other member. I'm not so responsible for that. I look after details.

"Dak's is a voice of one of The Silent Ones in a literal sense. He works quietly. He isn't one to shout or make obvious waves. His words are in his photos. Silent but powerfully moving when he wants them to be; the lap of a wave that erodes the stone cliff."

"So in your view, why all the secrecy? Dak said it all has to do with security for those attending."

"It does. First of all, there's the problem of so-called 'normal' safety for all those high-powered people who attend. With all the nuts out there waving guns and throwing bombs, if it wasn't top secret, can you imagine the security nightmare?

"Second, people can't stop you if they don't know what you're up to. Ask any kid who's kept on reading by flashlight under the covers after the lights-out call. And there's all sorts of people who want to stop us—'dead or alive,' as they say."

"What are you talking about? Dead or alive? You're exaggerating, of course."

"I'm afraid not. At times, it's been open season on environmentalists. Peaceful protesters with no more than voices and signs are murdered on a regular basis. From 2004 to 2014, over 900 environmentalists were killed. That's scary enough, but the real scare is the fact that only ten of the murderers went to prison. Remember Diane Fossey? Poachers in the African game preserves and national parks are still killing the rangers and scientists. It's everywhere.

"Sometimes we're targeted because of greed for money and power. Other times it's a religious thing."

Laurel was still not clear. "But how can a bunch of peaceful sign carriers be such a threat to anyone?"

"It's not them, personally, so much as what they might get done or get others to see. Some governor of yours in Wyoming took steps to stop using a science program that talked about climate change as a scientific fact. Followers of politicians like that would want to stop us for sure.

"Then there's the impact we'd like to have on so many major industries. Big businesses and wealthy individuals stand to lose it all. Fossil fuels are the obvious ones to go down the tubes. In your country, fossil fuel companies rip their pipelines through farmlands, wetlands, people's yards. If the land owners don't want to take the money offered, their land is confiscated against their will under eminent domain or some such bullshit. None of the big guys wants to give up seven- and eight-figure salaries and their golden parachutes. Then there are all their employees...that can put us in real danger.

"Religious factions, too. Some of them say any climate changes are God's plan, or that the Bible said there would be no more floods. Those and lots of others believe environmentalist are nuts. All it takes is one of them to become a radical."

"Dak hasn't talked about any of this," Laurel commented.

"There's a lot of things Dak doesn't talk about much, but he's *really* closed-mouth about his unshakable belief that, as the conditions get worse, anarchy and bad behavior will come out of desperation. Many have said that. Hell, it's already happened in bunches of places.

"But Dak goes a step further. He believes the danger of an all-out inter-intranational war between the 'haves and the have-nots'—which in this case is the haves against the environmentalists—is nearly inevitable. It may go on being fought with killings, but there's cyberspace, too. None of us can imagine how that might turn out. Wars over water, wars over food, while wars over corporate and governmental power go on at the same time. Hell of a mess...and I don't see how it can be stopped in his ideal Eden on Earth either.

"Regardless, Dak thinks he can—*must*—save the world. I tease him and call him an environmentalist spy, working in secrecy and paranoia. He hates that because it's too close to the truth!

"*I* just want to say, 'Hey, you stupid people, wake up! Clean up your act! You're killing us and yourselves!' Oh, yeah. And then I want them to actually do it! Like that's going to happen!"

Laurel couldn't ignore the differences in Dak and Lila. "For two people with such different views, it seems to work for both of you," she said.

"We get into some pretty hot arguments, but it does work. For a long time I didn't think Dak's approach was any more realistic than mine. I didn't think anything would work and we were all doomed. Well, Kiribati and several other nations still are doomed environmentally. But now I see a tiny glimmer of hope for others. Though the ones being lost to droughts and growing deserts rather than rising waters are possibly even worse off than we are.

"There's also the problem staring us in the face of what to do with 100,000 jobless homeless climate refugees from this country alone. How many are there, and will there be, in your country?"

Laurel had no idea. "Honestly, I don't know. Certainly far more than you'll have here."

Lila went on. "Even if Dak could get the whole nation of Kiribati onto a floating utopia, he still wouldn't have solved anything. The planet would still be going to hell. It would just be putting more and more fingers in the dike until the whole thing just crumbled. You've got your own climate refugees to worry about, too!"

Laurel dropped her gaze. "This is so embarrassing. I didn't know we had any until Dak told me about Alaska. I thought it was all some long distance future possible threat if ocean waters rose several feet. And that wouldn't be until after I was dead and gone.

"I had thought I was fairly well informed about it all. I even volunteered with some groups to help the environment. Have you heard the phrase 'Think globally; act locally'? Looking back, I can see that I, and nearly everyone I was working with, had the 'act locally' part down, but none of us were really thinking globally. How could we? We didn't have any idea what was really happening worldwide. Even acting locally was more like making *hors d'oeuvres* and thinking you'd just finished all the cooking for a complete banquet. It was just a drop in the bucket. It was important—I don't want to minimize what everyone was doing. It's just that we didn't know how much more needed to be done, or how many more people should be doing their part.

"After all I found out from Dak once we were traveling, I started poking around on the Internet, thanks to wi-fi services for tourists. I found out that the state of Louisiana has been losing 25 square miles of land every year. The fishing industries around the Mississippi Delta are being affected the most, so that should wake someone up. But it doesn't seem to have any affect at all."

Lila sighed. "Well, that's another reason the group isn't out there screaming about climate disaster and what we could be doing to stop it—trying to 'wake up' people. To make people understand how desperate the problem is, we'd have to hit them over the head with it. It's been done by others, and they were quickly labeled as alarmist nuts and ignored or shut up.

"Even if we could do that much, the next step would be to work to get the 'fixes' in place. All that alternative energy stuff, the clean-ups. But that comes across as too preachy, too controlling…too intrusive into people's heads and lives. Another turn-off. It all has to be done in ways that will be accepted. Or at least in ways that can't be stopped or avoided.

"I heard a line once—I can't remember where—but I remember thinking it was the perfect approach to wearing down those who don't buy all this or are unwilling to do anything about it. It was about being 'pecked to death by ducks.' That's a way that might work. We'll just keep pecking away at resistance to understanding that climate change is a deadly reality and resistance to taking action. But it would be way too late by then. Hell, it's already too late. Predictions are now for some massive global extinction."

Laurel was slow to respond. "Now I don't feel so inadequate in my feeble attempts from before. Every community clean-up at least brought some more awareness to the public."

"No effort is a waste!"

"Just one more question, and a change of subject: Dak has what I would consider a very…well, let me call it 'liberal' view. Is that common in your culture?"

"Yeah—you're talking mostly about relationships, I bet."

"Yes, I guess I am."

"The answer is a big no. That's all part of Dak's personal culture. Yeah, and mine too. I admit it. But not this culture here. Our personal ways of living have to do with some of the other cultures we've experienced, I guess. Mixed in with who we are ourselves. Not that all kids who wind up swimming around in a bunch of different cultures end up with our sense of morality! Hell, some of them are tight-assed oil barons now!

"There! Enough for now! Dress in progress!"

~

Laurel had returned to the hotel to find Dak already in the room, poring over notes and photos on his laptop. "Did you get the dress planning done?"

"We did. Lila knows a lot about her craft-or rather, art. She's an intelligent and creative young woman."

"Yes. And so are you."

He surprised her when he walked to the window and pulled the shades. The semi-darkness made Laurel feel less self-conscious. No explanations this time. Just a spontaneous moment and an easy lingering in bed. Laurel was still not completely confident when she and Dak made love, but it was not the usual dance where he took the lead, effectively reminding her of her lack of skills and knowledge. This was a simple moment of shared pleasure. Every time had been different with Dak. He knew this was a simple spontaneity she had never experienced with Mark. But rather than a "lesson," Dak, if pressed, would have called it a small gift to Laurel. If pressed more, he may have admitted to his own pleasure as well.

He had put his arm around her to pillow her head as she lay next to him, sheet pulled only partly onto her. "Dak, why is it always easier to talk after sex?"

"There is a release of oxytocin that helps…but everyone is different. Is it easier for you? Maybe there is a degree of intimacy needed before talking, and sex establishes that for some."

"Sounds logical. I'll have to think about it." *He always sounds logical in bed—and* about *bed,* she thought to herself.

"But you have something on your mind. What is it?"

"While Lila was working on my fittings, she was so open and easy to talk to. It was clear she has a liberal view of life and living too. So I asked her if the I-Kiribati culture has an open view of relationships, and she said it doesn't. She thought her more liberal views might have come from the exposure to other cultures mixed in with her own personal views. Does any of this make sense for you?"

"It does," Dak answered. "I was a TCK: a Third Culture Kid. I had a homeland and another place to call home. I lived between at least two very different cultures at all times. Then, like most TCKs, I formed my own cultural basis. Part blend, part bits of my own two cultures, part from other TCKs, and part from other places I been to. Now we've all become TCAs: Third Culture Adults. I'm the living embodiment of how our culture can be diluted to the brink of extinction if our people are scattered across other nations."

Laurel was fascinated by this new concept; the extinction of a culture. "Did that make you feel like you had no real home—had no real roots—or did it expand your sense of what having a place to call home can be?"

"In my case, some of each. And something other than either of those choices. Home became where my family was, but the family's homeland was where, in my case, the matriarch was. I came to realize how my grandmother was the glue that held my family and me together, and bound us to our sense of home. Our cultural roots were always there, too. For me, having that sense of home gave me a solid place to expand and grow from.

"The extensive traveling and being with so many different cultural backgrounds can affect TCKs in every imaginable way. But for nearly all of us, we develop a broader sense of what 'norms' are. Many form their own sense of morality that is cross-cultural or intercultural. That can help us to be a part of society, or it can separate us for being too open, too liberal, or out of the accepted range in some other way. Some do feel rootless. Some of those clamp down and become extraordinarily rigid. For some sort of artificial stability, I suppose.

"Sometimes we go along to get along. Sometimes we take on careers that require our unique cultural skills and comfort levels—usually in some international or multi-national position.

"But this problem of a nation of I-Kiribati being physically displaced to another land—or to no land, but something on the water—it will take all my skills and those of many others. I do think those that grew up as TCKs will be able to help the most. They will have a better personal understanding of displacement and keeping identity."

Laurel thought of her initial feeling of being overwhelmed with the responsibility of one relatively small business. This was so much bigger. "It must feel like a huge burden at times. So much to deal with!"

"Sometimes. But you can't know what direction to take if there are no clouds."

"What's that? Some sort of I-Kiribati version of 'every cloud has a silver lining'?"

"I guess it is, but for us, it's a literal statement, too. We navigate by our clouds."

Laurel wasn't sure if Dak was serious. "How?! Clouds are always changing and moving."

"So too are solutions and directions! The islands of Kiribati are so low that once you take a boat a very short distance away, they're no longer visible. But the water and islands reflect the sunlight back onto the clouds, causing subtle color changes there. Shallow water, islands, and deep water all show up as different hues."

Laurel began questioning her place at the meeting again. "I don't think that can help me! What can I do? I'm the exact opposite of being a Third Culture Kid. Now I realize how very narrow my background has been!"

"I think it's just your 'first time hesitancy' again. You are valuable for precisely that reason. You will have a fresh, new view of things that I've—*we've*—never thought of before. You'll see. But right now, we've got to get moving. We need to be packed and ready to leave first thing in the morning," Dak reminded her.

"I'll go and take care of the things I need to do to be ready…the dress and my hair. Details. I'll meet you back here. I don't know when, but it will take some time. I'll finish packing when I return."

~

Dak made sure he and Laurel arrived at their destination early in the day. They would have time to explore their surroundings on the little island and relax to be fresh and ready for the evening. They settled into their guest bungalow on the beach and decided to take a walk after lunch.

Dak, remaining barefoot, changed into a light shirt and shorts, hoping to walk in the warm water lapping at the sand. Laurel picked out something that would be cool while protecting her fairer skin from the sun—a cotton knit bra covered only by a loose, gauzy shirt and matching long skirt.

It was time together unlike their days and hours before. Forgetting why they were there, they explored the shells at the tide line. As they went, Dak told her their names of those small animals and how they lived their lives. Only when they were within sight of their room did the conversation turn back to the coming evening.

"Why did you ask Lila to make something for me that was a reflection of a sarong rather than an even less complicated line? The one she designed reminds me a bit of a sari, too."

"First of all, I didn't ask her to, we discussed it together. Besides, it's Lila's specialty. She understands it acts as a subliminal message. It's part of the whole package to sell people on an idea without saying a word. I know that must sound underhanded. Dishonest, even. But it's a very tough and competitive world. The lines of propriety have long since blurred. I'm not sure they ever did run more than surface deep anyway."

"You make me sound like a walking billboard or the flashing background music on some TV commercial."

"In part, you will be. It isn't meant to dehumanize you; it's meant to add another dimension to you and your abilities. Our concept is fundamental and inarguable. We are a nation that is drowning. Everyone at the meeting already knows that. But we cannot save ourselves alone, and so many others are in need of help too. We, you and I, must convince others to buy into our product—our 'product' being the importance of finding ways we can save ourselves, we I-Kiribati. It will take more money than we can produce on our own. We need a very large start-up fund or some very good ideas on how to proceed without the funding.

"That will require group members to trust our people, trust our concepts, trust our knowledge, and believe we are worth saving. Sadly, that might mean saving us before so many others who are also about to be lost in one way or another. That, I hope to avoid, if possible.

"So here's where you come in. First of all, you're female. Every parent used to tell their child, if you're lost, find a policeman. But now, these days, parents tell their children to find a woman, preferably one who has her own children with her, but above all else, the woman is the only safe, nurturing, trustworthy image left in today's cultures. Subconsciously, people will believe you before they will believe me or any other man in the room, as long as the rest of your image is strong and intact.

"And for that, you'll just have to be yourself. You're in your 40s. You're old enough to have some life experience. You won't be talking from the foolish dreams of a twenty-year-old. You're a well-educated and successful business person, so you speak with authority.

"Beyond that, I am convinced the role of women is pivotal in this quest. Even, no, *especially* women in third world nations. It's one thing for a powerful female political figure to make policy changes, but when billions of women worldwide take small steps that save them time and energy and reduce their carbon footprint in the process, we will have made real and tangible strides. It's women who will be struggling to provide food and water for families, so it's these women who hold the future of so many in their hands.

"And the dress? It's a token of respectful reflection and appreciation of the worthiness of the cultures without being just a copy. Being worn by an American, a Westerner, it's a subtle, understated reminder that peoples of the South Pacific are a respected part of the world too, not just a separate crumbling tourist destination shown in photos on a wall. Think of it as the Butterfly Effect dress!"

Laurel's insights were reaching a new level. "When you explain all the things that are going into this, I can see what a hard sell this has been—is going to be. I understand why you took business and marketing courses. But your goal is first to save Kiribati, and then all else—all other places and people—come after? Aren't other places in desperate need too? Do we have to ignore everyone else?"

"Yes and no. I don't want it to come to that. I don't want anyone sacrificed for another, but I don't want us pushed to the side because we are a tiny speck in the ocean, either. Is there a hierarchy of who and what is more important to save in the short term? In reality, there have to be choices. It can't all be done at once. Who, then, becomes more 'valuable' or 'valued' or 'worthwhile'? And who will make that decision, and based on what standards? Hopefully, we will find and promote changes that will immediately help those like the I-Kiribati but also have a far-reaching positive effect on the rest of the planet at the same time.

"Even with such life and death decisions, politics, economics, and even emotional appeal are no longer separate...if they ever were. They are constant influences. Some nations understand this better than others and have hired ad men and public relations experts, while others seem to know you can't win the hearts and minds of others through military force and violence but either don't care or don't know, and who only consider how profitable war is. Everyone is clamoring for one thing or another. And, being tiny, I feel I—or we—have to put out an exceptional effort."

Laurel didn't want Dak to know the full extent of her conversation with Lila, so she was very careful about her wording of the next question. "So let's take this to the extreme fantasy level. If you had unlimited funds—won the all-time largest lottery ticket in history or something—what would you do?"

"I think it would have to evolve as I went…as the people settled into the changes and we all decided what would work best as a next step. I know…that's a guiding principle; part of a mission statement, if you will. But I believe—no, I *know*—having philosophies in place is as important as the physical structures. It's those beliefs that give shape to the structures in a very real sense. So when I talk about what I'd do with unlimited funds, I *have* to talk about the intangibles at the same time."

"Of course; that makes perfect sense," she agreed. "Especially knowing you."

"Any large construction site begins with a separate office building, often a temporary hauled-in trailer, to act as an informational, instructional, and directional hub. In our legends, Nareau is a giant creator spider. So I would begin with two fairly large interconnected floating island structures with a portion below water level. They could be disconnected and function independently if necessary. And they could be anchored or able to drift in a major current. I'll explain why this is essential later. They would, symbolically, be Nareau's head and body. One section would house a take on the traditional *maneaba*, or meeting house, for planning, gatherings, and so on. The other, well, the other is even more of a fantasy."

"Go on," Laurel urged.

"I want to build a cultural and educational center. It would be a quality school that would prepare our children to be caring world citizens but would also train them in their own culture and traditions—give them a sense of ancient identity and pride. The school would include an international Montessori approach, and it would have a marine education component, an observatory, and strong art and music programs with a generally holistic approach."

"The Green School influence..."

"Yes, I suppose, but there's more. We must put my grandmother there. Somewhere there. She would know how to keep the culture alive, and she knows the old culture that must be taught to the youngsters."

Laurel made the mental note that Lila was right. Dak made no mention of Tibu ever getting too old to be a driving force.

Dak went on. "I think she's getting ready for a move of some sort anyway. She knows none of us will be able to stay on the atolls much longer for any number of reasons. But I'm getting off track.

"Right now, Kiribati isn't much of a draw for tourism, which would help our economics. It's very far away from the usual tourist routes, and every year there will be less to offer tourists. But if the spider could grow its legs—and there is already a plan by one architect that comes very close to this—one leg could be a series of village homes, another could be shops, another tourist cabins, another a base for climate change education and sea care open to all nations, another would be purely agricultural—but there would also be agriculture to some degree on each leg. Each independent section must be self-sustaining and not harmful to the environment. If this could be built, we could become a draw for ecotourism. And for the newer disaster tourism—for disaster junkies who want to see places that are in a process of destruction before they disappear."

"That does sound like quite a fantasy," Laurel said with some reluctance.

"Well, yes and no. Imaginative, but not impossible. So many facets of this are already on the market, or on a drawing board. But it would need a unique group to put it together. Money aside, the planners—ideal again—would have to include a psychologist, an environmentalist, a biologist, an architect, an engineer, a botanist, and so on. So educating today's youth must become a top priority whether or not we can save ourselves.

"And, believe it or not, there are already groups working with this scope in mind. Remember that Seasteading Institute out of California is working on a floating habitat that would house 50,000. I think it's time to talk about collaboration with some of these organizations, or perhaps begin a new type of consortium altogether. Perhaps through the United Nations or some other large parent group. But there are pros and cons to any decision to be hashed out."

"What about that free-floating or anchored aspect you said you'd get back to?" Laurel asked.

"Oh, right. That opens up a very complex set of considerations. First there's the present Kiribati itself. Before it's covered with water, people will be reluctant to leave. Moving aboard the new structure will be slow, so it will have to stay anchored nearby where families can come and go, see it, visit it, and visit those who have already moved.

"Then, what will they do for jobs? Will they have to learn new skill sets on top of all the other adjustments? Would that be too much for them to bear? How can we use their present skills to make a new artificial island nation survive? 'Artificial' is probably a term never to be used. It doesn't sound very reassuring on any level.

"Psychologically, will people need to see the last grain of sand disappear to have closure? Will they feel the need to stay in the same geographical location where they are familiar with the atolls and the sea?

"And what about the increase in severity of storms and storm surges? Will the new islands be able to withstand that, or will they need to move away from the old locations? If we need to move them, is there any practical and safe way other than the natural flow of the currents?

"If you become adrift on the currents, out in international waters, are we, legally, still a nation? Would we lose claim to those waters? What if we float into another nation's water's? Can they take over our island?

"We have no army. Will we be at the mercy of pirates or anyone else who may want to take over the entire floating nation? Can we become a United Nations protectorate? Will the United Nations still exist in forty years? Could we hand pick a dozen nations to sign an agreement to protect us? Why would they agree to it? What would be in it for them? Would they expect to have a say in our government?

"Do we even worry about what might happen, what might be the situation in our world in thirty or forty years? After all, we couldn't possibly predict the future or prepare for every possibility even if we wanted to. But on the other hand, *not* looking forward at possible consequences is what got us into the climate change mess in the first place."

Laurel was seeing little hope by now. "That sounds depressing! When you started talking, it was all so creative and exciting. By the time you finished, it was crushing. You're only one person. Why are you doing this? Why are you even trying?"

"In part, we've talked about it before. If you look at the whole picture, it's too overwhelming. But if you find one tiny place to begin, one thing you can do, then you have a starting place. If everyone picked a starting place, there would be a huge change in no time. Like your Amish barn raisings. And like those barn raising groups, I am not alone.

"My motivation is strong, too. First of all, you've forgotten, my grandmother put me on the mission. I don't want to minimize that.

She's quite a force. But there is more. Losing your homeland, *allowing* the loss of your motherland, is, well, spiritual matricide. I would also be allowing the death of my—*our*—culture and self-identity.

"Because of the position of the International Date Line, Kiribati is the first place on earth to see the new day, and the first day of the new year. It is both the symbolic and very real new world beginning. If I can make *any* difference, I must. With my people, we will sink or swim together."

"It still sounded like a completely overwhelming responsibility until you included the rest of the population. Can you win them over? Will they help you?" Laurel was hopeful.

"That's the easiest and the hardest part. Easiest because they don't have much choice; if they stay, they and the nation will eventually all drown. But hard, too, because the entire population, including myself, would be in mourning for their country—their very national identity. There would be depression, anger, resistance, and despair.

"That wouldn't be the only difficult thing. If they come on board with me, my responsibility to make good decisions is incredibly heavy. But then again, I wouldn't carry the burden alone. The people and the president are ultimately responsible. And the president is very aware of the full impact of the problems and possible solutions. But, of course, he can't do it all alone. I, ultimately, hope to be a useful advisor, if nothing else."

Laurel had her own ideas on that. "I don't believe that. I don't believe, with all your research, with all you know, with all your hopes and dreams and creative ideas, you would be happy being only an advisor. I think you want to do that, and it will be an essential position, but I also think you will need to be contributing something tangible. Your island idea is too well-thought-out for you to sit at a table and just talk."

"Maybe. Maybe that's why I need your time and ideas. Maybe that's why I need you to brainstorm with me. As I said before. I can't do this alone, and I'm not talking about the money. Though I admit, I need that too."

"There must be plenty of I-Kiritbati that you're already talking to."

"There are. But that doesn't show them that there are others in the world willing to help us. We need a fully international group behind the projects. If we could get all the backing we needed and the project was ready to go, there are two more ideas I think would be good. First, to 'officially' open and then complete the project on the following 12th of July, the date of our Independence Day. And second, our flag has a frigate bird on it. That bird will be extinct about the same time as our nation. I would also figure out how to get a breeding population going somewhere.

"And here's another job for you. Just because I've done this research and put these ideas together, it doesn't mean I've come up with the best answer. I can't be attached to this plan if it isn't the best thing to do. I will need honest feedback. Who knows? We might find a set of uninhabited paradise islands out there for sale somewhere. Not likely, but the point remains, we all have to remain open to change, whether it be the cause of the problems or the solution."

"Are you talking about Kiribati or life?"

"Yes!"

"Ah...your grandmother's progeny. I wonder about people like her. People in our culture go to expensive universities and pay high tuition fees to take all sorts of courses and come out with much less wisdom than your grandmother. How did she learn so much? Or should I say, so many of the right things?"

"It's the paradox of these times. More knowledge and less wisdom. We can work on the answer to your question as soon as we save the planet." Dak sat back. He seemed exhausted from the effort of talking about the complexities of the problems and solutions.

"I see this whole climate change problem as being a vehicle to wake people up; to force them into a kind of mindfulness they didn't have before. As an extension of that, I don't think you should think of your ideas as a fantasy on any level. The technology is there; dedicated people are there. There must be a way to make it happen. I think the answer will be like a paperclip. It will be so simple, so effective, we'll wonder why no one thought of it before. A whole idea—a *holistic* idea. Sometimes answers come to me when I wake up in the morning. I know I can..."

They had circled back to their room and stepped inside. Dak leaned closer to her. "I can't talk about this anymore."

"What?" Laurel stammered.

Placing his hands on her shoulders, staring at her lips, he repeated, "I can't talk anymore."

Frozen in place, Laurel watched his eyes as he took an eternity to move the final inches. Moving his hands from her shoulders to her head, he kissed her mouth for the first time. Again and again. Slowly savoring each moment.

This was not the same Dak Laurel had known—except for the quick change of subject. He pulled himself away, whispering, "Don't move." He moved painfully slowly as he unbuttoned Laurel's light gauze shirt and slid it off her shoulders, letting it drop to the floor. She stood in the cotton knit bra she had put on in the morning. Waiting. Dak's hands studied her waist, hips, the shape of her buttocks, her legs under the long, loose skirt. Running his hands back up, the material flowed over his arms. He gently guided her panties down to her ankles as she remained motionless but breathed heavier. A hand lifted one ankle, and then the other. The panties vanished.

Beginning at the back, Dak ran both thumbs under the elastic of her bra that encircled her. He gently lifted from under her breasts. Laurel felt them drop, liberated from the restricting piece of clothing, sending a shock wave of heat. Her knees nearly buckled as the sound of her own throaty moan startled her.

Her arms lifted as Dak slid the bra over her head. Taking her hands, he directed them to his own clothing, breathing in her ear, "Keep your eyes closed. Just feel."

Laurel unbuttoned his shirt while he kissed her again. Her hands were pulled up to his ribs. She could feel him undressing himself. She wore only the long skirt when she was lowered to the floor.

She felt the material brush her legs as he raised it, kissing her navel, kissing lower and lower, her wetness telling him she was as ready as he was. Dak pulled the skirt off and rolled her over. Pulling her hips up, he aimed for her G-spot with his thrusts. He began with deliberation and then grew faster and faster.

She was on her hands and knees, only aware of the sensation inside. She felt a hand reaching past her hip to between her legs as his thrusting grew. She squeezed her pelvic muscles, tipping the balance and throwing them both into ecstatically explosive orgasms.

Falling onto the floor beside Laurel, he gathered her up in his arms. He held her for a long time before he kissed her hair, too lightly for her to feel. He pulled the discarded skirt up over them as they dozed off.

~

"Dak. We need to get ready soon."

Still groggy, Dak managed a response. "Mmm. Yes, we do." He sat up, gathering consciousness.

"I need to ask you something. I need to know what changed for you. It was different this time. I need to know if it was something I did or said so that I can understand how I might use that again."

"It was different because *you* are different. You're changing—or emerging as the person you've always been just under the surface."

"I can't disagree with that, but it doesn't answer my question. This time began differently. *You* were different. We were in the middle of a conversation, and you had nothing planned. It seemed genuinely spontaneous. I need to know what triggered that."

Dak let out a heavy sigh. "I've never talked with anyone about this before, so I'm not sure how to explain it well. All men—and women—are different. Different things excite them. On top of that, anyone will react differently to different stimuli. There are many things that might excite me, but in the case today, my sapiosexual side was tapped. I know, it's a word you've never heard before. It's not commonly used. It's a person who finds intelligence sexually stimulating. It doesn't happen all the time, but when it does, for me, it is always unexpectedly sudden and very intense. So it's nothing you can plan or do on purpose. That was part of your charm—your attractiveness—today. It's just who you are coming through."

"Who I am?"

"Your innate intelligence, your ability to think creatively. You're tapping into a level of wisdom that's new and exciting. And that excitement is contagious."

"I never heard of anyone being sexually turned on by intellectual stimulation before."

"Smart is sexy. I don't know how it happens or where it comes from, why it works for some and not for others. But I do have some theories.

"I think when we're young, we buy into the concept of 'sexy' that is stuffed down our throats by what we see in ads, in books, and in the movies. It's all body-focused. Which, in some ways, makes sense, since the sex act is about using your body. But it's your brain that controls your body and your body's reactions. Everyone's body is different and provides an element of 'newness' to your brain's perceptions that fuels excitement.

"After so many bodies, some start to realize there is a person there, a person with a brain that controls their sexual reactions too. But it goes beyond that. That other person's brain also comes with unique beliefs, abilities, and life experiences. Their mind, then, becomes the source of a new and expansive dimension of sexuality."

Laurel caught on. "Maybe age has something to do with it, too. An accumulation of life experience teaches you the definition of 'sexy' is far broader than the deodorant and car ads tell you. And—"

"And if we don't stop intellectualizing this, we're going to have to delve into it physically again. Shall I hit the shower first so you can take as much time as you want after me? After I get ready, I'll be on the patio. Meet me out there when you're ready?"

"Yes, thanks."

~

Dak watched Laurel as she emerged confidently into the cool open air of the early evening. *A new butterfly that will, indeed, have far-reaching effects,* he thought. "Fantastic! You even move differently!"

"Of course I do. Because I'm afraid the dress will unravel somewhere. Lila put it together so quickly."

"It won't. She's very good at what she does. You must feel like a new person."

"No. Strangely enough, I feel like this is the way I should have been feeling all along."

"Well said. Well said."

Without a thought, they easily slipped back into the roles of business partners and entered the dining area. Dak introduced Laurel to several people. She was consciously aware that he offered no explanation of why she was here or what their relationship was.

At first, Dak introduced Laurel by only giving her name. If the conversation progressed, he explained she was an American entrepreneur and idea person with an opportunity to expand public consciousness in her geographical area by hitting new target populations. Her first thought was that it sounded over-the-top, pretentious. Her second thought was that, at its core, it was accurate. In her position, she could, potentially, reach customers, business people she conferred with, wholesalers, even employees and their families.

Laurel had been by Dak's side all evening. During that time, she transitioned seamlessly and unconsciously from being introduced as what she felt like was a tag-along to interacting as an equal. Having found her footing, she had picked up on topics she had researched. She then found points where she could hold her own, not so much sharing information as asking pertinent questions and skillfully drawing on others' fields of expertise. It was the art of polite conversation raised to a fine art.

Dak watched her. Laurel was practiced at this type of banter, probably from the years of gatherings with Mark's business associates at social functions. She was in her element even with those who had extensive backgrounds in climate change. And she was learning more and more as the exchanges went on.

~

The host took his place at the small podium where a tiny microphone curved upward.

"Good evening to all of you. I would like to acknowledge the disruptions, hardships, and risks being here may have entailed for you. We thank you for coming in spite of any hindrances.

"To begin this meeting, I would like to use an old saying. 'There's good news, and there's bad news.' We could have said that at the opening of any of our meetings. This time, however, the good news is better than it has ever been, and the bad news is worse.

"First, the good news. The media and the efforts of groups and individuals have brought a new level of exposure and knowledge of climate change to the public. Never before have so many begun to understand the full scope and immediacy of the problems the world's populations, and life systems, face. Never before have so many organizations and institutions made so much progress in defining the problems and finding solutions.

"Climate change is no longer considered the flawed theory of a misguided few that it once was. By no means has the battle been won, but we are solidly on the road to worldwide attention to the matter.

"Conversely, there is also the bad news. Many respected scientists believe it is simply too little too late. They now talk about only slowing the progress of the eventual catastrophic end to life as we know it on Earth. Therefore, it is clear that our focus must shift as well.

"In the past, our group's approach has been to take one focus, one point of concentration, for our quiet efforts—one cause that would ripple through populations like a small tsunami. Both because of the changes that have taken place in today's world and precisely because of that powerful ripple effect, we can no longer take that approach.

"Allow me to explain with the example just two phenomena: war and cancer. Both, on the surface, and as covered by the media, seem outside of the determination of human interference. Humans do claim to struggle to get both under control and end them. In the process, industries grow around those endeavors, and profits soar. Both war and cancer become the driving force for enormous, highly lucrative business machines.

"Is this beginning to sound like some conspiracy theory? Let's first take a look at the economics of cancer. Worldwide, there are about 15 million cases a year right now. Many charities collect funding to back research to find medical treatments to cure cancer. In many cases, a large percentage of those funds go directly to the high-paid executives. The rest of the funds go to cancer research, often in labs owned by already wildly profitable pharmaceutical companies.

"If a cure was found, 15 million people a year would still be getting cancer. They and their families would still be suffering, and the pharmaceutical companies would be making record-setting profits selling the cures. Hospitals would be built specializing in the curative treatments, and new oncology departments would flourish.

"Wouldn't it make more sense to eliminate the causes of cancer? Eliminate the suffering and struggling with the burdens of having a loved one stricken with a life-threatening disease for those 15 million families? No drugs to take with debilitating side effects, no declarations of bankruptcy due to medical bills, no loss of jobs due to illness. No cancer in the first place.

"Some estimate we could eliminate more than 80% to 90% of all cancers right now. Today. Because we know what causes them. The problem is, it would also destroy the world's economy. Look at a just a few items on the long list of known carcinogens from the American Cancer Society's website: alcoholic beverages, benzene, engine exhaust, diesel, formaldehyde, outdoor air pollution, shale oils, and tobacco—smoked, smokeless, or secondhand.

"To eliminate just those known carcinogens would decimate the alcoholic beverage and tobacco industries and the farming industries that grow the ingredients for those, as well as the mining and fuel industries, which would, in turn, destroy the automotive, trucking, and transport industries, leading to the collapse of the retail sales and marketing of all products delivered by those methods, including food, leading to widespread starvation, desperation, and the anarchy that would follow.

"In addition, those mega pharmaceutical companies that are presently making over 700 billion U.S. dollars a year in profits would crumble, causing far-reaching economic ruin. On the other hand, failing to take action of any kind will guarantee the continued destruction of the planet's health.

"And what about war? War, violence, and climate change are no longer separate topics. Climate change is causing droughts, famines, and the spread of vermin and disease. Wars of protest to governments that have not helped their people are becoming commonplace. Wars of competition for resources to stay alive are equally common. It will only get worse."

Laurel noticed Dak's restlessness at this point but remained fixed on the speaker.

"I offer this as an example of the care we must take in our endeavors to save that which is being destroyed and those who are dying. Nothing exists in isolation. We must also look at the far-reaching effects to ensure our cures don't kill more than we save. Although, admittedly, I am less concerned about drug profits than the planet's survival.

"We cannot snatch away the causes of exhaust fumes, air pollution, and so forth without also finding a way for the industries dependent on that old paradigm and system to thrive on a new and less dangerous way to exist and profit. For this reason, to this purpose, choosing a theme and direction has become too critical a responsibility for a small handful of us. This time, the appeal is going out to *all* of you. This time, our direction is to find a direction.

"To assist with that task, and as a follow-up to last year's meeting, there will be informational sessions for you to attend before deciding on any new goals. These are a direct result of some of our previous efforts to monitor the visions and progress of certain institutions and companies. These will include the findings on The Seasteading Institute and Blue Revolution Hawaii, both based in the United States, Shimizu Corporation in Japan, DeltaSync from the Netherlands, viability of OTEC energy systems and its proposed center in China, Cuna del Mar proposals, Interpol's Pollution, Wildlife, and Fisheries Environmental Crime Groups, the Evolver Network, One Community, and several others.

"In addition, there will be reports on various groups and committees, including the Intergovernmental Panel on Climate Change, the Earth System Governance Project, the Global Environment Facility, and others. Some of these have proven to have points that are sound, while others are teaching us what to avoid. The work of a handful of individuals will also be reviewed.

"Then, separate groups will be given the time allotted according to the schedule. Details will be given to you after the morning meal.

"Each group will then join two others to refine, clarify, and agree upon a core theme or direction. The third and last meeting will be to present and finalize your conclusions. From those meetings, individuals will be chosen to present ideas to all of us.

"Our group has expanded in both number and in diversity. We now comprise nearly every imaginable background, whether it be in ethnicity, education, business, or life experience. Our number of problems to tackle has grown as well…but so has our greatest resource; an ever-increasing number of innovative minds and dedicated hearts. It is with confidence born of that knowledge that I turn this meeting's task over to you.

"Beginning at 08:30 tomorrow morning, we will meet back here for breakfast. Thank you, and enjoy your dinner!"

Dak turned to Laurel. "What do you think?"

"I can't wait until tomorrow. I'm energized in a way I didn't expect. And I'm curious to see how the meal will be handled. There are so many different ethnicities and religions here."

"That was figured out years ago. Meals are served buffet-style, as you can see from all the covered chafing dishes on the long table. When we get there, you'll see everything is carefully labeled with the name of the dish and all the ingredients. Easy and effective. If it's something you choose not to have, move on to the next choice!"

~

After the dinner, Laurel and Dak returned to their room. They had reached a level of ease in one another's presence. Now, sharing a space was not the strain Laurel had earlier feared it would be. Conversations came and went easily. But Laurel was well aware this ongoing intimate time would not last much longer. She would use the moments whenever she could.

"Dak?"

"Mmm?"

"You once told me that some escorts get training from older women. Did you? Or is that too personal?"

"No. I can talk to you about it. I did learn from an older woman, but it was before being an escort was even an idea for me. I was very young, and she was my first lover…and quite a bit older than I was. She was very knowledgeable and taught me well—about so many things. It was from her that I learned we have to explore to discover what works best for us. And we can't be afraid to ask for it. We did a lot of exploring and asking that first summer."

So Dak was not a sexual genius, nor a man of extraordinary innate talent. He was just a man who was fortunate enough to have met the right woman and the right time. Laurel wanted to know more about that time. Who was she to him—a friend? A teacher? A lover? But she only asked, "Did you ever see her again?"

"We remained close friends. But she was killed in a boating accident some years ago. I still see her husband and children when I can. And her children's children now."

"Oh...I'm sorry. Did her husband know you had been lovers?"

"Of course."

"Wasn't he jealous?"

"No…but this could be a long discussion best saved for a later time."

Will there be a later time, or is this getting much too personal? she wondered, but only for a fleeting moment. She knew very well it was too close to home for him.

He turned the inquiries towards her. "Let me ask *you* something, if it's not too personal. You were raised in New England—a land of 'puritanical' views. From what I've gathered, your own household was a conservative one. But you don't have that mindset. Do you?"

"Now there's a question I've never been asked before," Laurel said. "I think for some—maybe many—puritanical repression is supposed to keep one safe. But instead, it can eat at your insides, leaving nothing but a hollow shell of a person. I missed internalizing that kind of rigid reserve. To some extent, I lived it for a long time, but it hadn't eaten away my ability to grow out of it—my need to grow beyond it. For me, now, it's better to approach life sensibly and logically but with reasonable caution when called for. And at my age, I have no time to waste."

"But you still have an outward reserve. You don't always show your emotions. You'd be good at poker," Dak countered.

"That's probably true. But it takes one to know one. You're not exactly an open book yourself. I think I learned to stay guarded as a child. It just seemed easier at the time. And I was too busy taking it all in."

"As a child? What were you like then?"

"No one has ever asked me that before. Well, let's see...there's a Norman Rockwell painting that describes me as a child far better than I could. It's called *Girl at the Mirror*. She's sitting on a child-sized stool in a pure white, lace-trimmed slip. The viewer sees her from the back. The girl is staring at herself in the mirror. She sees her real self there, in spite of having put her hair up like some movie star's magazine picture barely visible in her lap. She is surrounded by a dark unknown, but there is the clear reality of who she is, undeniably, in front of her.

A proper little lady, constricted into an almost fetal position, feet awkwardly big, knees drawn up and together, forearms hiding her chest, chin touching inwardly curled fingers. Her dolly still there but pushed aside. Her face says it all. Will she be this pure, pale, plain Jane all her life, she wonders? She knows there's more to the world. She knows there's more that she can be. But will she?"

"Did she?"

"I think she's still in transition. More like the little girl in his painting called *Shiner*. Look it up and draw your own conclusions," Laurel smiled.

~

The next morning, there were many presentations to be held. Since they couldn't attend them all, Dak suggested they attend as many as they could separately. He chose to attend the sessions related to organizations and corporations. Dak was presenting information as well, but Laurel had already heard his concerns and readily went her own way.

Laurel was enthralled by the simplicity of a concept first envisioned by a young man when he was just 19. He and his supporters were confident the oceans could be cleaned of plastic waste before it killed more of the waters' inhabitants. In addition, the reclaimed plastic could then be cheaply converted to fuel. Laurel wondered why there was no mention of biodegradable plastic for future use and elimination of the problem altogether.

Another speaker out of California presented a PowerPoint program on the use of fungi to eliminate land-based pollutants, produce medicines, make safer insecticides, and grow food. Laurel learned how hemp plants could provide a sustainable resource for making textiles, paper, building materials, food, and cleaning products. And she listened in dismay as statistics revealed why and how economic and corporate self-indulgence encouraged wars and undermined healthy food production.

Laurel attended presentations telling of Sweden's economic successes that grew in proportion to its world-strength carbon tax programs, Germany's green building codes, France's ban on fracking, and its successful investment in renewable energies. She heard of Colombia's concentration on health and promotion of biking for transportation, China's push for renewable energy, and the rising economy and decreasing fuel consumption in British Columbia.

It was a long and heady day. By the time Dak and Laurel rejoined for the late dinner, both were anxious to share new insights.

Dak began. "How did it go for you today? Anything of particular interest?"

"Yes and no. There were talks about specific things that I found both new to me and promising for practical use. But, no, it wasn't the individual bits of information that struck me the most. It occurred to me that no one is putting a large variation of things together into one major approach or project. A holistic approach. I'm trying to think of a way to do that. I want to devise of a way to combine the things I've learned from you, the speakers here, my own Internet searches."

Dak was pleased she had become so seriously invested in the cause of climate change but was afraid she would be discouraged when she found she had set an unsurmountable task for herself.

"That sounds like quite an undertaking. Do you think such a concept is even possible?"

"I won't know until I try," Laurel said.

Fatigue and a need to process the implications and conclusions in their own minds soon quieted their conversations. Each found a spot for themselves and went over their notes; Laurel's in her notebook and Dak's on his ever-present laptop.

The second day was scheduled with discussion groups. Priority crises and feasible plans to counteract the negative impacts were pondered and evaluated. Spokespeople were chosen, and groups reformed with new members from other previous groups. Each final reshuffling coalesced and distilled into fresh organic structures of intellectual and creative power. Individuals were chosen by the host and his assistants to present their views for the final day.

When Dak and Laurel headed to their room, Laurel seemed more energized than Dak expected.

"You look like you're bubbling over with something."

"I can't wait to tell you," she began. "I managed to think of some ways to bring more facets of all this together. When I brought up the idea of a major project in the first group today, they were very positive and even said I should be the one to take the lead for the next round of groups!"

"And did you?"

"Yes! And once I began, pieces started to fall into place more and more. The responses were equally more enthusiastic too. People began adding their own ideas too. It was an amazing day for me!"

"So are you going to tell me about it?"

Laurel hesitated. "Not yet. I want to finish it up on my own. *Do* it, perfect it, on my own as much as I can first. I've already taken so many parts of this from you and the others. You don't mind, do you? It's the first time in a long time that I've felt this sort of achievement."

Dak saw a new sparkle in her eyes. "Of course not. I have organizing to do too."

They both went straight to their notes.

The third day was the official last day of the meetings. Some attendees would stay an additional day or two to cement plans and network with others, but the morning would be the culmination of the efforts of all those there. The final four presentations would provide the direction and goals of the entire membership for at least the coming year, with one being the major focus. Through the years, Dak had reached many with his pleas for a way to save his nation. But he was never a final presenter—nor did he expect to be. His was a personal quest. This was a time for goals that would be international with worldwide impact.

Laurel had taken more time than usual to dress and ready herself for the day. At breakfast, she quietly flipped through one of her little notebooks again and again without more than a few words to Dak.

"Are you okay? You've been very low-key this morning. Preoccupied."

"What? Oh. I'm fine. Never better. Just so much to think about. And this will be over by noon. In some ways, I've been away from home far too long, but in other ways, for me, this is ending far too soon. There's so much more I want to know about. More I need to think about."

"Makes sense. You won't mind, then, if I leave you to finish your coffee on your own while I gather some of my own notes?"

"Not at all. That would be perfect."

Dak had one last chance to speak with a man from a construction company that specialized in off-shore drilling platforms. He wanted specific figures as to how much battering from storms, winds, and tsunamis this type of architecture could withstand, and what it was about the design that gave it the supporting strength.

The earliest part of the morning had been left without formal structure. Then, as on the first evening, the entire body of members met together to hear the four final speakers.

Dak and Laurel heard the first speaker give a compelling plea for the elimination of carbon emission fuels. Since the dawn of the machine age, the cumulative effect had brought humanity to a deathly point, he had said. He offered solutions such as wave-driven energy production, screw-designed wind generators, and even using human waste to produce energy. Laurel couldn't imagine any argument against any of it.

The second speaker focused on non-chemical food production. Non-polluting energy would be a moot point if humans didn't survive due to lack of proper food. Beside the organic approach, this speaker included architectural examples of high-rise condos and apartment dwellings that were designed to use gray water from washing and bathing to grow a family's crops on vertical structures.

Laurel leaned toward Dak as they applauded. "My own house has become an embarrassment. It's far from energy efficient, and I don't grow enough of my own food to count for anything."

"Plenty of time to work on that when you get back," he said as the applause faded.

The third speaker began by citing the wars and conflicts going on at that very moment that had their roots in droughts and general lack of clean water. The phrase "the coming water wars" was now obsolete. "Water wars are here as entire nations are running out of water," he said. He offered several possible solutions.

Dak leaned toward Laurel and said, "That sounds like quite a priority issue."

"Yes, but it's still only one facet of the bigger picture."

Then came the announcement for the final speaker. "We've scheduled this speaker last for a reason. This is the person who has the broadest goals while targeting specific, unique crises. Laurel Bradford."

Dak snapped his head to face Laurel. She didn't give him so much as a glance as she rose and walked forward. She needed to maintain her focus. She had told him how well her presentations had gone but he didn't expect this. She took her place with an easy grace. If she was nervous, it didn't show.

He had spent the previous days telling her she had something to contribute, bolstering her self-confidence to participate. She had taken it all to heart and bloomed. He had thought nothing could shock him, nothing would surprise him, when it came to women. He had been wrong.

As Laurel walked from the table to the place where she would face the entire assembly, she found herself reliving that first meeting when she took ownership of Mark's company. She remembered all the things she had told herself then; she couldn't show the least bit of nervousness or overcompensate and seem arrogant, there were no enemies here, all would be well. She needed only to be herself. She had done this once before.

Laurel took her place. With a soft smile, she paused for a brief moment as she looked at the faces in front of her.

"I know I'm the last one to speak before lunch, so I promise to keep this short." There was a warmly responsive undercurrent of laughter. She had their attention.

"Let me introduce myself. My name is Laurel Bradford. I'm from the United States of America, and I'm an ordinary, average person. Until very recently, my thoughts and beliefs about climate change were restricted to those of the average person; that is, limited and tucked far behind everyday concerns and activities.

"Yet, here I am today. Thanks to so many others, I've come a long way. But I am only one person. While the Earth is being destroyed, too many others remain blissfully unaware they are already squarely in the path of devastation. So how can this destructive inertness of the average person, across the globe, be ignited into action? I have looked to my own awakening, what I've learned from so many others, for clues. Added to that are the contributions of Dak Gordon and so many others here today. I give them full credit for all the knowledge that I have only put together into one comprehensive idea.

"It is clear we must stop trying to convert anyone to our way of thinking. It hasn't been particularly successful. We can abandon the desire to convert others. It builds resistance. Instead, we need to get everyone—enemies, friends, polluters, the greedy, the tree huggers—all working together towards mutually beneficial goals.

"Naive? Yes. Definitely. Impossible? Perhaps not. Some say greed got us here. Greed for power, money, prestige, and comfort. That same greed can get us out. Knowing that power and profits are strong motivators, a two-step process, taking profits and power into account can be successful.

"How can greed and profit save us? Make saving the world, saving the poor, saving the environment—make it all profitable. Not just marginally profitable, but *solidly* profitable. Then, those that only care about their own business and their own profits, even the purely greedy, will be on board with the purely altruistic and green tree-huggers.

"The concept is elegantly uncomplicated. A few ways to go about finding profitable goals can also be relatively easy. On a local scale, here is one example already in place: African elephants are being poached to the brink of extinction. This has gone on in spite of the boycotts on ivory and conservationist campaigns against it. The profits are too alluring. However, there is the tourist trade to consider, as well. People come to the big game lodges to see elephants. When those African nations and local village people realized there was more long-term profit in protecting the elephants, the tide against poaching began to turn. Former poachers were hired to keep other poachers at bay. Helping to protect elephants keeps tourism thriving. Live elephants are simply more lucrative than dead ones.

"As our host and opening speaker said, we must remain cognizant of the fact that, like elephants, poachers, and tourists, 'Nothing exists in isolation.'

"We know we cannot snatch away the causes of exhaust fumes, air pollution, and climate change without also finding a way for the industries dependent on that old paradigm and system to shift toward, and thrive on—a new and less dangerous way to exist and profit, just as poaching can be abandoned for tourism.

"If consumers see there are cheaper and cleaner ways to provide themselves with energy, they will insist on access to those. This causes a natural consumer-generated boycott of the expensive pollution-producing products, spurring industrial changes. Profits are still made, consumers are happy, and the planet benefits.

"Why, then, has this not yet happened in the nations that are causing the worst pollutants and worst climate change? First, too much of the general public doesn't know this is possible for them now at this very moment. And second, the alternatives are not always readily available to them. Corporate barons will continue to suck fossil fuels out of the earth and pollute the air, land, and water as long as it is made profitable by consumers still buying into their products. These corporations have yet to see there are other means of producing profits. But, with the public's insistence, corporations can and will quickly change.

"So what do we here in this group need to do? We need to prioritize our concentration and efforts. We can encapsulate all we need to do into four interdependent goals.

"First, we—as in 'all living things'—need to survive. We need to survive on the most basic life or death level.

"Second, we need to minimize struggle for resources in order to eliminate causes of violent competition.

"Third, we need to guide corporate and personal greed toward sustainable and benign profits.

"Fourth, we must energize and perpetuate the movement towards awareness of problems and the implementation of solutions.

"While survival is the top priority for all, survival from immediate disasters is not the problem that we, in this group, need to concentrate on. The storms, droughts, and floods are there for all to see, bringing immediate rescue work. The survival we *do* need to work on is long-term survival. Not just survival due to shortages of food, water, and clean air resulting in the on-going pollution and climate change, but also survival from the inevitable destabilization of governments, chaos, anarchy, and bloodshed that we already see in the battles for basic needs. Without taking that factor seriously, we could, quite literally, be saving the world environmentally, only to have it annihilated by the effects of humanity's violence against itself.

"Therefore, we cannot just 'fix' parts of the environmental disaster; we must also address survival from climate change while addressing survival from competition for remaining resources. People with nothing are desperate people who can easily turn to violence. People who are making profits in desperate times can easily become people of desperate actions.

'Simultaneously, survival must include a restoration process where there has already been damage. And we must make survival, restoration, and profit-making support the continuation of the movement.

"Can we do all this at once? We must. We have no other choice. Time has run out. So *how* do we make all this, these four goals, simultaneously possible?"

Laurel leaned forward. She looked at the faces in her audience. Then, in a lower and slower voice, she said, "I have a plan."

Laurel straightened up. Raising the volume of her voice, she continued.

"I propose we find a nation. Find one that is on the very brink of extinction to become the showcase for both desperate needs and viable solutions. That much is easy; there are now many. But there is only *one* nation that can serve marketing and public awareness like no other, thanks to its real and symbolic positions. What better choice for a nation to save on a completely new level, by new methods, than the one that is, quite literally, the first in the world to see the dawn of each new day, and the dawn of each new year? Not only that, this one nation can also be considered the center of the planet, spanning not only the old and new days and years, but also all four hemispheres. This single perfect choice is Kiribati.

"Kiribati is also poised to be the first nation to become extinct due to climate change. Between higher storm surges washing away homes, entire villages and food sources, fresh water wells turning brackish, and lack of adequate waste management, all life here is in immediate peril. In round figures, the population of over 100,000 is large enough to serve as a complete symbolic nation for all others, yet small enough to make saving it possible. Though smaller in population, this nation also covers an area of ocean the size of the continental United States. Such a vast space will open the visions for an infinite number of creative possibilities.

"But time is very quickly running out. The land is becoming uninhabitable. Whole villages have already disappeared. The national bird on their flag is becoming extinct, crops are suffering, and fishing is being ruined. And the waters continue to rise. It is clear all I-Kiritbati must, in some way, evacuate.

"That leaves us with an enormous opportunity to truly see in the dawn of a new paradigm for existence, survival, and even the very definition of a nation. With technology and experts *that already exist,* with cooperation rather than competition, we can support the survival of this nation while fulfilling all other goals as well.

"We can use saving this one nation to bring attention to the problems everywhere, provide an opportunity for positive public relations for profit-centered businesses, and show methods of restoration and preservation for what does remain while promoting peaceful co-existence and public awareness for now and the future.

"We must not just face the new dawn here, but leap wholeheartedly into the new year and the new age of survival.

"I propose we support an international, worldwide, commercial competition that will generate both advertising and new contracts for the businesses involved. This competition will be an educational tool for the public as well, by also supporting all the media coverage that is possible. A chance to make history is in our hands.

"What kind of a competition can do that? This international competition will be to build the beginning of the physical structure for the new Kiribati, village by village, city by city. Some contestants will choose to build floating islands; others may design platform-based villages, much like oil rig companies already use. Others may choose to anchor structures into the atolls and islands that were once dry land. The plans may be for an entire village or a series of add-on individual homes and other structures that can be joined to form a village.

"The rules will be simple: each new structure or village must be self-sustaining in every way, culturally sensitive to its target population, and non-polluting. While in process, this can generate a huge new market of eco-tourism and eco-education through international educational institutions for the I-Kiribati. Toward this goal, the showcase structure should also have an underwater viewing area to make the sea and its inhabitants visible to all. Visible and *near*, not distant, unseen, unknown creatures.

"Miraculously, all components needed for such a project are already firmly in place. Let me emphasize that once more: *we already have the know-how to do this*! There are already institutions that have studied 'seasteading,' architectural firms that specialize in building on water, experts on preserving cultures, and others who have already considered the questions of governmental controls and personal safety. There is already the technology to produce sustainable clean energy, clean water, and healthy food. There is even at least one company that specializes in the workings of international competitions specifically in the field of architecture.

"And through this competitive project, we can take the fact that nothing exists in isolation and use it to our advantage. Let us look at another successful business model. McDonald's has been a success worldwide, in part, because someone there understood a very important marketing tool. If you can hook children while they are young, you have them for life. On this marketing principle, I also make a motion that we contact authors to write children's books on climate change and on this competition in particular. There are also writing competitions already in place that can open to this topic and to this project. We must strive in our educational endeavors to show there are better ways to run corporations that are still profitable, and keeping schools in the loop with this project will help to do that.

"Worldwide, real-time interviews can be provided to schools via the Internet, along with written and photographic blogs and publications that follow the project's progress. We must contact universities and urge their professors to assign the study of, or suggest doctoral theses on, transplanting cultures, psychological effects of losing one's homeland, political and personal security of future floating nations in international waters, restoration of what is still salvageable of the land, and complete non-polluting self-sustainability in aquatic settings and on shorelines with rising waters.

"This group here today knows it is too late to waste our energies fearing climate change; it is already upon us. If we must fear something, instead, we fear the blindness of masses of ordinary, average people drowning in the mob psychology called 'today's society.' But fear is a useless drain. It is imperative, for our most basic level of survival, that we take that fear and transform it into life-saving action—not just support, not just goal setting for a future not yet here, but definite and immediate action—now. It is this project that will not just represent the dawn of a new era for the entire planet, but also raise awareness worldwide, provide an opportunity for financial prosperity for those involved, show ways to restore present damage, and, in the process, save an entire nation of people.

"I make a motion—no, an impassioned plea—that this group consider modifying their total silence and ask for the support of philanthropic organizations such as The Giving Pledge. I beg that this group consider openly promoting and initiating this project, this competition, with all of its supporting profit-making projects to wake up ordinary people into saving an entire nation while showing the way to save the remainder of life on Earth.

"This is not only a critical turning point in survival, but also a moral crisis. We have fought for the survival of the rain forest, endangered species, and animal habitats. How then, in good conscience, can we turn our backs on an entire nation of 100,000 suffering, drowning human beings?

"Thank you."

Laurel began to gather the notes that she had barely glanced at as that familiar moment of stillness froze the audience in place. But which way would opinion go this time? She expected Dak to break the silence first. As if on cue, he rose to his feet and began to clap. Then others joined him, all standing and all increasing the pace and volume of the applause. Only then did Laurel raise her gaze. And breathe.

She began to walk back to her seat, gauging the reactions. Were they just being polite? No. Heads were bobbing in affirmation and smiling in approval. But she knew she was merely a vehicle to present the summary of all she had learned from others over the past days and weeks.

When she reached his side, Dak embraced her and whispered in her ear, "Stand until you make eye contact with the whole room."

Laurel gave a modest wave of thanks to those around her and smiled as she caught their eyes before sitting. The applause subsided. As the leader began to speak again, she glanced toward Dak. He was staring at her, smiling.

Laurel, Dak, and the others were served lunch. Dak ate quietly, but it was not his usual mealtime silence. He watched as others streamed to Laurel's side. He listened as they gave words of encouragement, added ideas of their own, or asked for the names of the companies that could promote and build "her" project.

Later, when they had a moment alone, Dak said to Laurel, "I don't know what to say. I had no idea..."

"I didn't intend to keep you out of the loop in the usual sense. It was something I needed to finish on my own."

"I understand perfectly. And may I say, with admiration and immense gratitude, *bravo!*"

"And that's all you need to say. Thank you. But, as I told those there, I only put it together. All the parts came from you and the others. Now we wait to see if the idea will be accepted by the group."

Dak gave her a warning. "As urgent as this needs to be, committees will take time to do evaluations. You'll get an indication of real interest very soon if they ask for all your reference material."

"Speaking of time, I need to pack. It won't take too long."

~

It was their last night on the island. Laurel had finished her packing and sat under a leaning coconut palm to watch the sun. Before, she would have looked at its fading glow as if it were sinking in the distance. Her world was a bigger place now; instead, she wondered where it was rising just past her line of sight.

The rustling of fronds above her harmonized with the rushing of the swirling bubbles by the shore. Her body tingled with awareness. She closed her eyes in an effort to memorize the sensations; warm touches of the wind; the smell of the salt air; a chirping insect; the sound of tide-tossed pebbles rolling in and out with each wave; the texture of the ground beneath her bare feet.

Soon this would be gone. *She* would be gone—back in New England, staring at this month's picture on a calendar entitled *Paradise Shores*. Which was real? This now? The well-cropped and angled photos there? Was there any place, any *thing*, real enough to plant her feet in? To depend on for the rest of her life?

Of course not. That had been her mistake in her time before Mark's death; thinking she had reached some kind of "life goal" and wondering where the discontentment had come from. She had, in effect, been concentrating her efforts on stagnation rather than the journey up a path. Her path.

Laurel straightened her back and concentrated on the last of the sunlight on her closed eyelids. If thoughts arose, she transformed them into dragonflies that fluttered away. Finally, her mind was still.

When the last of the light was no longer discernible, words in her head returned. *Nothing is intrinsically real unless we pay attention to it and give it meaning. It is all a collection of different realities.*

Laurel opened her eyes. The earth's single daytime star had transformed into an open universe full of small lights that only clear and pure air could reveal.

Laurel thought she was hallucinating. An entire galaxy had fallen into the sea. Stars concentrated in undulating ribbons, washed up on the beach, paused, then slid back into the sea. She took the few steps to the water's edge and realized she was witnessing something she had only read about. It was bioluminescent plankton. She tossed up a splash with her toes; the spray of water ignited with the living sparks.

Laurel walked back into the bungalow. Dak was sitting at the writing table, working on photos. "Come look," she said as she took his hand and led him to the stone-paved patio and just beyond onto the shore.

They stood shoulder-to-shoulder for several minutes, watching the living light twinkling in the water.

"Dak, Megan will be back before long, and you'll be leaving."

"Yes?"

"I'd like to take advantage of that time. I'd like to learn as much as I can before you're gone."

Dak felt as though he was missing some cue. "Go on..."

"I want you to teach me the way the older woman taught you."

"She was a rare mentor. But I will do my best."

"Will I ever get to the point where I can just do this, enjoy this, with someone and not be going through some learning process?"

"Let's hope not. Learning new things about sex and about ourselves and others should never end."

"Yes, I agree with that, but sometimes now I wish it didn't seem quite so...proper? Quite so educational."

"There was a time, not that long ago, when you found the 'almost clinical' approach good for you."

"That was then; this is now. Time to move on."

"So you won't mind if I use the word 'cock' instead of 'penis'?"

Laurel chuckled. She knew Dak was attempting a lighthearted joke, but even that still sounded didactic. For all his physical openness, he would not—or *could* not—let any emotion show in the context of a relationship. "As long as it's in private, I think I can handle that! I need to begin to feel like I know what sex is like with people who are not so attuned to me—what sex is like in the real world. Am I making any sense?"

"Of course. Let's go back in. I'll tell you what some men like."

"Tell me? Or show me?"

Almost affectionately, Dak put his arm around her shoulder and guided her back toward their room. "Maybe both. Did you ever get into oral sex with any man?"

"Do I have to admit I didn't? And not with any woman, either!"

"Do you have an interest in that?" he asked while he began undressing her.

"I never thought I did until recently. I see how affectionate and loving Rachel and Megan are. I've seen the way they look at each other when they think I'm not there. I am intrigued. I've found myself watching other women who are obviously together. Women I don't know."

"I'll be happy to explain my approach while you tell me how it feels. And, if you like, when we get back, I can arrange for a woman to join us. Or just to be with you without me. Someone you'll never see again, if you would prefer that."

"I can't rush this much more than I already am! This has been a complete change for me—for my life. So one step at a time!" Laurel was undressing Dak.

"I'm just letting you know the choices—*some* of the choices—you could make in the future."

"*Some* of the choices? What else?"

"If you want to explore, there are fantasies, role-playing, 'talking dirty' as some call it, threesomes, or with four, women, multiple women, bondage, oral sex, anal sex, Tantric sex, rough sex, having sex in public places, S&M, pornography, sex toys…"

"Wait! Stop! I get the picture! I'm getting overwhelmed by how much I haven't experienced!"

"Being inexperienced is merely a temporary condition, easily remedied."

Laurel thought Dak was going to laugh. But he didn't. Not quite.

"If you have the opportunity to experience a woman, you might like to know that, in some ways, there are basics that don't change. You have to enjoy a woman's body. If you do, she will sense that and respond. You have to love the color and texture of her skin," he said as he ran his hand over her body, not pausing at any one place. "You have to love the smell of her," Dak went on as he breathed in her hair, down her neck, the side of her breast, across her stomach, and down to her pubic area. "Where subtle scents are released."

Dak was right, he was enjoying her, and she was responding. She pulled his head to her face. His scalp had a faint aroma that reminded her of almonds. "I never noticed before, but I would know it was you even if I was blindfolded."

"You have to love every crease on her body," he said as he drew a light line with a finger, first under each breast, and then in the shallow furrows where her thighs met her body. He retraced the motion with his tongue.

Laurel was too aroused to be a questioning student.

"Now. The longer you can stay where you are, the more intense your orgasm might be."

Dak took Laurel's hand. "Feel what I do," he told her as he took her middle finger into his mouth. Dak guided her in pressure, areas, speed. While he talked to her and while she followed his directions, Dak kept Laurel aroused by touching her, drawing the backs of his fingers here and there, squeezing, releasing, moving on.

His fingers moved to her hair, drawing slow swirls on her scalp, then grabbing handfuls and gently pulling—a different place each time, rousing her higher with each tug. "Ease off. Now watch."

She slid up beside him. Dak took her hand and guided it to herself. "Go ahead," he said, "while you watch me."

Laurel was as wet as she would been had he already come inside her. His eyes were closed. She touched herself as she watched him. "Next time, try this with your tongue," he said.

Laurel imagined her tongue gliding everywhere his finger went—slowly around, below, over, flicking here, caressing there. Then, "Watch..."

She was climaxing, but her eyes were fixed on Dak. Laurel was still watching intently as muscles tensed and quivered in his body and then relaxed, leaving his limbs as flaccid as his penis.

His eyes were still closed when he spoke to her. "Have you ever had multiple orgasms? Can you come more than once?"

"I've never tried. Next time," was all Laurel could say before she drifted off into a deep and satisfying sleep.

Dak opened his eyes. She was breathing deeply but silently. He turned away from her but kept his back against her warmth.

Part Three

After Dak and Laurel left the little island, the plane ride to Hawaii was long. Laurel welcomed the time to sit and process all that had gone on since she left home. Dak welcomed the time to rest.

"We should try to adjust our sleeping times every day from now on to arrive at hours that sync with Boston when we get there. It will still be hard, but it will help."

"You're serious? Right now it seems like a mathematical problem bigger than the problem of the jet lag itself."

"Very serious. If you ever had to adjust your body for an eight-hour jet lag, you'd be willing to try anything. Stay hydrated, and don't depend on alcohol to make you sleepy. If this isn't the right time to sleep, wake me up. Otherwise, I need a nap!"

With that, Dak leaned over and pulled the shade down over the bright window with a snap. Laurel dug around in her carry-on and pulled out a small notebook and pen. It was the one she had been carrying during the entire trip, and she had to flip through most of it before she found some blank pages. She set up a simple grid with days and hours to figure out when they should progressively shift their sleeping hours. Or at least try to.

Other thoughts kept interrupting. She glanced over at Dak. Her assessment of him had changed so drastically from the time the subject of hiring him first came up to his serious work in her furniture company until now. They had reached some sort of level of friendship, though not in the usual sense. She still asked no personal questions, and the simplest intimate details of his life were lacking. No...the intimate details—his hopes and dreams, his aspirations—were an open book to her, and maybe only her. What others would consider benign information—say, where he spent his non-working time—was still a mystery.

She had underestimated him in the beginning. She probably still did; his full capabilities were unknown to her. But she had also underestimated herself. No—she had never truly attempted to judge what her full potential might be.

Her personal life would be taking a different direction—that much had already been inevitable at Mark's death. Laurel still didn't know where her own personal path would lead in the end, but she was now ready to find out. Even anxious. She was well aware that she was about to enter a larger new world outside herself as well. Her company would not remain the same. It couldn't if it was to survive and thrive as a business. Its purpose and mission statement would have to be changed. It was time for another meeting, once she got over the jet lag, and once Megan was back at work.

Laurel was exhausted and elated. So much needed to be "fixed." There were so many seemingly insurmountable problems and so much opportunity for...what? She couldn't imagine the possibilities ahead.

Her mind drifted as the plane's engines droned. Laurel remembered a conversation she had with Dak when he explained why he wore no aftershave, soaps, or anything else with any scent. The last time she when to a toiletry shop, it was like going to the produce section of a grocery store. All the deodorants, shampoos, soaps, lotions, perfumes, and even candles and air fresheners had food scents: cucumber-ginger, green tea-jasmine, cranberry-peach...

Dak had once light-heartedly described her former life as "vanilla." At the time, she thought he had meant it was colorless, bland, flat. But maybe he had meant there was an unseen underlying flavor; a warm, rich undercurrent imparted by the mature seed pod of an orchid. He had a knack for seeing more in women than they saw in themselves.

What would he call it now? More importantly, what would *she* call it now? Laurel leaned toward ice creams. For a while, it might have been Rocky Road. But now? Mocha Almond Fudge with a Coconut Sauce Ribbon. She liked the coconut sauce addition. To her knowledge, it didn't exist. Yet. She drifted into a light sleep, thinking of other invented flavors-to-be.

Laurel and Dak were jarred awake as they touched down in Hawaii. The airport was a turmoil of concrete, steel, glass, people, and smells. She had never noticed the onslaught of clashing odors in a bustling city setting like this before. Now it assaulted her senses.

The two days in Hawaii were to be a decompression stop on the way to the familiar life back in New England. There was no discussion about it, but these last two nights before returning home would be spent in the same room. They didn't need to give each other the wide berth of privacy as before.

They leaned on the railing of their balcony overlooking the hotel pool and beach. There were tourists, elbow-to-elbow. Dak spoke first. "I know the area fairly well. There are some shops that sell the types of things we've ordered for the store. Would you like to go see what they charge for them here?"

"Let's go!" Laurel was already picking up her notebook and bag. She slipped on the secure money belt with her valuables, dropped her phone in her pocket, and headed for the door. Dak acted as tour guide, and Laurel recorded prices of items for future reference.

Afterward, they returned to the hotel. Dak suggested they find someplace reasonably quiet to rest and begin getting used to crowds of people again. "Might as well," Laurel said, finding an outdoor table on the edge of the cafe area. They ordered iced tea, more to hold their place there than because they were thirsty. "Do you mind if I turn our discussions back to that academic style again for the moment? I have some questions."

"Good," he said simply.

"The last night we had together—I assume by touching ourselves, the point was to find out what feels good to the other person by watching what they do for themselves. But you didn't watch me."

"Yes and no. And maybe. I've heard some say it's good to ask your partner how they give pleasure to themselves because they know what feels best to them. While there could be some helpful information in that, in reality, the process doesn't always transfer that well to a partner. Physiologically, psychologically, it might be related to the inability to tickle yourself. Touching yourself and being touched by someone else in the same way don't necessarily produce the same results. Even the same sort of touch by different partners won't feel the same. But

I did purposely show you what feels good to me. How did you feel when you were watching?"

"Honestly? Well, let me put it this way. I'm beginning to understand why some people enjoy pornography so much!"

"There you are! How about being watched?"

"With the right person? Why not. It's still too new to me to really say. And I noticed you used the genderless 'they' rather than 'he.' Keeping all options open?"

"Exactly."

"It's time I started taking some responsibility for my own 'education.' So I suggest we finish this tea and head upstairs. You can show me more of your 'tricks' before we leave."

~

It was going to be another long flight. The plane changes were a welcome relief from the constriction of the aircraft rather than an annoying delay. Laurel was thinking more and more about getting back into a work routine. She was well aware her time with Dak was shorter than ever.

"Dak, have you thought about the missing money at the furniture store?"

He could have criticized her for jumping back into work topics so soon. Instead, he followed whatever track Laurel needed to be on. "On and off, but I've hardly concentrated on it since we left. But it's obviously still on your mind. What do you find difficult or unusual about all this?"

"A lot. First of all, I trust my people. At least, I trust the ones that seem to have any contact with the funds. And I've not been able to find any trickle of money from anywhere in our system. Then, of course, the amounts of money that go missing seem too small to be worth the risk of being caught."

"Hmm. Then think about what would make it worthwhile, and think outside the box—outside the system. And check your figures…

are the amounts randomly different every time, or is there a pattern? Are the times monthly, random, or patterned? I hate to cut this off, but I didn't sleep well last night, and I need to be on my game when we land."

"Of course. No rush on this anyway. I've waited this long." Laurel was again left to her own resources to figure it out.

~

They landed in Boston with a harder thud than expected. Back on the little private island, it was her idea to energize the "green movement" and save a nation. But here? Now? What was she to do? She couldn't go back to the narrower world she had once lived in so comfortably. She couldn't un-see what she now saw all too clearly. And she couldn't take the rest of her life to decide.

Dak had gone on to his own place; she still didn't know where he was staying. Rosa and Gus had picked her up at the airport to bring her home. She was more than ready for her own bed tonight. She felt a major transitional phase of her life was now behind her. She took comfort in that. Now she could relax and let it all blossom in whatever direction she cared to nurture it all with no traumas or upheavals.

Greta, all smiles and little whines, prancing in place, was waiting for Laurel. And Laurel had missed Greta, too. Laurel would have more conversations in the coming days with Greta, helping her to clarify her own ideas and mental meanderings. But now, just a familiar chair and a furry ear to scratch would do.

She dragged a bag inside while Gus and Rosa each brought another. She couldn't wait to get in the door. With bright anticipation, she stepped into the living room and stopped in her tracks. "This is awful!"

"What?" was the only response Rosa could muster.

"What was I thinking when I decorated this place? I don't remember it being so dull. So drab. So downright depressing! How could I have not seen it before?"

Rosa, relieved the dissatisfaction was on Laurel's own shoulders, said dryly, "Can we wait until tomorrow before we start repainting?"

Laurel's comeback was quick: "Since tomorrow's the weekend, I won't be going to work. So, yes. We can start then."

That night, Laurel fitfully battled jet lag. Her body and her brain were in two different time zones. She gave up more than once, getting out of bed only to find she could no longer stay awake after an hour or so. She went to the kitchen to begin her day at 4:00 am. Since more sleep was impossible, she was determined to stay awake until at least 9:00 pm.

Laurel had been told coffee wouldn't help much, but she put on a pot anyway. She took all her notebooks from the trip and spread them out on the kitchen table. She began going through them, but this time, due to Dak's influence, she was copying and grouping items into folders on her laptop.

Rosa came padding in to find Laurel still busy with her notes. "I'll make you some breakfast," she said, already busy with pans and plates. "When Gus is up and ready, we'll show you what we found upstairs in that storage space."

"Okay," said Laurel, deep into her task. She put everything down when breakfast appeared under her nose. She hadn't realized she was so hungry and shoveled it in gratefully.

Gus appeared, wearing paint-spattered overalls. "Miss Laurel, did Rosa tell you about upstairs?" He still called her "Mrs. Bradford" at work, but now they were at home.

"Not really. What's up? Did you find it needs repairs?"

"No. I'll explain how we found it."

"It?"

"Yes. Rosa went up the stairs—they're kind of weak and small. Not very strong."

Rosa, fearing Gus was getting off track, nearly yelled, "Just tell her!"

"Yes. Well, Rosa went up and found it has drywall already up. And it's painted white. Ready to fix up for a room, not just storage. A nice window, too, and built-in shelves at one end. So we started taking measurements. The room was too short."

"Too short?" Laurel echoed.

"Yes. By about eight feet. At first, we thought a wall had been dropped closer in because the roof is at an angle. So we went outside to look at the roof. We could just see the corner of what we thought was an attic vent. But the room doesn't have space for an attic vent."

"Wait a minute! Are you saying the room was bigger and part of it got walled off? And there's space with a vent behind it?"

"That's what we think. Come look," Gus urged.

"And there's shelves on that wall," Rosa quickly added.

"That doesn't make any sense. Why would anyone do that?" Laurel mumbled to her groggy self as much as to Gus and Rosa.

The stairs proved to be as flimsy and rickety as Gus had said. Laurel, undeterred, was followed by Gus, and then Rosa. Laurel stood transfixed. "This is much too small."

Rosa, a bit wild-eyed, added, "But look at the shelves. A whole wall of beautiful bookshelves. That's a lot of work to keep anyone from tearing through a wall. Do you think there's something bad hidden behind there?"

"Probably nothing so dramatic. Maybe there was sagging or damage they tried to hide before they sold the place."

Gus had an easy solution to that mystery. "Who lived here before? Let's ask them."

"I'm afraid we can't. The owner is no longer alive."

Rosa asked, "Was he a bad person? With things to hide?"

Laurel told them the little she knew. "No, he wasn't bad. But we were told that when he retired and had this house built, he was already beginning to show signs of paranoia. He thought people were after him. As the years went by, he became more and more strange and isolated, reclusive. What they call a 'conspiracy theorist.' He was sure the government was up to no good and experimenting on the public. He even thought the jet trails in the sky were dropping viruses on us. The real estate agent said he would not have died if he had gone into a hospital to be treated, but he refused. Some cousin that kept an eye on him had him taken in when he was too weak to protest. But it was too late. He died in the hospital within days."

"So did he hide his crazy books and papers up here on these shelves?" wondered Gus.

"That still doesn't explain the wall," Rosa was quick to point out.

Laurel had been staring at the bookcases. "I know what this is. I've gone to enough home shows and through enough interior decorating magazines; I've seen this before. There's a door here somewhere. A section will swing in or out. It's on hidden pivot hinges. Or maybe rollers. Feel around. Try to move something."

Within seconds, Gus nearly fell into the hidden room when he pushed on a shelf. All three laughed and cheered. When they peered in, they saw it was fully furnished. When all three were inside, Gus looked back at the door. It was reinforced and could be securely bolted from the inside.

"It's a panic room!" Laurel realized. "This makes perfect sense, knowing about him. Look—there's a phone line. And a sky light. It's not an attic vent at all. It locks, too. And here's a toilet. There is a water line to the sink, but it's only cold."

"What's this?" Gus had found a pile of chains and small boards. "It's some kind of ladder with big hooks on one end. Why would he need this when there's already a ladder over there by the wall?"

"It has to be a second way out," Rosa offered. "The skylight. He could reach it with the ladder, open it..."

"And then use the chain ladder to get down," Gus finished Rosa's sentence.

"Primitive, but effective. But this place doesn't look completely finished. Maybe he was working on something else, too. What should we do with it? We could put in better stairs, make the room out there into something useful, and then you could use this for storage. Take a look and see if there's anything worth keeping, and then we'll start throwing this stuff out."

Gus found the rolled-up bundle stuck behind the desk, not hidden, but pushed in just enough to keep it from falling on the floor. It was a roll of table-top size blueprints—lots of them: floor plans for the house, elevations, schematics of the building's electrical systems, diagrams of the surrounding grounds. Lots of penciled notes on nearly every movie-poster sized page.

"What do you want to do with these?" Gus asked Laurel.

"I suppose they might come in handy. Let's keep those." Laurel looked around the room. "There's some interesting junk here, but nothing I need. If you find anything you want to keep, feel free."

Gus was fascinated by the skeletal renditions of the house. Now he knew what it meant when people said a house had "good bones."

"Miss Laurel. Does this mean we have a basement, too?" He pointed to one of the frayed pages. It was an inside elevation of their apartment addition with a big square blank under the first floor. "Let me see. It certainly looks that way. But where's the access?"

"Here?" Rosa pointed, poking her head around Gus.

"But there's no stairs there. It's just a small closet. Maybe they changed the plans."

"Maybe like he changed the room upstairs!" Gus offered.

"Maybe so. Let's go look."

The three clamored downstairs like a bunch of school kids being let out for the summer. Then they were at the closet. There was nothing. Without warning, Rosa yanked up a corner of the carpet. And there it was: a crude rectangle of plywood with a hole drilled near one end, just big enough to get a finger in.

"Go on, Gus." Laurel told him. "Pull it open!"

He didn't have to be told twice. The wooden stairs that led downward were plain and basic but much sturdier than those that led to the second floor. They wasted no time in going down. This time there was nothing but dust. It was disappointing. They were suddenly adults again, but it had been fun while it lasted.

Laurel's adrenaline dropped like a rock to the bottom of the ocean. "I have to take a nap," she said as she gathered the house plans, rerolled them, and headed off to bed. She slept deeply, but only for an hour. Maybe it was the coffee she had had. Maybe the jet lag. Either way, she was awake again. She turned to the coils of plans she had dropped on the bed and flipped through them again.

The front of her home looked plain and rectangular like any colonial. But hers had parts that looked like later additions on each end and the apartment toward the back. Wherever the structure departed from a simple box shape, there were steep and complex roof lines, mostly on the back and not visible from the road. It made for untapped, dead-space attic possibilities. Not that she needed more storage, but Laurel was curious if that could be a future selling point. What she found on the plans was section after section with hidden access. It would be fun to look for them, but she had no delusions about finding anything interesting after seeing the empty basement space. And even the most paranoid person would only need one panic room. She would look for them later. Or another day.

Laurel staggered toward the kitchen, thinking adventure seemed to be in hot pursuit of her now…since Mark's death. Or had she just been blind to so much around her before?

Speaking of not seeing, she was more than ready to redecorate those bland color schemes in every room. *This could be a monumental undertaking,* she thought. Laurel plopped herself down at the kitchen table while Rosa made a salad for her lunch.

"Rosa, I've got to do something with this place, but right now I don't know where to start. So much to do. Here, at work, other community projects. But just look at this kitchen. It's as white and sterile as an operating room. The stainless steel appliances just make it worse."

"I can fix it in one day. Maybe two." Rosa hadn't even looked up from slicing the cucumbers.

Laurel thought about it. Rosa spent more time in here than she did lately anyway. *Why not let her loose? How bad could it turn out to be? Oh, God. Not fluorescent yellow, though.*

"But Rosa, it would take more than a day just to paint the walls."

"I wouldn't paint the walls. They don't need it. I would make it different. I'll start Monday. You stay out of the kitchen until I'm done."

Rosa had already made up her mind that she would get the go-ahead.

"All right. I'll give you until I come home from work Wednesday evening. If it's not done, you have to agree to finish it before the next weekend is over. If it *is* done, I'll take you and Gus to dinner, anywhere you want."

"Anywhere?"

"Anywhere. Here's the household credit card. Go for it!"

Rosa chuckled as she plunked the salad bowl in front of Laurel. As she turned to walk toward the sink, she broke out in full laughter.

That sounded like Dr. Jekyll…or Mr. Hyde. It was a thought she did not share with Rosa.

~

Laurel, busy with her own endeavors, didn't notice that Rosa was gone most of Sunday. She was out buying things. She brought home a couple of flat boxes, quarts of colorful paint, various bits of wood, hardware, and live plants, all of which she tucked away in their apartment where Laurel would not see them.

If someone had asked Rosa what she was about to do, the list would have been short: window shelves with plants, a painted border, a tablecloth and napkins, a mat to stand on, a couple of things on the deck. She got busy the minute Laurel left for work Monday morning.

The big double windows over the sink faced south, making them sunny all year. Rosa installed removable tempered glass shelves there, resting on simple white wooden brackets. She added pots of aromatic rosemary, mint, basil, parsley, chives, and cilantro. Every time they were trimmed to use in a dish, they would fill the air with their scent.

On the deck outside the window, she carefully positioned a fully functional chiminea so that it would be squarely visible from the kitchen window. She began seasoning it with small, cool fires, easily monitored from inside. The chiminea was flanked by two trellised planters, each holding a young flowering vine.

Inside, the plain nook with a built-in desk now had a goldfish aquarium just at eye level. Only by sitting at the desk could one hear the mesmerizing gurgle of the bubbles.

Rosa deftly hand painted a border. It was mostly shades of green leaves with occasional tiny goldfish-orange buds and small yellow-centered flowers. It was a flame vine, the same one on the deck in the planters. Rosa added small details—touches of brown on the major stems with delicate curling tendrils forming curves reminiscent of those in a chambered nautilus shell. The fine spirals dropped down to the window frame and around a door.

The once-cold bare table was covered by a bright print tablecloth, with stylized but not-too-feminine flowers, in colors reflected in the border or complementary to it. Was it Indian? Was it from South America? Yet the flower shapes were not unlike some colonial crewel work.

The new napkins were each a different solid color, but they were the same colors found in the tablecloth: green, red, orange, and yellow. One lined a fruit bowl, brimming with dark avocados, bright citrus fruits, and yellow bananas. Darker green, thick mats now protected weary feet in front of the major work areas.

They were simple changes, really...but the effect was nothing short of explosive. The white walls were no longer sterile, but brilliantly clean.

Wednesday evening, Laurel arrived at home and found Rosa and Gus waiting for her before she got out of the car. "So are you here to tell me you didn't finish the job yet?"

"No, it was done hours ago."

It was not with complete confidence in Rosa's taste that Laurel entered the kitchen. On the other hand, Gus, following behind, was wearing a broad and confident grin.

"I can't believe this! It's so cheerful, so lively—so full of life! It's bright, but not gaudy. I absolutely *love* it! Let me look at everything.

"The glass shelves in the window let the light in—those are pots of herbs! Oh my God! Look at the deck! It's like part of the kitchen! That ceramic oven—the terra cotta color goes with the border in here!

And the planters too! Are those the *exact* same flowers in the border?"

"Yes; my friend had some. Hummingbirds and butterflies will come for it."

"I thought that was a stenciled border, but it's hand painted! Who did that?"

"Rosa did!" Gus had been waiting patiently to answer that very question.

"What an eye she has! Touches of just the right colors in just the right places."

Laurel looked around more carefully. She noticed the oversized steel stove and refrigerator that once dominated the room were now barely noticeable. *The art of distracting the eye. Dak would understand this work of art!*

"I had no idea! You've obviously done this before. It's truly beautiful. I guess I owe you that dinner. Have you chosen a place?"

"Yes, but it's a surprise."

"Okay. I'll wear my new black dress and be ready to go. Saturday night good for you?"

"Sure, but no new dress. This is for casual clothes. Nothing fancy."

"I'll be ready."

Gus would be driving. "We'll leave early—4:00 in the afternoon."

"My goodness! It must be a long distance away."

Neither Gus nor Rosa said anything to Laurel's remark.

Saturday afternoon, Laurel was ready. It was exciting, this new adventure with Gus and Rosa. She had no idea what they had in mind, but that only added to her delighted anticipation.

They clamored into Gus's car. The long ride Laurel expected never materialized. In less than a half hour, Gus was slowing down in the middle of the block in a residential area.

"Where's the restaurant?"

"We're here! And you're going to have to help cook!" Gus could barely contain himself.

"And where exactly is 'here'?" Laurel asked, genuinely confused.

Now it was Rosa's turn. "My sister Valentina's." They were climbing out of the car when the front door flew open. "And there's Camilla and Olivia, Hugo, David, Leonardo, Liam, and Alicia."

"Liam?" The question was out before she could think. Laurel didn't mean to pry, but all was well. Rosa was unflustered.

"Short story. I'll tell you later. Doesn't matter; we're all family one way or another."

They put Laurel to work chopping and cutting; to what end, she had no idea. The house was full of noise and hugging and happy chaos. She lost track of which names went with which faces, and no one cared. Making small talk with Rosa's sister, Laurel said, "Rosa's quite an artist. She painted a border in the kitchen this past week, and it's truly beautiful."

"Yes. When she was young, she sold many paintings and drawings. She did some murals, too. She was a professional. But then the kids came along. I think she misses it sometimes."

"Maybe she'll get back into it now that the kids are grown." Valentina did not respond.

Pots were done boiling, the oven timer had rung, and the drinks were being passed around. Dinner was served. The air was rich in delicious smells and sounds of joyful abandonment. Little ones automatically spoke English with Laurel, telling her the names of each dish. Adults sometimes lapsed back into Spanish, but at no time did Laurel feel left out.

Gus and Rosa laughed most of the way home. They had fooled Laurel, who had thoroughly enjoyed it. Dinner was supposed to be her gift to them, but it was theirs to her.

"So now you have a family, too. Just like Liam does. Whenever you want," Gus assured Laurel. She would call Valentina tomorrow to thank her—and to keep in touch.

Once back, Laurel grabbed a glass of ice water and went to her room. Her world had cracked open once again. More people, more cultures, and different ideas and beliefs had once again rushed in when she least expected it. Some unseen hand was hurtling her forward.

She lay flat on the bed for a sense of grounding, stability. Her eyes had nowhere to go but up. She hated that tray ceiling. The thick molding around the expansive recessed square hid indirect lighting. It looked heavy enough to kill her if any of it ever came loose. She felt the inner ceiling's white solidity pressing down on her. It was suffocating. She should let Rosa loose on it. Really put her creativity to the test.

~

The next day was Sunday. It would be her last day to acclimate before work the next day. She would get her clothes ready for the week. But what else? Laurel refused to fall back into her previous routine. She could do better. Do *more*. Do something else.

It was Rosa's day off, but Laurel saw her coming home in the late afternoon. "Rosa! I have a challenge for you. I'd like to pay you overtime to do some more of your magical painting."

"Another room?"

"Well, not the whole room. My bedroom is large but when I look up at the ceiling it feels like it's going to crush me. I know that sounds silly. Maybe because I've spent so much time outdoors lately, and being inside is—well, it feels like I'm trapped. Maybe. I don't know. The point is, do you think you can do anything to make it less suffocating, just by working on the ceiling?"

"Move whatever you'll need into another bedroom for the week. I'll be done in a few days if nothing unusual gets in the way."

"It's a deal. Keep track of your time. I'll pay you overtime."

"No. Maybe the next time."

~

When Laurel went back to work, she thanked Megan and the others that had covered for her while she was gone. They had all reassured her that they had missed her but had done fine without her.

There were only a few decisions they had been reluctant to make on their own. It had gone so smoothly, she was almost disappointed. However, it did make her next moves easier.

Laurel told Megan she was planning changes. She went through the basics of the ideas that were the most solid, adding that if all worked as planned, she would have to be promoting Megan to a more responsible—and better paying—position. When Megan didn't jump for joy at that prospect, Laurel's intuitive reaction was quick. Laurel added she would like to first put Megan in charge of working out details for having a small day care group so that toddlers and nursing moms would be looked after. That did it. Megan bought into the whole concept of the Bradford Village's more global addition and couldn't wait to get started.

With that much accomplished, Laurel hit the financial books again. She briefly reviewed her findings for accuracy. She recalled her discussion with Dak one day when he said he had "one or two ideas." She thought about what else he had said as they rode back on the plane.

What would make it worthwhile? Repeated small amounts over time…but that would take too long and merely magnify the risk. But multiple small amounts at once might be worth it.

Laurel made a quick graph of amounts and dates. With this visual, it was obvious. There was a very distinct pattern. Different amounts cycled through a nine-amount pattern. Shortfalls came every two and a half weeks and began within days after she had gone to the bank the first time. Laurel had gone there for help and, thanks to Tony Moreno, had gained a better understanding of how Mark had handled the store's books.

She thought again...*multiple small amounts at once would be worth it. Outside the box—outside the system—becomes outside the company's system, leaving the bank. Eureka. The theft must be occurring at the bank. Only there could small amounts be taken from multiple sources, making enormous amounts possible. It has to be Tony. Who else would know enough about me? Who else knew when I took over and knows the company so well? He met me and thought I wouldn't understand enough to ever notice. He underestimated me.*

Laurel wanted to go screaming to the bank—to John Renson in person. But she was trying not to be led by an outburst of emotion. Not in this situation. She would first run this by Dak, to see if his conclusions were similar.

~

When Laurel spoke with Dak, he said he had wondered if the problem did not have its roots at the bank. Laurel continued with confidence. She wanted to bring Megan in on it so that the three of them could go to the bank together, and maybe—no, *certainly*—bring the company's attorney.

Dak watched and listened as Laurel's mind hit high gear. He interrupted her. "I don't think I should be there."

"What? Why not? You saw it before I did!"

"I only had hazy inklings; you figured it out on your own. And my place here is only temporary. Megan is the one who should be at the forefront on this. She's the one that will be taking over more and needs to present that imagine to the bank...and the attorney."

"Yes. I should get this on the schedule as soon as possible while Megan is still able to go to the bank."

Laurel talked to Megan and their attorney. A meeting was arranged. The attorney would be present but would let Laurel take the lead.

John Renson was predictably horrified. Stammering and stuttering, even. He would lead a thorough but quiet investigation and get back to her immediately. He was nearly groveling at Laurel's ankles for allowing him to be the one to contact the authorities, thus keeping his own reputation intact.

~

Laurel saw Dak at work, but they hadn't talked much during that first week back. He was preparing for his leaving, and Laurel was catching up. On her way home from her furniture store, she wondered, yet again, where he went after work. Where he stayed. Where he slept. What he did. He once said he had reason to be back in the area in the future. What reason? It couldn't have anything to do with the group or the project—he would have said. She wanted to learn so much more before he left forever. Or would he come back? In some ways, they had become so close. Yet in others, he was still a mystery. She considered following him some evening.

But who was she kidding? She wanted to learn more about sexual techniques from him, but what she *really* wanted—now, today—was just more sex with him, with or without the academics of it. It was a desire she couldn't explain. She longed to have sex with Dak, but in a way that was different. She wanted to leave the learning for another time. She wanted to be able to finally just enjoy the experience…but not with anyone else. Not yet. She wanted it to be with Dak. There was no desire for a romantic relationship. And there was still too much she didn't know about him to be called "friends with benefits."

So what was it? They had shared something very rare and intense. There were the secrets. They had shared unspoken parts of their lives and themselves. There was more, too. Matters of life and death. Life and death on a worldwide scale. Laurel wondered about the life-long links formed by men who fought side-by-side in combat. Was this something akin to that?

~

With Gus by her side, Rosa was waiting for Laurel when she came in. "It's finished."

Now having an idea of Rosa's talents, Laurel was anxious to see how she had tackled this problem. The three of them went to the bedroom door. Gus opened it and stepped back. Laurel peeked in before entering. She saw nothing different, nothing moved, nothing out of place. Well, she had told her to work on the ceiling specifically.

Laurel stepped in and looked up. The ceiling was gone. The entire tray section was now a paned skylight. There, above the large glassy squares, was the dusky evening sky with a rose-golden glow still visible in the west. No. It wasn't possible. She looked again for several seconds before she realized what Rosa had done.

"This is unbelievable! How did you do this?"

"Gus helped. He fixed the lights in the moulding around the edge. If you turn this on in the morning, the lights are there on the opposite side. Just a little light and a soft, warm color. It looks like dawn; here, this switch, and it's bright mid-day. I just painted the sky and put shiny lacquer over it to make it look like glass. Three coats. We both worked on the crosspieces to make it look like windows. I added the tops of those pine trees at the edge. I had to use a tree that would look the same all year."

"There's a tiny bird in that tree!" As Laurel examined it more closely, she saw Rosa's signature attention to details. The crosspieces had screws, and there were hinges and a locking mechanism. "We'll have to talk about this. You must want to do more than this. Your talents must be aching to get out! Think about it, and we'll see if we can come up with any ideas over the next week or two.

"Have you done any paintings in your apartment?"

"Only where it didn't show."

"What did you paint?"

"I painted what I missed about my birthplace. But only in the bedroom!"

"Could I see it?"

Rosa was hesitant. "Okay..."

It was a parade: Gus, Laurel, Rosa, and Greta. At some point, Greta realized where they were headed and took the lead. Laurel's anticipation grew with every step. What would Rosa do in a place she thought no one but Gus would ever see? And what did she miss?

Gus cracked the bedroom door, reached in with one hand, and

flicked the light on before flinging the door open with pride. Rosa held back. She had done this without asking specific permission. It wasn't her house; it was Laurel's.

Even after seeing two of Rosa's works, Laurel still could not have imagined what she saw. This must have taken weeks to complete; there was still a faint smell of wet acrylics. Every single square inch of both walls and ceiling were covered. Like Laurel's bedroom ceiling, a sky was realistically painted overhead. There was vegetation, distant scenery between the leaves, birds, insects. The line between ceiling and walls no longer existed.

Laurel's first thought was of Gauguin. She had read somewhere once that he had, perhaps in a syphilis-induced stupor, painted the inside of his hut with miraculous scenes. But this was no Post-Impressionist style. It was Rosa's own version of realism portrayed with a mastery of line, form, and color. Laurel thought she recognized some of the plants—the pitcher plant vines, orchids and bromeliads nestled in protective banana plants, and a fan-leafed palm, all at the edge of a tropical rainforest.

An entire ecosystem hid in the vegetation. Tiny frogs, colorful spiders, and insects; a bat hid under a large curled leaf. Rosa was not just a painter, she was also a self-taught biologist. Ideas bombarded Laurel's brain. A conservatory or greenhouse attached to the new and coming Bradford store project where Rosa could grow her beloved plants and paint them to sell. Students who would learn from her. But these were Laurel's rampaging thoughts. Would Rosa even consider so much notoriety? Where would the money come from to build this? It was a mental outburst of emotional creativity that Laurel had some trouble reining in.

"Rosa, this is the most beautifully astounding thing I've ever seen. There's so much here, but it doesn't close the room in or make it seem smaller. It seems endless. We really have to talk about this—doing something with your talents. Would you consider that? Exploring some possibilities?"

"No...Gus and I work together. I can't do this big stuff without him."

"Gus, too. We'll all talk about it. Why haven't you been doing this instead of keeping house?"

Rosa thought fast. She would not go into the details of her past, but she would not lie, either. For the first time, her voice had an edge to it. "Well, for one thing, let me put it this way: You've been to many nice restaurants. Think of ten of them. How many have Hispanic busboys clearing tables?"

"Well, I guess they all have at least some. A few have all Hispanic busboys. Why?"

"Same restaurants. Now. How many have Hispanic waiters?"

"I don't think any, but...*oh!* That's horrible!"

The point was made. Gus stepped in. "You should have seen what she did to the walls for the kids when they were little. They loved it. She's done very big walls outside, too."

Rosa shot him a glance. Gus said no more.

~

Before bed that night, Laurel talked to Greta about the conversation. "How blind I've been. I thought I didn't have a prejudiced bone in my body, and yet I never noticed Hispanics have basically been blackballed into minimum wage jobs in the restaurant business. Can people have really been that way with Rosa in spite of her obvious talents? I wonder what Gus's story is. I admire them even more now, knowing what they must have gone through, coming here to this country. How much worse it must have been there."

Laurel knew she needed to be doing the same thing she wanted Rosa to do—live her life in a new, more inclusive, more productive way. She would go through her notebooks, trying to make some lists of things to do and things she should address, both at work and beyond.

~

It had been two weeks since Laurel's return from the trip. All was in place. Finding this bank scam tied up all the loose ends. Megan was due any day. Dak was doing Megan's duties but had also worked with Laurel to start shifting those responsibilities to others. Megan could then take on more of Laurel's duties, and Laurel would be able to chart a new course for herself.

Then came the first phone call. "Hello, Laurel? This is Bill—we met about three weeks ago? I was very interested in your ideas."

"Oh! Yes! Bill! How are you?"

"I'm fine thanks. I just called to tell you, all have agreed—your ideas will get top priority."

"Oh! That's amazing!! What do I do now? What can I do to help?"

"Well, first, we'll need legal permission to use your presentation speech. We'll use it as a basic game plan and work from there."

"Of course! Just fax any documents I need to sign."

"Good. And we'd like to have any background information you have on the institutions, architects, foundations, whatever you used for research. Why reinvent the wheel? Once we look those things over, we'll need to get Dak and his people on board. Do you mind if I call him?"

"Please do! And then I assume you'll let me know when and what the next step will be."

When Laurel hung up the phone, she was catapulted back into that time, so recently, when she barely gave the store a thought. Her mind was back there, but her body sat at the big desk in her office. She still didn't have clear plans as to what she should be doing, but at least she knew there was no way she could slip back into her old, self-absorbed life. The desk that had once propelled her out of her grieving was now a block of stone that anchored her in place. She would pass it on to Megan. No; she would give the space—the *office*—to Megan and tell her to pick out a new desk for herself.

~

It was Megan who took the second call. She told Laurel that Mat had phoned. He said he would be an hour or so late. He sounded rushed, flustered, upset.

"Do you think he's all right?" Laurel asked.

"Honestly? He didn't sound like he was. Maybe he had an accident. But he did say he would be in, so I suppose he's not hurt."

"Have him see me when he gets in."

Megan didn't have to; he walked in and went directly to Laurel's office. Megan followed him in out of concern.

His Uncle Ari's shop had been burned to the ground.

"Mat! No! Tell me what happened! Is your uncle all right? Was anyone hurt?"

"No one was hurt. It really could have been so much worse. I'm sure you know there's been unrest against non-Muslims there for some time. Uncle Ari's employees have kept him well-informed, so they were already prepared to leave. There was a group from a different region that came in and burned his shop down. At least they did it when it was closed and no one was there."

"Where did they go? Do they have plans? Has he lost all of his resources?"

"You know, being forced out of places is nothing new to Armenians. He and my aunt have been sending money out of the country for a long time. More recently, they were keeping a bag packed that they could literally grab and run with.

"As far as plans, they already had a visa to visit me. They never had children of their own. I think that's why my aunt sort of adopted every employee that needed help. Anyway, of all the relatives, right now I live in the most stable place. They were going to come to seriously look at the opportunities for a permanent move here.

"They grabbed their bags and headed for the airport. They spent about twenty hours there before they got a flight out to Turkey. They spent another day in the airport there and are on a flight to Spain. From there, they'll end up here. Somehow. They're picking up whatever flights they can along the way."

"What happens when they get here?"

"They'll stay with me until I can get them set up in an apartment and then a job—or two jobs. And the permanent visas, green cards, or whatever. It won't be easy, but like I said, it could have been so much worse."

"What are you doing here now? Don't you have a lot to do to prepare for their arrival?"

"Well, yes, but there's a lot to do here, too. What I need to do at my place can be done after my work hours here. So there was no question."

"That's admirable, but now you have more pressing responsibilities at home! I know your uncle was in the furniture business, and I do have some connections, so I'll make inquiries—no promises! But I'll try. I'll wait until they are here and settled in. Even if I can get him an interview somewhere, I wouldn't want him to do it while he's still frazzled from his sudden flight.

"Take whatever time off you need. Ten years from now, which will be more important; that you didn't miss a day of work, or that you took care of your family?"

"Well, when you put it that way...thanks."

The following day, Megan called in. She said she was having Braxton Hicks contractions again. She had gotten so used to them, she had come in to work with them before. But this was different. They were stronger and not going away.

"Megan, where's Rachel? Get her! You're probably in labor!"

Twelve hours later, Megan delivered a little boy. They named him Dariav. Laurel was anxious to see him, but this was the time for the new family to bond. She would wait.

~

Dak was late coming in the next morning. He had gotten his phone call from the group as well. Laurel assumed that was why he was having difficulty being fully attentive to his role of furniture store assistant/consultant that day. But Laurel had her own agenda for him as well.

"I want to actually use you as a consultant. After all, we've been telling people part of your duties here include that. Besides, I won't have you available much longer since Megan will be back before too long."

"What did you have in mind?"

"Before we talk about it any more specifically, I want to show you some places. Certainly nothing as exotic as Kiribati, but probably something new for you."

"It is to be a surprise, or may I ask about it? Or them?"

"Sure. I can tell you more. They're basically tourist attractions around New England. But maybe not what you'd expect. It will take us a day at each location. One, Sturbridge Village, is a historical village set up exactly the way it was in the late 1700s and early 1800s. Everyone there dresses and speaks the way they did during those times. The entire village operates in a bit of a time warp right here in Massachusetts.

"It's probably impossible to find a day to go there—or the other two places—when there isn't a crowd. But that might be fine, too. I want you to see the people that go there and see what attracts them, why they like it so much. I'm talking marketing.

"The second place is in Connecticut, and it's similar in that it's also an historical site. But that one is a seaport—Mystic Seaport.

"The third has to do with the sea too, but we'll slide back into the present. It's in the same general location as the old seaport, but this is an educational aquarium of sorts. We'll probably go to the seaport and then find a place nearby to spend the night rather than drive back and forth."

"I could work on that. Sounds like we'll need reservations. Is one room okay with you?"

There it was. So much implied in that one question. Laurel tried to sound emotionally flat. "Perfect. We'll work out the details for dates and all. We'd better do this quickly, considering everything else that's going on. I think what we can observe in these places might give us food for thought for both your project and the store expansion for me as well."

~

Dak had shown the Pacific to Laurel, and now it was her turn to show him this small part of New England. She kept him focused on watching the crowds as much as seeing the sights. She pointed out the throngs of tourists, all eager to watch the craftsmen and buy their products. Many were from thousands of miles away, here specifically to see these places.

In the towns, side businesses had evolved from the original attractions as well. Gift shops, restaurants, hotels—they all had full parking lots and cash registers ringing, all creating jobs for local residents. The towns had profited from the taxes, and the local governments did their part to keep parks and sidewalks attractive, roads in top condition, and the traffic flowing. One success had spawned hundreds more.

Dak had been a spellbound tourist too but had also kept an observant and more objective business eye open. Back at Laurel's home, he was ready to examine the trip. "So! Now talk to me about what we saw. Or should I say, what you saw that we need to discuss."

Laurel was ready. "Glad you asked! You know I always carry around a little notebook everywhere I go. Sometimes I jot things down because they seem like they could be useful at some point in time, even if I don't know when or how.

"You know about hoarders? Once I watched a program on hoarding. A woman held up a bent piece of wire about six inches long. She said she couldn't bear to part with it because it looked like could be so useful for something. That's my notebook. I hoard ideas."

"In a way, it reminds me of my childhood photo albums, full of potential information just waiting to be decoded."

"I can see that! I want to take you through my thought process so this makes some sort of sense. I'll try to keep it short, though.

"Every now and then, I flip through my notebooks. I came across some old notes I had taken on Helen and Scott Nearing. They've been dead for years now, but they were quite the 'free thinkers' in their day. They left New York and moved to Vermont in the early 30s, and then to the woods in Maine twenty years after that. They were the power behind the back-to-the-land movement and stressed a pure and simple life.

"The point is, people clamored to work on their farm in order to learn from them. Sometimes they were overrun by people who were eager to do manual labor for them. Similarly, with the places we've just visited, people paid substantial amounts of money just to watch for one day. Then I thought of all the places where people actually pay for the privilege of working for someone else. And I don't mean some fancy dude ranch, either."

"What's a dude ranch?"

"Oh, it's a place where grown-ups can ride horses and play cowboy all day and have cocktails and barbecues in the evening.

"But I was thinking more along the lines of sheep ranches in Australia or New Zealand, or archeological digs and paleontology excavations where people pay to work. And students at universities who pay tuition and then serve or work as apprentices as part of their training."

"So you've convinced me—people will pay dearly to watch others work or even pay to work for others. And?"

"First I want to sit with you and pick your marketing brain. What exactly attracts people to the places we saw there? And what entices people to pay to work somewhere? Mmm. Maybe we need to work on the definition of 'work' in those settings. It might give us a clue.

"Anyway, now it gets a bit off the rails. We have Mat's uncle, who is talented and has managerial experience, needing a job, and we have international awareness of products, sales, economics, and devastating climate change. We need profits to keep the business growing; we need funds and a way to create public awareness to help Kiribati and the project; we need local and international exposure to make it all happen. We have photos of craftspeople and artisans doing wonderful things who live in endangered places, we have a business that needs to expand physically as well as conceptually, we have Rosa, who turns out to be an incredible artist..."

"Stop! You've just given me a long list of disconnected facts. Care to connect them all for me?" Dak interrupted.

"But I haven't even gotten to Lila yet!"

"All the more reason to stop to connect all this together before adding anymore to the vague jumble in your head!"

"Actually, that is exactly what I was hoping you could help me do. Could we create a profitable, separate business, in another location? It would be a new kind of place altogether—not just a new expanded furniture line as we had discussed.

"All products would be made from sustainable materials. They would be ordered and sold on the fair trade basis. It could still carry furniture, but product lines would be expanded to much more, depending, in part, on availability of appropriate quality merchandise and consumer trends. That would mean the stock would be fluid, changing. Maybe even seasonal."

"You know there are already some stores, even chains, that operate along those lines," Dak reminded her.

"Yes, I know. But this goes further. The store would be divided into sections, like a marketplace. Each stall-like area would be devoted to a different theme or need. Each stall would become a microcosm unto itself. Products sold will support people, projects, needs. Think of all those separate units at the historical places we visited. The blacksmith's, the cooper's, the dry goods store. Like that, but under one roof.

"Depending on what it was that attracted people, stalls would have photos, films, and, in some, a person creating a product and answering questions about his or her skills, where they are from and what cause they are supporting. Then, there could be workshops and classes for the public, showing them how they can do some of the projects or learn about the needs of the people being supported."

Dak interjected a bit of reality. "Frankly, it all sounds a bit loose in the way it would be accomplished and profitable. And it sounds like a huge endeavor, taking lots of capital."

Laurel was undeterred. "That's another thing we need to talk about. Would it? Or could we begin on a modest level, expanding as we go? Making it a non-profit organization is an option that might help too. It *should* be non-profit.

"Think about what we already have at hand. Ari Lazarian has run his own business all his life. He knows how to make furniture that is Western in taste as well as more traditional ethnic styles. He understands fair trade concepts and the logistics of import-export tactics. And he can supervise a multinational, multicultural employee base.

"But it shouldn't be limited to an international focus. We have areas of this country that are dirt poor with people who need jobs—people who have all sorts of talents. Think Appalachian wilding, whittling, music, story-telling. And native populations in Alaska. But I'm getting off track."

"As usual. *Way* off track."

"I know, I know. But bear with me. We have Rosa and Gus with their talents and connections to Hispanic traditions, products, and areas of needs. Rachel has the background with Bali and the larger Indonesian areas. And then there's Kiribati!"

"Stop right there. First of all, Kiribati isn't overflowing with trade items. There isn't much of a thriving cottage industry there. And you keep saying 'we.' Are you including me?"

"No! Well, I am hoping you'll stop in now and then to take a look and offer your 'words of wisdom,' but I'm not operating under any delusion that you might want to settle down and stay here, if that's what you're asking. The 'we' includes you in this initial planning phase… and even then, only if you want that. I'm talking about a bigger 'we.' Me, Megan, all the employees here already, and future ones.

"And as far as Kiribati not having much to offer, all the better. It can be used to emphasize the needs there. That stall would be more public education and less profit. But surely we can find someone from there who is willing to show what is done there. Like weaving palm fronds into those lovely crowns; everyone there seems to know how to weave something! Little toy animal figures, mats...there were women making jewelry and other small items from the shells…or those blouses that all the women wear. And your photos of how climate change has changed their lives.

"The Kiribati Project itself could be a wow-factor. Don't you think? It will draw some amazing entries for the competition. We could show those plans! Get more public support for that."

"Slow down! You're going *completely* 'off the rails.' By the time this is all in place, Kiribati might not even exist anymore!"

"Sorry! I was getting carried away. Again. These bursts of insights are still new for me. I haven't figured out how to handle them yet. But anyway, you can see how the possibilities are endless!"

"'Endless' is the first problem. We need to ease off and solidify ideas, assess the problems, evaluate methods and feasibilities. Think about supporting product lines. 'Support' in the sense of both what would support such a business on a financial level and what would support the bigger picture—subtly informing the public, assisting the causes…and what causes would you choose? What would be your central focus and mission statement?"

"That's a good question. The 'green movement' in general for a background theme, and then I'd have to research that. But kids have got to be an integral part. Maybe we could team up with some schools in the broader area. You're right. It all needs a unifying mission statement. That should be first to keep us focused."

Dak was more onboard with each thought. "I agree with that; and bringing in children is a key to both marketing and awareness. Well, it isn't an impossible plan, but it is monumental.

"And now you have yourself in three projects, each big enough on its own. Aren't you starting to spread yourself a bit thin? Can you carry this off? Emotionally and physically?"

"Three? Oh, yes…three—this, the Kiribati Project with the group, and the store as it already stands."

"See? You've already lost count! Step back and try a bit of objectivity and less passion—only for a moment. I'm not saying passion is a bad thing. It's essential. But, if you could do this, how would you manage it? I mean, *literally* manage it—as in, manage each endeavor as a business. Who would be in charge of what?"

"I have been thinking about that too. First, I would like to see a fresh face on a somewhat expanded Bradford Village Furniture Company with all the imported items we bought. Once that is up and producing a solid profit base, I thought I could promote Megan and have her take over. She could help to groom someone to do more of her present duties. I've already started that. I would then be able to reduce my responsibilities there to work on these other two things. I'd beg for your input whenever I could, of course! But Mat and Ari could help with formulating the newer store concept."

"You mentioned Rosa and Gus? But if you start pulling all those people, who is going to take over *their* present duties?"

"Well, that's why I'm brainstorming with you! But I haven't mentioned this to them. I'm not sure they would be interested. It's just a thought."

"Okay. Let me sleep on this for a couple of days and get back to you. In the meantime, you can be working on step one: getting the present business invigorated.

"I'm going to be away for three days, but you can call me anytime. I'd like it if you would. Let me know how it's all going."

Laurel stopped. "I see you're pulling away, too. No more letting me know days in advance?"

"Do you mind?"

"Is that a test question? Of course I don't mind! I'll be too busy to notice you're gone. How many women have told you that before?"

"Very funny. I have a couple of hours before I have to go. Shall we head for the bedroom?" Dak expected Laurel to readily agree as usual.

However, she was not ready to drop the thought of his leaving—or rather, his leaving yet not leaving. "Dak, I want to talk about your going away. But you won't be gone completely. You've always avoided talking about our relationship, but I need this clarified."

Dak became as still as stone. Laurel waited until the silence forced him to speak. "Are you talking about what expectations you might have for the future?"

Laurel was quick to give a direct reply. "Not exactly. I want to know where we stand in your eyes. Where we go from here. You know I'm not talking about anything romantic. It's just that we've been through some significant times together. Times that have meant lasting changes in our lives. I wouldn't be surprised if you could walk out of here and close the door behind you. You would send emails and make an occasional phone call, all related to our common interests, and never notice any difference in your usual pattern of existence. That isn't a criticism, it's just who you are. But you've helped me to open so many doors that have been so good for me, and I can't close any of those doors."

Laurel had the sense to stop there, not over-explaining, not defining her terms, but leaving the interpretation up to Dak. It did not help him to relax.

"Look, Laurel. Because of things in my past, years ago, I became very good at shutting down emotions when it came to other people. I found it was the ideal skill to hone when I began working as an escort. I learned to objectively watch women, pick up on nuances of gestures and expressions, unobscured by my own emotions. It worked to the point where I was able to get to know them better than they knew themselves. It became easier and easier with practice and became what enabled me to be exactly what they wanted and needed without encouraging any emotional connection. It has become such a part of who I am that I've forgotten how to turn emotions back on. I haven't had a real friend since I was a kid. You've come closer than anyone. Friendship is something I don't know how to do any more."

Laurel had listened to Dak, but she also noticed how he lost eye contact, slumped his shoulders ever so slightly, and clasped his hands together as if holding on to himself. She would have to be careful, or else risk losing this moment both for herself and for him. "Is that something you want to re-learn? Do you want to learn how to have friends now?"

Dak considered her question as seriously as she had asked it. "I think I do. I'm getting older. I've had some years of fantastic experiences. But I have to admit to myself, I've become a hermit in the process. That must sound strange. I have relationships with others in one job, show or elicit raw emotions in my photography job, and can't get my own emotions up to having the kind of easy friendships I had as a child. I do consider Megan and Rachel 'friends,' but I am still closed off to them in so many ways."

Laurel avoided any physical touch, but said, "Look me in the eye. If you are serious about this, I think I can help you out. I can be your liaison, your escort between your world and the experience of having friends."

Dak stared into her eyes, weighing her words and his risks. "Yes. I'd like to give it a try, anyway."

"Okay, then," she said without too much inflection in her voice. "We'll get started here and now with one point only. I understand your need for privacy, and even secrecy, but friends share information about themselves. Can you begin by telling me where you live? That's a very basic question, and I'm not asking for an address. Just a city would do."

Dak flashed Laurel the hint of a relaxed smile. This much he could do. "I travel too much to say I live in any one place. I have three tiny places in three cities. One is in Boston. So when I can, or need to be, I will be near enough to come to see you."

It was more than Laurel expected from him. "That would be perfect." She knew this was quite a breakthrough for Dak but wanted to give them both the chance to carry on from there—if they could. She added, "So if we talk by phone or email, I will ask you where you are. You can tell me the country or city. Would that be agreeable?"

"You'll probably have to remind me that an answer of 'on an assignment' is not enough. But, yes. It would be a start."

"Speaking of places," Laurel began, "do you have any photography events lined up?" The dancers had shifted. She was now leading, bringing familiar and easy topics back into Dak's conversation with her.

It had broken the mood for any love-making but this conversation made Dak far more ill-at-ease than Laurel had ever been in those first intimate moment s with him. He wanted to break out of his shell now as much as she had then.

They talked a while longer, and when he left, it was Laurel who reached out to him saying, "And friends hug when they say goodbye!"

He hugged her back. "Well, then I'll have to hug this friend, too," Dak said as he reached down, put an arm around Greta's neck, and ruffled the fur on her head, as if to reinforce his newly acquired ability to express a small friendly emotion.

Laurel waved at him as he got into his car but closed the door before he pulled away, leaving him to depart freely without a lingering wave of goodbye from her.

~

That night, before going to sleep, Laurel's thoughts turned back to her yet-untamed flood of creative ideas. *I can't keep calling it the new project or 'that plan.' Things need names to give them life and meaning.*

When she awoke, it was the Bradford Global Village. "Perfect!" Laurel said to herself, stumbling out of bed. She picked up the dry-erase marker on her bathroom counter and wrote the new name across the top of her mirror in bold letters. She kept the marker there to scribble things she didn't want to forget. That usually meant something to add to a shopping list or a question for Megan that came to her while she brushed her teeth. Now there was a title heading. Rosa would find it when she tidied the house later. And, being direct, she would ask what it was. Rosa would definitely tell Laurel exactly what she thought. Laurel counted on it.

Things were beginning to fall into place. People from The Group would be contacting her, so she would be helping with the project before long. The Global Village would raise awareness and promote fair trade practices. But what about involving children to help insure a long-term commitment to green endeavors? Laurel was, or would be, thinking and acting globally, but where was her acting locally?

Laurel reached for the rolls of floor plans for the house and spread them out on the bed. She knew what she wanted but had no idea how to make it happen. She had combined ideas and approaches to put together the new Kiribati Project. Why couldn't she do it again? She sat cross-legged with papers all around her. Shuffling, studying, shuffling. She reluctantly put them aside to get ready for work.

Laurel drove to the store but still had the house plans on her mind. She thought of the "secret" passages and spaces; she thought of doing something with them. Something "good." Nothing came to mind.

She went into her office and set up her coffee pot. Her phone rang. It was Megan. "Hi, Laurel! It's me! Check your email. I just sent photos of our boy!"

"Has Dak seen him yet?"

"Yes, he has! Dak said as soon as the weather is warm enough, he'll teach him to swim so that he can become 'the sea lion he's meant to be.' Whatever that means! He tried to find a heated pool for him now, but I stopped that!"

After chatting with Megan, Laurel opened the email. There he was. The dark hair and deep brown eyes—he looked much more like Rachel than Megan. *Sweet baby!* Laurel thought. She was already in love with him. How could she make his world a better place? How could she help insure he and his generation would even have a world?

The idea struck her like a bolt of lightning. She glanced at the clock. Just after 9:00. That was good; the offices would be open. She scanned the net for the university's site, its programs and courses. Laurel found what she was looking for. She punched in the phone number. "Hello. I'd like the office of the Dean of Engineering, please. No, I need to speak to him directly...thank you. Hello, my name is Laurel Bradford. I'm working with an international engineering venture, but I also have a more local opportunity to collaborate with your Environmental Engineering department. It could provide a hands-on alternate energy design experience for a student assignment. I think you might find it perfect for one of your Capstone Design classes. I would like to make an appointment to offer information on this, if you are interested. Yes…we're beginning an international competition for an aquatic-based, expandable, self-sustaining structure. But I could explain that as well. Perhaps some of your advanced students would like to submit designs for that too...of course, that would be fine."

Laurel readied her sell. She had all these odd spaces tucked under the roof lines of the house. Some connected, some did not. The structure could be retro-fitted with whatever alternative energy sources the students could come up with, under the supervision and approval of their professor. Since it was going in her home, they would discuss payment for materials. Yes, she was forty miles from the university in Providence, but it was an easy drive. And any student that could afford the tuition there surely had a car. It would be good for her and good for the students, good for the environment. And the Kiribati project would get both exposure and participants.

If Laurel was to explain the new Kiribati project, she needed a real name for it. She would get Dak to talk to the group for that. *Hook these bright young students while they're young, just like McDonald's. Then they'll pass it on to their kids.*

Laurel was beginning to feel she was no longer adrift. She was getting her house in order. In the evenings she would go over her expanding plans with her most trusted confidant, Greta. Megan was coming in part-time and helped Laurel look for a location for the Bradford Global Village.

John Renson called. Laurel and Megan went to see him the next day. He had gotten a trusted employee to track down the program that Tony had used to pilfer money from nearly every large business they serviced. Authorities were called, and Tony was quietly arrested at his own home. It had all been cleared up with a minimum of publicity. John was personally meeting with every company that had been targeted and fully refunded every cent. Most were not even aware of what had been taken.

"If you had gone to the police first, the bank would have been ruined. And, quite frankly, so would I. I can't tell you how much I appreciate the way you handled this. If there is anything I can ever do for you, anything this *bank* can do for you, please let me know," Renson eagerly offered.

"Thank you, but there's nothing..." Laurel began.

"Actually, there is something," Megan interrupted. "You know our reputation, and you know our business is solid. Ms. Bradford is poised to expand and begin a new concept store at another location. Could we discuss a start-up loan? At a low rate of interest? Perhaps with advertising on location stating the bank's support as a cooperative gesture?"

Renson had been listening intently and didn't notice Laurel's mouth hanging open.

"Yes, could we?" Laurel added.

So it was settled. Funds were there for the Global Village to begin. Mat Lazarian and his uncle Ari would be there to oversee its development, especially when Laurel was actively participating in the Kiribati project. Ari understood intercultural supervision and would still be able to make his furniture…this time, with admirers wanting to know all he could tell them.

~

Before Laurel met with the Dean of Engineering, she needed to look at the blueprints and the spaces in the house so she could speak with him about structural details. She decided that Gus and Rosa should be familiar with them, too. One by one, they found panels where solid walls should be, backs of closets that swung away, and another built-in bookcase door.

Most places were nothing extraordinary. Electrical outlets and lights, a chair, a table, some small bookshelves. Papers and books on conspiracy theories, on hiding things in your house and yard, on surveillance techniques, and common odds and ends that might be found in any office or sitting room.

But then they tracked down the space off the master bedroom. The blueprints showed the area, but the access point wasn't as obvious. It took some serious searching this time, but they did succeed. This time, what they found was unexpected at first. But, on second thought, it should have been no surprise. There was a large swivel chair and a bank of screens. A flip of one switch, and they all sprang to life, feeding pictures into the monitors from every corner of the house, and outside as well.

"Gus, do you have your cell phone on you? Let's see if we can find any of these cameras. Let's start with this one in the kitchen. You go down and we'll talk you through until we see you looking at it."

They found pinhole cameras in hard-wired smoke detectors, decorative metal embellishments on crown moulding, and in a ceiling light fixture. Some also had audio. Laurel's bedroom would have been off-limits to any students anyway, but now there would be a way to monitor their whereabouts if she felt the need. Or, if she heard noises in the house, she could easily check every room. Besides, it would be an unnecessary effort and expense to tear the cameras and monitors all out and take them away. They would stay.

Laurel met with the university's Dean of Engineering, who couldn't wait to see what her property could offer the students. He was equally intrigued by what the advanced students could contribute to the "New Kiribati Project," as it was now officially called. Megan was spending more time at work now that the day care was up and running. Dak was there less and less.

Laurel knew he was still in town, and he came to continue her "lessons" when he could. She would be working with him on the New Kiribati Project, so they would be in touch for some time to come. Laurel knew Dak also visited Rachel and Megan; he still worked for Rachel at times, so she thought nothing of it.

The dean from the university had set up a time to come to Laurel's home to evaluate the possibilities there and get details about the architectural competition. He brought two people from their Center for Environmental Studies. Laurel was drawn to both the man and the woman. It would be a good working relationship.

Rosa would be there during the day to act as a liaison between the students and professors and the household. They were interested in the entire structure, but Rosa and Gus insisted on their privacy, to which Laurel readily agreed.

Laurel was busier than ever, but she was learning to delegate to her trusted staff. Little Dariav was learning, too. He was sitting up by himself under Greta's watchful eye during his frequent visits.

Greta had learned as well. She, Laurel, and Rosa had kept up with their refresher sessions, and Greta had accepted the students without concern—all but one, that is. Following Greta's indication, Rosa kept track of the girl's whereabouts. Within days, Emily was found trapped by the snarling dog in Laurel's bedroom—a space clearly designated off limits for students. The girl stood holding a bracelet from Laurel's dresser top. "I just wanted to look at it! I wasn't going to steal it!" Greta wasn't going to let her put it back on the dresser, even if that *was* Emily's true intention.

Rosa spoke with the professor. It was made it clear that student would not return. The sweet-faced young woman did not take it lightly, ranting at Rosa that she had "messed up" her life.

"Not me!" Rosa said to her. "You made your own choices. Besides, it is not me that is throwing you out of this house and your class—it's the school's rules." Within a couple of days, the rest of the students had already settled back into their routines.

~

On the other hand, Laurel had no chance to fall back into her own routine. As promised, she would be in Kiribati for the Independence Day celebrations in a few months. She looked forward to it and had kept in contact with Lila over the past year. For their differences, they had much to share—and Lila was positive and upbeat, and she made Laurel laugh.

"Come on, Greta. Time to tell you how things are going. You're a lot cheaper than a therapist, you furry sweetheart." It was easy to slip into thinking of Greta as a friend. She was attentive and always happy to see Laurel and any friend that came to visit.

Laurel got ready for bed. She was feeling something. Something familiar from her distant past. What was it? She laughed out loud. It was contentment. She climbed into bed; Greta followed suit in her own bed nearby.

Laurel was deeply asleep. Something nudged her awake, snuffling. "What's the matter, girl? Do you need to go out? That's not like you. It's after midnight. Are you okay?"

Greta answered with a low, quiet, and very distinctive growl. She was in a semi-crouch, creeping out the bedroom door. Laurel was instantly alert. She grabbed her cell phone, ready to call 9-1-1. But it couldn't be an intruder; she had an alarm system.

Greta vanished in the darkness. Laurel was on her feet nearly as fast, phone still in hand. Within seconds, there was a blood-curdling scream. It was a man. *Gus is in trouble!* was her first thought.

Then she heard the man again. "Get this fucking dog off of me! Get your goddamn dog! It fucking broke my wrist!"

Laurel could hear thrashing and growling. Within seconds, she was there. The man was wildly trying to land a punch on Greta, but she was tugging one way and then the other to avoid his blows. Laurel screamed at him, "*Freeze* or she'll tear your throat out!"

"Okay! Okay! Just get this fucking dog off me!"

Laurel gave the order, and Greta reluctantly let him go. The man was cowering in a corner, holding his right hand to keep it from flopping. Greta kept guard. He wasn't going anywhere. "You move, and you're dead," Laurel said in a calm, deep voice as she dialed 9-1-1. She was terrified, but she wasn't about to show it.

Then she saw the gun on the floor. She had seen enough cop shows on TV—she kicked it well away. That's when she saw Rosa and Gus standing wide-eyed, frozen in place, staring at the gun sliding toward their feet. Gus was holding a large kitchen knife, ready to throw it. Laurel didn't see that his grip was one that revealed both practice and power.

Rosa stood speechless. Her hand was to her chest, touching the oddly shaped drop of gold that hung on a fine chain around her neck.

Laurel was giving the dispatcher the address and telling them to come to the front door. "Yes. I'll stay on…No, it isn't. Just a minute... Rosa, go unlock the front door!"

When flashing red lights lit up the windows, Laurel took Greta and put her in the apartment. The officers rushed in, but by now, the man was begging for any emergency services he could get. He had seen the amount of blood he was losing from the compound fracture, and the pain was intensifying. Inexplicably, he suddenly looked up and screamed at Rosa, "This is all your fault, you fucking bitch!"

As the police entered the room, the man began to whimper. With tears rolling down his cheeks, he told himself, "My life is ruined."

Rosa and Gus looked at him as if he were speaking a foreign language.

Before dawn, they had the full picture. The man was Emily's boyfriend—the girl who had been found in Laurel's room and asked to leave. He had come "just to scare" Rosa, but the police had recognized him. He had previous arrests for DUI, petty theft, and assault. He had pulled telephone lines outside that he hoped connected the security system to its base. If not, he would have been in and out by the time the company phoned to check on the house and then called the police. The gun he had was stolen, and the police had no doubt his intention was to do more than scare someone.

Greta had protected her family with uncanny intelligence. She had taken it upon herself to awaken Laurel and then investigate without a sound. When she saw an arm with a gun coming around the corner, she leapt for it without any warning and without any command. As Zack had predicted, she bit down hard enough to crush the wrist and refused to let go, even when the man managed to land a couple of blows. It had only made Greta crush harder.

Gus was petting Greta. He said to her, "A dog is reliable. You can count on a dog." Laurel remembered. They were the same words he had said to her before Greta came to live with them.

The four of them—Gus, Rosa, Laurel, and Greta—were up all night. Laurel phoned Megan's desk and left a message that she would be in after noon. She would explain when she got there, after she had a nap.

Even without any sleep, Laurel couldn't settle herself right away. She lay on her back and looked at the "sky" above her. Every time she thought things were finally settling into place, something else would happen. Now this. She would call the security company tomorrow and tell them how ineffective their system had been. *No doubt, they'll want to gouge me for an upgrade. I'll think of something else*, she thought. *Maybe I can build off of that bank of screens and cameras already in place. Maybe...*

She thought about Dak and his bodyguard services. *What good would his martial arts and muscles do against a gun? Everything is relative, even security.*

She drifted into a stream of consciousness. Dak, perfect in so many ways. He was the perfect gentleman, always anticipating her needs, the perfect person for the roles he filled in the company, ideal for security...emotional security, his strong emotional love for his country, his grandmother. His inability to take the emotional strain of watching Tibu age, his unemotional approach to love-making, Lila's observation of his inability to talk about the coming increases in violence. Laurel saw that for all his talk of security, he really meant personal confidentiality. He had no sense of feeling secure when it came to his own emotions.

He was, in short, a human being like everyone else. Granted, he was a unique, talented, and finely tuned one. What she gained from her relationship with him was not to be minimized, but he was still a person with his own issues. Did she expect something else? Something else...the New Kiribati Project. Had he really thought of everything? Or did he leave out those things he couldn't face in his own life? Lila was right—he had made no mention of accommodations for the elderly, disabled, and infirm. What else was a tender point for him? Conflict leading to violence. He had never come close to mentioning a police force, a jail, dealing with piracy on the sea. She reached for the notebook by her bed and jotted some notes to cover with group members.

What am I leaving out of my life? What am I not seeing? It's all already too much sometimes. Now this, too. This break-in. It was even Dak that got me to bring Greta inside at night. Dak is gone—for the most part. Where do I go from here? Who do I turn to now?

Laurel looked up again at the clouds above her bed. There, in their glossy undersurface, she saw her own reflection.

About the Author

To create this tale, R. Vania has drawn on years of experience working in the fields of international education, cross-cultural adaptation, and medical psychology. She now has the opportunity to devote her time to research and writing. A theme that is constant for her is the belief that nothing exists in isolation.

www.ingramcontent.com/pod-product-compliance
Lightning Source LLC
Chambersburg PA
CBHW020557180626
46810CB00007B/2541